Parikshit Aagneya
Gets To Live Forever

Immortality, a blessing or a curse?

For Parik, the son of an ancient goddess, the price is very high, indeed. His mother, in a fit of anger, cursed him with immortality. The price he's forced to pay? Each time he's reborn, he must undergo an excruciating death.

If that weren't bad enough, everyone around him must also die, so that Parik might be gifted life once again.

This is the story of one of Parik's rebirths, and the tale of the people he has come to care about. They see him as a god, come to save their city. Only Parik knows the truth.

Everyone around him will die, so that he alone can live.

Consumed
Farley Dunn

THREE SKILLET

CONSUMED, Dunn, Farley L

First Edition

 THREE SKILLET

www.ThreeSkilletPublishing.com

Cover by Farley L Dunn

All characters are fictitious, and any resemblance to actual
persons living or dead is purely coincidental.

This book may not be reproduced in whole or in part, by
electronic process or any other means, without permission
of the author.

ISBN: 978-1-943189-01-4

For Nate-Nate:

Yes . . . life's demons are real.

1

FATE STALKED THE DARKNESS, and still, the city slept. It's said that all things must die, even the wonders of the world and the great cities of the ages. Nothing is immortal, the wizened mages whispered.

They were wrong.

However, that wouldn't save the city. Not this night.

THE CITY'S GRAND TEMPLE gripped the sides of the mountain, a lumbering dragon against which the walled citadel nestled as a pup might huddle at its master's feet. The Holy Edifice had been built centuries before, and the city had grown around it, a massive organism feeding the sanctuary's hungry coffers.

The vibrant moon far overhead brushed gentle fingers down the city's elegant stone avenues. In courtyards and pedestrian malls, fountains sang their liquid melodies, the gift of distant reservoirs and towering aqueducts. The inhabitants had long since been lulled into complacency, and rightly so. This was indeed a city of the ages. The fathers and grandfathers of those who rested within its cradling arms had laid its stones, and not one had ever been overturned from another.

It had endured for ten generations and surely would endure for many more. Such were the dreams of those that resided within its walls.

NESTLED AMONG THE NIGHT-SHROUDED ramparts, stone steps shivered in the shadows. Dust rose from mortarless joints, only to settle slowly back once again. The ground underneath the city's foundations stirred to life, and that was as it should be. Let the city's inhabitants rest in the remaining time they had left, for their world's existence was drawing to a close. Within the darkness, an age-old curse had awakened once again. Even the stones felt the evil that was coming to life.

Parik knew of the power that gathered beneath the bedrock. It drew together for him. The power would come to him, do to him as it wished. It would bring him renewed life, although it was unwanted life, and in doing so, it would rain death upon all he knew.

"Muse?" Deep and resonant, his voice called into the room, echoing in the hollow space. He stood from his blanket in search of his woman. She'd be distressed. The shaking of the stones always drove the Muse from him. It was the wretch his Muse had left behind, now returned to herself once again, who would be awash in pain. She'd be frightened, and he had no wish to see her suffer.

"Muse?" he called again. It was the only name by which he knew her.

Hearing a whimper, he stepped to the girl, and he knelt in the shadowy darkness and took her face in his hands. He looked gently into her eyes to see them filled with fear. He knew those eyes, yet they no longer knew him. What she'd been to him, she could be no more.

"Please don't be frightened," he murmured. He reached a hand to caress her hair, a familiar action, then withdrew it just before he touched her.

He felt dust brush the back of his neck, knowing it to be the grinding of stone upon stone, and he looked up at the ceiling far overhead. This woman would die. When the power came, the people around him always did, and there was nothing he could do about that.

She didn't have to die afraid, however. He could do nothing else for her now that the power had started to gather, but comfort was the one thing he could provide. She surely desired relief from her fear more than anything in the world, and if she desired it, he could give it.

With gentleness in his fingertips, he reached and touched her temple. In that connection, he felt the warmth of power draw from his hand, and the fear on her face melted away.

"I was afraid," she whispered, her eyes studying his face. "I'm now not afraid." Even so, she remained still, and after a moment she shivered.

"I wouldn't have hurt you."

The man sighed with his exhaustion and stood, his body glistening in the dimness of the moonlight leaking into the interior of the room. Against other men, he was tall, and even the age that held him in its grip couldn't disguise the power that resided underneath his skin. A stray ray of light found its way through yet a new crack in the ceiling, and where it filtered through the dust-laden air to illuminate his hand, the tip of one finger glowed. He glanced down, noticing it in the light, aware it no longer ached, and knew it as yet another sign that the Muse had fled far away.

His sudden weakness, the tiredness he felt, was more than the age in his body. It was the curse at work. It was the fingernail, and it was a decision that had been forced upon him at the beginning of all that had ever been.

MANY EONS AGO, HE was known as Parikshit Aagneya, Tested-One Born-from-Fire. The mortal son of a goddess, he'd spurned her incestuous advances, refusing to become his mother's lover.

Wrestling for escape, even as she'd cursed him to eternal misery, the yellow tip of her Second Hand's fourth nail had come loose in his fist. It was from her Healing Hand of Life, and he'd immediately understood that to ingest the nail was to claim part of her power for his own.

He'd stolen the tip of the Goddess Lamahätsu's most precious fingernail, and she was furious.

So, with triumph on his face, even as fear raged in his chest, he'd swallowed it whole, feeling the surge of unimaginable power rush through him. For a moment, his feet stumbled in his flight. He looked back, fearing Lamahätsu would be upon him. She stood as if transfixed, however, and he paused to watch. Her Fifth Arm of Death brandished fire and lightning, while her Two Arms of Love traced patterns in the air, knowing he'd see. Laughter danced on her face, and longing was in her eyes.

It was longing for him.

The Goddess of Life, the fire-breathing seductress who had birthed the fires of the world from her womb, desired one who was formed in the Fires of Creation, and those fires were hers. As she'd once birthed the world, she had given life to Parik, knowing that as he grew, he'd become ever more that one who would be there to satisfy her loneliness. As a child she'd doted on him, but it wasn't a child she needed. She had waited—not always patiently—as he'd approached the chasm separating childhood from manhood. Only then would he be ripe for her needs.

He had known, although sensed was more accurate than known, really, as the mists of the evening will suddenly be there, their beginnings unnoticed until they're fully around a man.

As his body leaped in a matter of months from child to man, she became ever more affectionate. She teased with him, her ministrations aimed at drawing him out. When she gathered him to her, her Two Arms of Love caressed his newly muscled shoulders, running down his chest, and stroking his lengthening legs.

However, he'd also seen how she'd bristled, how her Fifth Arm of Death had flashed fire, and her storms had lashed the world when he became interested in the mortal girls of the villages. The realization had come upon him until there had been no doubt. Parik's mother, Lamahätsu, the Goddess of Life, had birthed him, yet she also groomed him to be her consort, her vessel of satisfaction.

Despite his respect for her powers, Parik knew he'd never allow himself to be any of those things.

In preparation for the final days of their relationship as mother and child, Lamahätsu had prepared a banquet of sumptuous proportions. It was to be served on the great stones that rested on the beds of coals that had erupted from the bowels of the earth in the time of creation. The forested bowers of her boudoir smelled sweet, with branches of pine spiced with the aphrodisiac cinnamon of the lower reaches. A crashing waterfall stood in the distance, its billowing flumes at Lamahätsu's beck and call.

Parik had grown tall, and his back was straight with the strength of impending manhood. His beard had yet to grow, but his voice ran deep. Lamahätsu's desire for him already waxed strong. It bled from her voice.

"Parikshit, my son, I've prepared a Meal of Celebration. Come to me." Her voice had purred as she called to him, although it sounded more like the rumble of distant thunder across the hills. "Tonight, a dozen seasons and a half more have come to fruition. We will celebrate together." Her smile was the first flash of the sun's rays through the storm's breaking cloud cover.

The storm was ever-present, though. Experience had taught Parik that.

"Celebrate, Mother?" The feast and its attending bowers of greenery, obviously intended for an amorous conflagration, one that would require the quenching waters of the mountain snowmelt, had not escaped the son's attention. "You are the ageless Five-Armed Goddess, the Womb of Creation, the Bringer of Life. The world celebrates you every day."

He laughed, but he'd also watched her Two Arms of Love. They were moving in the ways they had moved when he'd first bridged the chasm to manhood, and they were motioning for him to draw near to her.

"Ah, the old names." Her laughter was the ripple of rain on a summer stream. She moved his direction, and in her Two Arms of Life, she held a platter of red pomegranates. "I've grown these especially for you. Do you like the color? Take a bite, my precious Parikshit. For companionship." She stroked a pomegranate with one of her Two Arms of Love, picking it up to hold it out to him. The distant thunder rumbled her sultry words. "You care for me, do you not?" Her Fifth Arm of Death toyed with her raven hair, drawing it out into spiky snakes that stayed where it left them.

"You're my mother. You birthed me from your

womb. Of course, I care for you." He reached for the pomegranate, and as he took it, he observed her eyes. They crinkled in anticipation, and lightning flashed across the skies.

"Eat, my son." One of her Two Arms of Love reached to stroke his shoulder, running up under his leather vestments. "Eat and be mine."

In the moment of his mother's touch, Parik's suspicions were no longer mists in the farthest reaches of his mind. The haze of qualms that had haunted him over the past half-dozen seasons solidified, and without warning, he was in the pine and cinnamon bower. His vestments were thrown off to one side, and he lay bare. His mother stood above him, and her raven hair writhed with anticipatory need. Dark clouds roiled across the sky, and lightning flashed from her eyes. She laughed, and thunder crashed through the heavens.

"No mortal man has been for me what you will, my precious son. Many have tried, and I've killed them for their failure. You, Parikshit, birthed of my womb, will now be the one to rule at my side." She laughed again and reached toward him.

Parik had been horrified to find the motion of her hand made him prickle with need. He tried to struggle, but his limbs were fastened by some unseen mechanism to the pine boughs underneath his back.

"Ah, my son. Don't fight. It was the pomegranate, you see." The rain on the summer stream rippled again, more violently this time, barely heard in the sensations flooding through Parik's loins. "It's only half the magic, though. Once we are one, your very essence will return to me, and you'll want me as much as I want you. We will be drawn together, companions always." She ran one of her hands along the side of his neck, tracing his collarbone, and sliding it sensuously across his chest and arm, stopping when she reached his wrist. He smelled the trees around them begin to scorch, singed by the fires of Lamahätsu's blistering passion.

Parik yelled his defiance, and then he was once again standing, holding the pomegranate, with his mother's hand underneath his vestments. The touch that had been the treasured stroke of a mother's love was now the vile contact of filthy lust, and he felt his body cringe. He returned the pomegranate to the platter, and as he turned to withdraw from his mother's side, the sky darkened; and the rumble of her voice became the lightning crackle of a gathering tempest.

LAMAHÄTSU SENSED THE CHANGE in him. After all, she was also the Giver of Death as well as the Essence Eater. In her divinations, she'd sensed he might hesitate; and although the future was never sure, she knew men as men didn't know themselves. She knew Parik even better. She understood his every nuance, the very shading of his essence, and she'd seen his vision even as he'd seen it. It had been hers to give, although it had been an unintended gift. She wanted him voraciously, needed him intensely, so much so that she'd let her control slip, and her desire had erupted into his thoughts.

When darkness had crossed his face, she knew he

was revolted. He wouldn't partake of the pomegranate, no matter how much she plied him. He'd seen its purpose, and without it, the bonding wouldn't be complete. When she saw him gather himself to leave, she read the intent in his movements, in the finality of his facial expressions, and she made one last stab to keep him. If he'd just stay, she could employ other machinations to entrap him. She could. She knew it. She was the Goddess of Life, the carrier of the Womb of Creation. She'd birthed Parik, and she would have him.

"My son," she pleaded, and her voice softened to a gentle breeze, as it rustled the trees in the distance. Her Fifth Arm of Death smoothed her wild, raven hair, and her Two Arms of Life reached to him. "I've always loved you, my Parikshit. Please stay. You are safe in my bowers. Trust me." She lied well, too, although there was the faintest hint of keening in the wind as it spoke her words, and it told of her dishonesty.

"Son?" His voice was brittle with disgust, shattering her hope of reconciliation. He'd been birthed by the Goddess of the Beginnings of the World. His words carried power of their own, even if it wasn't a supernatural one. "Am I your son or your intended companion, one you only desire so you are not alone?" His eyes were hard, and while his couldn't shoot fire and lightning, and there was no Fifth Arm of Death hovering above his head, his green orbs, darkened with fury, nonetheless flashed with slicing daggers of hate.

"My son," her brook of a voice burbled. "You are my most treasured possession. Please stay." Her need still burned in her, and as much as she tried to control it, forcing herself to let only the sweetest facets of her Many-Armed Self through, she still needed her son's touch. She couldn't be satisfied without it. For eighteen seasons her longing had built up, and now she was learning the frustration of denial. Her body needed this man she'd birthed for this express purpose, and the brook became a torrent barely contained within its banks. "The feast. It waits. Please stay that long, my precious Parikshit."

PARIK HEARD THE ROILING undercurrents in her words, and he was repulsed. "I think not. I will go, Goddess. I think I'll go far, and I don't think I'll return. You've been a parent to me up until this day, but no longer. I'm not prepared to be your consort. I bid you farewell, Mother Goddess, Life Giver." He tucked his vestments to his waist with one bent arm, and he gave a small bow. Then he turned to exit his mother's presence forever, knowing he'd never return.

"You'll die out there." The screech of a hundred crows assaulted his ears. "Without me, you'll die, Parikshit. You'll live a mortal's life, and you'll die at the end of your time, old and broken. Is that what you want?"

He stopped, but he didn't turn. "Die? If I stay here, I'm dead already. How can you think to taunt me? Death by companionship or death by old age. The choice seems clear to me. I'll take old age, Goddess Mother."

"Parikshit!"

Thunder rumbled his name, and a violent gust of

wind whipped around him. In the maelstrom, dust and stone pelted his flesh.

"What now, Mother?" Parik faced her, and the change in her appearance frightened him. He'd never truly seen her as he saw her then. She'd been irritated with him before, most notably when he'd taken his first love from the village, but this was different. This was anger fueled with desperation, and there was something more, something much more.

Sparks flew from the tips of her hair, and violent, roiling dust poured from between the rocks at her feet. The ground shook, and Parik stumbled as he shifted his balance to regain his footing. Fear wouldn't, however, force him to her bower of pines and cinnamon.

"Parikshit." The shifting stones at his feet spoke his name. The rising dust whispered of adoration, even while it brushed his legs in an obscene dance of lust un-filled.

"What is it now, Goddess? Will you kill me as I stand? Is old age not enough for you?" His heart beat in fear, but he wouldn't let her see. He kept his back straight, and he spoke to the commanding presence standing before him with defiance in his words. "Do as you will. I was created in the fires of your womb, and if you choose to take me, then take me as I stand. I won't stop you, and I couldn't even if I wished to do so."

The ground moved again, and new, deeper cracks split the place where he stood, sending new waves of dust billowing into the air.

"Parikshit!" This time darting lightning demanded

his attention, and the goddess that was Lamahätsu began to glow. "You are my son, youth-man that you are, and I wouldn't have you die." Underneath the building thunder, she murmured, "That wouldn't serve my purposes. You are more important to me than all the powers I wield."

Her Fifth Arm of Death stretched its five fingers into the sky, and five lightning bolts flew from them. With a cracking shockwave, rain and hail began to litter the ground, beating the bowers of Lamahätsu's boudoir, and shearing in twain the great stones that were heated by the coals from the Fires of Creation.

"No, I won't kill you." Repeated thunderbolts slammed her words into the hillsides. She laughed cruelly, and a mountain in the distance erupted into flowing lava, showering the surrounding villages with flaming ejecta. Her body growing ever larger, and with her brilliance shining ever brighter, she pointed her five arms at him. "I will give you life, Parikshit, immortal life." She cackled, and the trees of her boudoir burst into flames. "I will give you *life*, Parikshit."

"Life? I have life. Immortal life? Spare me, Lamahätsu, Mother Goddess. Keep your immortal life, your empty gift. I don't want it." He sneered, even as he felt the tickling of sweat on the hairs within his armpits and across his loins.

"It isn't a gift, my son. It's a curse. You'll live forever, my paramour, until the fires at the end of time devour the very rocks upon which we stand." Lightning flashed angrily around her, dancing her words to him.

Lamahätsu was now twice as tall as her son, and the light that shined all about her was blinding.

"How can such a thing be possible?" he scoffed. "I've none of your powers. I'm a mere mortal. Will you turn me into a god to stand beside you? How can you curse me with such an empty threat? Your words are hollow, Mother. You are the one who's eternal. Speak the truth to me, or let me walk from this place forever."

"Forever?" Lamahätsu's five hands were in constant motion by then, and a reddened, glowing sphere had formed in their midst. It seemed that only by their constant motion was the glowing thing kept contained. "Look for your Muse, my son, for your Muse will keep you safe. He must keep you safe, for if you die, he dies. Or he may try to kill you just for spite." Lamahätsu's laughter cackled once again, and the searing lightning that was her voice blinded him with its brilliance. "Yes, you'll live forever, even as you grow old and die, and in your rebirth, each time you'll take untold thousands of mortals with you. This is your curse, my son, to be reborn over and over at the cost of every living thing around you."

Parik laughed disparagingly, even as sweat coursed down his back. He didn't know if his mother could do this thing, but she might try. She was the Goddess of Life, and she did have Two Arms of Life, Two Arms of Love, and a Fifth Arm of Death. Yet, in his disdain, he rebuked her, brandishing his defiance.

"I won't have your curse, one where you can pursue me lifetime after lifetime. I've loved you as a mother, but I love you no longer. Let me die of old age while you live forever. I wish only to be gone from your presence."

"My presence?" Lamahätsu now towered as tall as the trees, and the ball her hands contained had taken on a green hue, one lit with yellow fire. The resounding timbre of her voice crushed the grasses and shattered the branches of the remaining trees. "We will be bound throughout the ages. I will live only as you live, my son. You are still mortal, after all. Your immortality will come only in your rebirth." She leaned forward and held out the glowing orb to him as she smiled. "Come, partake, Parikshit. I have a pretty present for you, a parting gift, so to speak."

The ground shook violently as she stepped forward, throwing superheated dust up from the bowels of the earth. Parik was pitched from his feet. As he clambered up, he realized he must have been entranced to simply stand there as Lamahätsu reared before him and prepared her curse. Angry with himself, he turned to run, only to feel a massive hand wrap itself around his body, with one finger at his throat, two across his torso, and another crushing his legs. A whirlwind spoke into his ears.

"My gift. You must not leave without my gift."

The fingers against his torso pressed hard, and Parik grabbed at the hand. In his fury, the yellow nail from his mother's fourth finger broke off. Lamahätsu released him with a wail, and he dropped to his knees as she howled in pain, drawing her bleeding hand to her side. Without understanding why, he knew he must ingest the poisonous nail—he must—for it would bring him a measure of strength against the goddess.

When he turned, fearing she'd seize him again, there stood Lamahätsu, with her Two Arms of Love weaving a goddess' magic in the air, her Two Arms of Life holding the glowing sphere, and her Fifth Arm of Death brandishing lightning and fire above her head. A red stain ran from the fourth finger on her Hand of Healing.

Then, with her Two Arms of Life, she threw the ball at him. Just before it engulfed him, a crashing torrent of thunder across the hillsides wrapped her final words about him.

"Remember your Muse. Look for him—or her!" She laughed hideously as the fire-laced green orb engulfed him. Parik's torso was overwhelmed with burning sensations that surged throughout his body, intensifying as the glowing ball was absorbed into his skin. He collapsed to the ground, writhing in torment. When the burning faded, and he could open his eyes again, Lamahätsu was gone, and he was alone.

STANDING IN THE STONE chamber with the woman at his side, the old man Parik had become sighed heavily. He knew what lay before him. It was time to be reborn, and many would die. He'd continue to live, and others would perish in the process.

All he could do was make things better when he could.

The moonlight once again caught the fourth nail on his right hand, and it glowed yellow, the same color once seen on an old goddess' hand, a goddess who hadn't been present in goddess form in more seasons than any mortal could count.

Parik could, though. He could count the seasons. He didn't need to know the number. He'd lived every one.

2

CHIARINA LUCANUS TUGGED the small, warm body of her brother tighter. The shaking in the ground distressed her. When he turned in her arms, groaning, she comforted him with a whisper.

"Patience, small brother. The morning comes. Perhaps the people will be more generous. We will have food, then." She paused in the darkness as the stones in the building shifted again, and once the dust had settled, she kissed his cheek. "Perhaps you won't be hungry when you sleep tomorrow night."

She was certain he would be, though. With her crippled leg, it was sometimes all she could do to drag herself from this abandoned room she and her brother called home. It was shelter, but it was also off the main avenue through the city, and not many people walked the side street where she sat with her bowl. She dared not go farther from their room, either. Her brother was very small, and he couldn't be left alone, not even on the chance she might find additional coins on a more heavily trafficked street. Small boys—abandoned small boys—were sometimes sought out for use in religious practices—sacrificial ones—that took more from the boys' small bodies than any religion had the right to demand.

As she turned on the hard, stone floor, pain lanced through her crippled leg and up through her loins. She groaned, damping her responses to the mind-numbing torment as her brother stirred and moaned in her arms. The pain was worse since she'd been visited by the goddess. When she was just a girl, the pain was bad, but she'd been able to push it from her mind. Now, though, it was too much, sometimes.

The first time the goddess had visited her, Chiarina had been on the street by her bowl, unsure what was happening. She'd been frantic that she was dying in a new and horrid way. As her fingers had pressed against the pain, she'd screamed, falling to her side and letting the sensations flow where they would.

For weeks she'd lived in terror, but when an old serving woman from the temple stopped by, one who visited regularly in her white tunic with its red stripe, bringing Chiarina alms, the old woman explained the goddess' monthly gift. She also told the crippled girl that she was sorry she must still beg, but with the pain, she couldn't be accepted into the temple's holy order. To carry the basins of water to cleanse the supplicants' feet, then to stand and listen to their absolutions—a duty required of the temple serving women—wasn't an easy task.

With the old woman's words, Chiarina knew her hopes of joining the temple for her livelihood were dashed, and that meant Thaddiaos would continue to sleep hungry most nights.

Closing her eyes, Chiarina thought of the man who had stopped and spoken with her from time to time over the past season, occasionally dropping coins in her bowl. He was tall, with his hair pulled sternly from his face, rolled and in a catch sack at the base of his neck. Often his head was also draped with a cloth.

His eyes were old, although they smiled at her.

Chiarina might be just at the cusp of womanhood, but she knew faces. The man had a very old essence inside of him, and she could tell he'd lived a very long time, far longer than his crinkled eyes suggested.

The woman who sometimes walked with him wasn't old. She was quite a beauty, although what Chiarina envied wasn't her face. She wished for the straight legs the woman walked upon, ones that didn't pain her when she moved at night, or force her to crawl wherever she went. Chiarina envied her for that. What she didn't envy her for was what she saw in her eyes. Just like the man, the woman was very ancient, an old nimji, an elemental forest creature that should have merged with the new religions many lifetimes before. Nimjis, however, didn't take young boys for sacrificial rites, and the two had never tried to claim her Thaddiaos. Still, she always made him hide inside no matter who came by, so they wouldn't know of her brother. It was a risk she couldn't afford.

A scrabbling sound along the wall caught her attention, and smiling through the darkness, Chiarina reached inside a small pocket in her tunic. She pulled out a dry crumb of bread that was too small and too old to satisfy her or even Thaddiaos. She tapped the stones along the wall, setting the breadcrumb on the floor just beyond the ends of her fingers. Then she tapped again in an odd, irregular pattern. After a pause, she heard her pattern repeated. Keeping her fingers very still, she waited as the sounds grew closer, and when they stopped, she felt the shiver of whiskers on her fingers. That was when she knew her offering had been accepted, and she lifted her fingers to run them across the furred head.

She'd never seen the creature, but she knew it was like her in many ways. It was often hungry, it made friends rarely, and it was crippled. She knew that, because she'd felt of its legs, and one of its front legs was malformed, just like hers. She guessed that was why she saved bits of bread for its nightly visit. She felt a kinship to this creature. Then, after making its trade, allowing a gentle touch in exchange for its meal, the rat would be gone for the rest of the night, its crippled body making the same irregular tapping on the stone the girl had used to call it for its crumb.

After the building was silent again, Chiarina lay very still, listening to the world around her. It was when the floor began to move again that she closed her eyes and tried to squeeze the tears away. The moving floor made the stones shake, and the shaking stones made her afraid. After all, if the stones could move, what would keep them from falling on top of her, and if she were gone, then who would take care of Thaddiaos?

That frightened her very much, indeed.

MOVING HIS HAND FROM the moonbeam, the fingernail's glow faded, and Parik knelt once again to the woman's side. She was quite beautiful, really, although she wasn't his. She could never truly be his. The Muse had only been using this vessel, taking the young woman as her own, and Parik had really lain beside his Muse.

In the beginning, many lifetimes ago, existing with the Muse had been difficult, disconcerting, even. At times, deadly; frightening; without apparent connection.

He always knew the Muse, although he couldn't search her out. The Muse found him. Parik just knew she was there—or he was—when she—or he—showed up. When she was gone—or again, when he was gone—the Muse was simply that. Gone. Parik didn't know what caused the Muse to inhabit one person or another, or to leave that person. The Muse refused to answer those questions.

Still, he knew the Muse had saved his life as often as she—or he—had tried to take it. He'd fought the Muse, too, even killed him once, although after that, Parik had learned that the Muse couldn't be killed, only the Muse's host. That was back in the early days, before his first rebirth, and he'd been fresh to his mother's curse. Assured of the Muse's death, he'd gone on a three-week drunk to celebrate.

He'd believed his companion a close friend, and he had been before the Muse had taken him. Parik wasn't as proficient at recognizing the Muse then, and when the man had suddenly changed, Parik put it off to a bad fortnight of gambling and lost coin, or perhaps there was an unsuspected change coming in the weather. What was clear was the new quality in their relationship. Verbally confrontational at first, the coarse bantering soon escalated to physical challenges, and then the threats started. No matter what Parik did, his friend wouldn't be placated.

One night on the road, after much carousing, Parik hired two wenches to join them in their room. It was when they lay together with their wenches between them, with just candlelight to see by, that his friend began to tell Parik things this friend had no way to know. The friend began to goad him, telling him of the great Mother Goddess, and how she had a son she'd attempted to take as her lover, only he'd spurned her. When Parik laughed, telling him it was just an old story, his friend had pressed him and ridiculed him, telling him in great detail what he should have allowed the Mother Goddess to do to him, and what he should have done to her in return.

By that time, Parik had heard enough. Angry, he

stood up and yelled for his friend to leave the matter alone. He had no idea what he was talking about. There was no Mother Goddess, and even if there were, she had no son. She wouldn't have taken him as her lover in any case, because he'd have cursed her to the fires that sprang from her womb in the creation of the world.

His friend leaped to his feet to look Parik full in the face. With a leering grin, he gloated. Then he spoke the words that took Parik's blood to a height he hadn't known existed.

"Remember your Muse. Look for him. Do you not know me, Parik?"

His friend had turned to his things and grabbed a long-bladed knife, and in two quick motions, sliced cleanly into the chests of both the wenches. As they gurgled their last breaths, their eyes wide with shock, his friend laughed.

"Your mother wanted you, but you give yourself to wenches like this, instead. How fitting that all the females you take should die horribly, just as the Mother Goddess did when you denied her. Would you like to be next, my friend, Parik?" The man had then brandished the blade in the candlelight, its blood-coated surface gleaming wetly.

In one smooth motion, Parik stepped to his scabbard, and his own blade was in his hand. Crouching, he parried with the man he'd once called his friend.

"Tell me how you know these things. Has a wygrog visited you? Is that why you've changed?" His old friend seemed as a weredemon that parades as a man in day and steals his essence at night, leaving unnatural knowledge in return. Parik flashed his clean blade as a warning, listening to the women as they finally quit their death throes in the room's dim light.

The friend sneered. "Has a wygrog visited you? Do you not know me, Parik? I'm your Muse, and I might kill you tonight. What's one more death, after what you did to your mother?" He twisted his hand in a gutting motion. "Like that? Do you want to die swiftly, Parik, or slowly like these wenches? I'll let you choose. With haste or ease. Make your choice. Quickly, now." He stepped onto the bed, his feet moving casually over the two women whose lives he'd so callously taken. Then he dropped in front of Parik, backing him to a corner.

"Stay back," Parik called, falling against the wall, knowing he had no retreat. "You've been my friend. I don't wish to hurt you."

"Ha! I'm not your friend. I'm your Muse, and I'm not sure I like you very much. Look at the gift you gave this girl. She spent her final evening with you, and she lies dead because of it. What manner of gift is that? At least your mother gave you life, not death. How could you be so cruel? Your Muse seems to think you don't deserve to live. Come taste my blade, and you shall enjoy the special gift you've given these wenches."

Then, with quickness unparalleled by anything Parik thought him capable of, the blade was at Parik's throat. His friend leaned hard into him, pressing his chest into Parik's, his breath warm on Parik's face.

Parik whispered, "This Muse is real, then?" He

needed to be sure.

"Real enough to kill you. Do you wish to die?"

"No." Parik's eyes narrowed, and in a sudden burst of muscles, he threw his arm around his friend.

The man's eyes grew wide, and his body went rigid for a time. Then, with a cough, blood began to foam from his mouth. The blade at Parik's throat fell away and clattered to the floor. With a moan, the man who had been Parik's closest friend fell backwards onto the floor, his eyes blank and blood running down his chin.

Parik stood for a moment with his eyes closed, holding his hand close to his side with fingers spread. Then, taking stock, he looked around the room. Leaning forward, he grabbed his friend's shoulder and rolled him over enough to pull his knife from his side, wiping it on the bed linens as he stood. He also knelt and picked up his friend's knife, knowing it as easily might have been red with his own.

Pulling his tunic on, he rifled his friend's clothing to collect whatever coin he might have, leaving it neatly stacked on his friend's chest to cover the cleanup. Then, grabbing his own things, he stepped to the door and let himself out.

That was the first time he'd killed his Muse, not realizing his friend was locked somewhere still inside. It wouldn't be the last time, though. However, the Muse never died, just moved on, and Parik had learned to do the same.

Parik touched the woman's chin as she sat in front of him, and when she looked up at him, he questioned her,

"Do you remember your name?"

"The city?" She reached and touched the wall, the coolness of the stone seeming to surprise her. "I'm in the city?"

"Your name?" Parik brushed the hair from her face. He'd done so many times in the past season, but she was no longer the person he'd bedded. The touch carried a memory for him now, but no emotional attachment. Parik had also learned to let that go as soon as the Muse was gone. There could be no emotional attachment when the woman didn't know who he was.

"Zekiye." She paused, and even in the darkness, Parik could see her smile with her returning memory. "Zekiye, daughter of Romy the sheepherder. Do you know Romy?"

Parik wished he did. Then he could send this woman home. She'd have a reason to leave, and she might be saved. The others in the city wouldn't run, though. They knew their city was safe. It was built of stone, and stone was forever. If there was danger, they could run into the walls of stone, and the walls would protect them.

Parik knew better. The walls would kill them. He lived in a city of dead men walking, and there was nothing he could do about that. Now that the power had started to gather, he couldn't even leave to draw it someplace else. It would hold him as tightly as when he'd seen himself in his vision lying in the Mother Goddess' boudoir with its green pine and cinnamon bed. The spell that he'd foreseen there could hold him no more tightly than the one that held him wherever the power started to gather, and the power had started to gather. The Muse taking flight was proof enough of that. The earthquakes were another confirmation. Most of all, though, it was what Parik felt in his inner being. His life was reaching its end. He'd soon walk anew upon the face of this earth, and there was nothing he could do about that.

3

"PARIK, YOU KNOW I love you." Once, many exist-
ences ago, she'd told him that.

"Sure, Muse. You love me. You've also tried to kill
me in more lifetimes than I care to count." He turned on
his side and stroked the Muse's face. She'd been someone else last week, an older woman who was a senator in
the city government. Parik didn't know what satisfaction
the Muse had gotten out of that, but she'd pushed some
new and quite extravagant legislation through the city's
legal system, laws that had guaranteed rights for female
citizens of the province.

"Kill you? No." She giggled, but the repeated sound

wasn't that of glee. Rather it carried the off-key chords of maliciousness greatly enjoyed. "I wanted you to see that I could, that was all. You need to appreciate how fragile life is. When you live forever, you tend to forget."

He sighed, then after a moment murmured, "A lot you would know about that."

He lay back, his eyes tracing the low ceiling. The senator had lived in better quarters, but she also had a husband and grandchildren who regularly came to visit. Parik had only found the Muse during the final weeks of that game, and now she'd become a free woman with coal black skin and the most exquisite carvings in her flesh. Even her earlobes had been stretched to allow great, brass rings to be inserted inside.

She reached long, ebony fingers to his chest.

"I could become a man, again. Would that interest you, Parik? I could become a man, and I could come to you. Would you like me to do that, come to you as a man?" She giggled once more, her playfulness clearly meant to goad.

"I wouldn't like for you to come to me as a man." He pushed her arm away. "I've had quite enough stimulation for one night, thank you, temptress. I would just as soon you leave me in peace." He sat up and repositioned himself, separating his body from hers. He turned to appraise her new look. "Black becomes you, Muse."

"It adds variety, you mean." She ran her hand up and around her neck. "It still feels like skin, though. Delicious."

"As a man, do you find your interest in men, still, or in women?" He watched her face, hoping for a moment of honesty.

She ran her fingers down his arm, pausing at his elbow. Then, taking his hand in hers, she held it gently, an unspoken question in her eyes. When no answer came, she released it and stroked his arm once again.

"I," she paused for emphasis, "always find my interest in you, dear Parik." She smiled. "Always."

He laughed. It was the cryptic answer he should have expected. "I'm hungry, Muse." When she grabbed his hand again, placing his fingers between her lips, he pushed her away. "For food. Fruit, perhaps. You haven't answered my question, though. As a man, Muse. Tell me. I must know how your desires fall."

"Why do I still chase you?" Her lips pouted, and she grabbed his hand once more, massaging the knuckles. Then, in seeming randomness, she brushed her touch over his fourth finger, finally stroking the nail there.

"I've yet another question, Muse. Answer this if you won't answer the other. What is it that fascinates you so about that finger? You seem taken with it. You worry it day and night. It aches, besides, any time you're near. Leave it alone." It was old Lamahätsu's power, or at least the remains of it. He'd not forgotten even after all these years, and he wished it left in peace.

"Pshaw." She pushed it away, reaching to his face. She trailed her fingertips around his lips, then up and over one ear. She touched her lips to his and whispered, "I find this more fascinating, but you are unwilling to work with me. So, we rest, and I must banter with you."

"Banter?" Parik leaned away. Reaching for an apple, he checked it for worms and bit into it. After swallowing, he continued, "You don't banter, woman. You avoid my question. Men or women? Tell me, and I might be yours, yet."

"Be mine? You are mine, Parik."

"Thief." He looked away, setting the apple aside and hooking his hands behind his head.

"Thief? I've taken nothing of yours. I will now, though." She leaned over, reaching across his body as she took the apple. On her return she looked to see if there was a change in his manner, one suggesting the possibility of continued amorous affections, and she sighed when she saw there was none. "I have your apple, dear Parik. I've stolen it. Now, I'm a thief."

"You've stolen your answer from me. Tell me, Muse, or I'll leave your side. You've piqued my curiosity, and I won't be denied. I must know." She rarely divulged even the slightest information about herself. It had become a game of theirs for him to try to learn something new, no matter how trivial.

"For this I will tell you." She grabbed his chin, smiling, before running her hand down his bare chest. She wrapped her long fingers sensuously around his wrist and brought his hand to her face, pressing it against her cheek. Then she squeezed it tightly until he placed his own hand over hers.

"Easy, Muse. I'm mortal, after all, even if you are not. If you injure me, I must heal. I can't simply take a new body to inhabit for a time." He let out a sigh of relief when she released her grip on him.

"You'll give yourself to me if I tell?" Her voice was petulant, as if he made a habit of promising and then not following through.

"Give? No—"

"No?" She slapped his stomach, and hard, interrupting his words. "You would tease me?"

"I can't give more." He laughed, although the sound was hardly that of amusement. "Our ardent endeavors throughout the night have been pleasurable but exhausting. Besides, the day has already begun." He glanced at the wooden slats forming the walls. The wood was placed with gaps between to facilitate circulation, and already the noise of the awakening city came through.

"What should I care for the morning?" She pursed her lips petulantly, but her eyes had gone soft.

"It will be hot during the day, and morning is here."

She laughed. "Have it your way, Parik. When I'm a man, I'm drawn by manly desires, and I long for women. Yet, even when I'm a man, I remember being a woman. So, while I'm a man, I still desire you."

He looked at her for a time, placing in his mind what she'd described. "Yet, you never . . ." He paused and looked at the ceiling, daring her to fill in his unspoken response. He grinned before glancing to her face once again.

"I never what, dear Parik?"

"You've never come to me as a man. Instead, you always try to kill me when you are a man."

Her laughter tinkled. "Jealously, dear Parik. If I came to you as a man, you would rebuff me—"

"I would." The words came as a sharp interruption.

"You agree much too quickly, my lovely man." She pouted, grabbing his hand once again and worrying his fingernail. "When I'm male, I can't come to you, and I'm insanely jealous of those who can. I want no one to have you if I can't, and since I can't kill all the women in the world, it's much easier to kill you."

Parik snorted as he let out a full-bellied laugh at her reply. "You've stabbed me, put poison in my food, and pushed me off sailing ships because I enjoyed other women. How do you know I'll survive? I do remember old Lamahätsu's curse even after all these seasons. My Muse will live only if I do. Do you not know that, Muse?"

She was quiet for a moment, letting her fingers dance along his thighs. Then, she smiled brightly, her teeth white against the blackness of her skin.

"You've never died, no matter what I've done to you. I've saved you each time."

"Saved me?" Parik was incredulous. "I remember the people who saved me, Muse. The pig keeper's daughter, or a lonely serving woman. Once, even a mer-woman pulled me from the sea and set me on dry land. You've never saved me, Muse." He laughed. "Those are the women I truly love. They rescue me out of the good-ness of their hearts, not because some ancient goddess pointed them my way. I know you, Muse, and you would never do that for me. You take and take, but you never give. Your one redeeming quality is consistency. You're always here with me, whether trying to kill me or woo me. One way or the other, I know you'll be at my side."

She reached for his hand, stroking his arm. Her lips, full and sensuous, brushed his neck. "I told you what you wanted. May I now?"

He laughed. "Not so fast, Muse. As a woman, what are your interests?"

"Parik," she chuckled softly. "As I woman, I always have you."

This time she didn't ask when she slid next to him, and it did seem that, after all, he could develop an interest in her desired activities once again. It was later when he was asleep that she whispered the rest of her words to him. "I am the pig keeper's daughter and the lonely serving woman, Parik. I'm even the merwoman who saved you from the sea. Only when you're at death's door do you fail to see me for who I am. Only then do you love me because I'm a woman. Only then are you truly mine."

She drew her jet-black body next to his, and she draped herself over his sleeping form. Together they lay silently in the heat that already ran rampant, and it wasn't even fully morning. Soon, all was still as bars of sunlight traced the low-ceilinged room, the Muse joining Parik in sleep. Later was time enough to rise, but for now, rest was needed.

A SMALL NOSE SNIFFED along the bottom of a wall,

and deep within the new layers of dust lingered the familiar smells that told the rat where to go. The stones along the city street were well-known, and at each crack or unmortared joint, the small animal hesitated, taking in new information, if any was available, learning the latest signals for the path it traveled daily.

The rat would have considered itself very lucky, indeed, if it only knew what luck was, for it had two very consistent food sources. At one location, it always received a morsel of very dry bread, and at the other, the more generous of the two, it could count on a small pile of grain. It preferred the first, because the only price it had to pay was to allow the girl to stroke its fur and occasionally run her hand over its poor excuse for a leg. At the more generous dining location, the man who fed it continually attempted to get into its poor little rat brain.

However, the rat was content to limp along with its irregular little tapping pattern, only dimly aware that there was a better life out there that rats with four good legs were permitted to live. The three-legged rat had little idea of that, and it scurried along, content for the most part in its rendition of a successful rat's unchanging days.

"ZEKIYE, DAUGHTER OF ROMY the sheepherder, please come lie down. The night is still deep, and daylight won't come for many measures of time. You must sleep." Parik motioned to her, his movements clear in the brightening moonlight. "You may have the mat. I won't molest you there."

He needed his rest. He could save no one in what was building, but he could help a few, help them to face the coming devastation with as much serenity as any dying person could possibly know.

"Zekiye," he repeated. "The mat." She shook her head from side to side. "I can leave the room if you wish." He'd get no sleep that way, but then he'd get no sleep if she sat huddled in the corner, either. At least one of them would be able to rest.

He saw her stand in the dimness of the room, and satisfied, he made to move toward the door. Before he could open it, she called to him.

"Stay. If you don't mind. Please." Her voice was a near-whisper, almost as if she were afraid she'd be over-heard. "I'm frightened alone. I feel I can trust you. Sit with me."

"If you wish." He chuckled ruefully. If she could truly trust him, he'd have rebuffed the Muse so she would have been freed. However, Parik knew better than that. The Muse more likely would have taken the girl to a brothel and offered her freely to any comers. It had been kinder to the girl to take her in and give the Muse her way. At least this way, he knew she'd been treated with tender hands.

"You must sit with me," the girl pleaded.

Moving to her side, Parik was surprised to feel her against his leg, and he realized she was resting her head in his lap. He smiled. The Muse had done just that many times, rested her head this way. There must be some-thing of the person that came through even as the Muse had possession, either that or something of the Muse lingered after she left her host. However, this girl was free. He knew of few that the Muse had taken twice. Come the morning, if the city existed that long—and Parik felt it was far too soon for it to fall—he'd see if the girl could be convinced to make her way back to her home.

"I remember I was to be married."

The voice interrupted his thoughts, and Parik looked down, surprised. "Married?" He'd never thought of that. The bodies the Muse inhabited were just that, bodies that showed up and were there until the Muse ventured on.

"I remember a long white dress, one with openwork along the sleeves. My mother let me try it on, and I was so excited. I ran to my friend's house to show it off."

"What happened, then?" Parik remembered the dress. It had been torn and used to stop the bleeding when the girl's time had come. Somehow, that saddened him. To him, it had been just a white dress. To this girl, it was her future, probably one hand-stitched by a caring parent.

"I don't know." She shifted on his lap, putting her hand under her head. "The season doesn't feel right, though. Time has passed. My hair is longer." Parik didn't say anything. "Have we been friends all this time?" Her meaning was quite clear. *More than friends* drifted through her whispered question. She tilted her head to look up at him, moving against his leg.

At her innocent touch, he felt the beginnings of desire, forcing it from his thoughts. He shifted his position, certain she must be able to tell, but she gave no indication she was aware of his discomfort.

"You can tell me, if we have," she implored. "My great-great gran was taken by the goddess once. She was no more than the daughter of a pig keeper, but she woke up in the arms of a man who said she pulled him from a deep ravine and nursed him back to health. My great-great gran didn't remember a bit of it, but everyone around her said it was true. That's how my great gran was born, and she never had another father."

In that moment, an overwhelming ache overtook Parik. He did remember the daughter of the pig keeper and her sudden question when she awoke. He'd thought it just disorientation. They had been together for weeks, already, when she questioned him. She was reassured when her family supported his story, but he had no idea she'd become with child. He should have known, he guessed. That meant this girl was his child, or, to be more accurate, the distant daughter of his child. He was her father—after a fashion—and if she hadn't told him this, he never would have known.

She gushed, her voice suddenly breathless with giddiness, "I know it's true, now, about the goddess. The goddess has taken me, and I've been with a great man. Tell me so before I return to my people. They'll understand."

He stroked her face without moving more than his hand. "When you arrive, will your man take you back? Will he marry the woman whom the goddess allowed to be with another man?"

"I don't care," she said with sudden desperation in her voice. "If you don't tell me it's so, my people will think it anyway, and if I return with a child, they'll remember my old great-great gran. My child will be revered. Please." She grabbed his hand, the one with the fingernail that glowed, and she stroked it, her eyes drawn to it in the moonlight.

"Why did you do that?" It didn't ache with her touch as it had the past season and a month. His breath caught with the intenseness of his sudden need.

"What? I did nothing except take your hand."

"My fingernail. Why did you stroke it?" His blood beat fast, but he had to know this thing.

"It glowed in the light. I was fascinated. You, I think, have been blessed by the goddess. If I'm blessed with a child, I'll call him after you, and all will know he's blessed of the goddess. What shall I call him when he's born?"

"I'm no one, and you are far from the truth to think I've been blessed by the goddess."

"No One's Son." Her voice tinkled with laughter, even as the muskiness of the night laced her words. "What a name that would be! You mustn't force me to call my child No One's Son. He'd be horrified." She slid closer. "What's your real name?"

"I'm known as Parik."

Her laugher was high and melodious. "Parikson. Parik, the son of Parik." She brought his fourth finger to her lips, whispering her words, "Blessed by the great Goddess of Life, from whom life flows eternally. Parikson, the son of one who is the most favored of the goddess."

Parik's thoughts were far different. Cursed by the goddess, he thought. Not blessed, Zekiye. No, not blessed at all.

4

CHIARINA OPENED HER EYES to rays of light filtering through new chinks in the wall. Each beam lighted uncounted motes of dust that still hovered in the air. It was clear the detritus from the stones that had shaken during the night had yet to completely settle. The lack of ventilation in the close room didn't help, either. Perhaps the heat of the day would pull the dust up and out of the open window slits at the top of the walls.

She touched her brother's face to wipe a layer of dust away, only to have him shift and cough at her touch.

A scrambling sound caught her attention, and Chiarina looked to see a slender tail twitch as it disappeared through a small crack where two stones didn't quite meet. It was the most she'd ever seen of the elusive, three-legged creature, and it pleased her immensely to have caught sight of it. The dust it stirred in its passing pleased her less. It was all over the room, and she'd have to remove it before Thaddiaos could be allowed to play. It would make his cough worse.

Thaddiaos coughed again, harder. Then again and again. Chiarina patted his thin back, knowing she couldn't go look for herbs to ease this for him, and with no coins in her bowl, she had no money to buy him food. The coughing would have to be endured, but that didn't mean she wouldn't hurt for him each time his body was wracked by the fist inside his belly.

"Hungry, Chini." The small voice whispered the day's most immediate concern into her ear. "Please, Chini. Will there be food today?"

"Maybe, little brother." She patted his back again, then began to rub the flat of her palm down his side, aware how each of his ribs was sharp beneath his skin. She tried to show him a bright smile, but she couldn't hold it. So, she teased with him. "I'll try to look especially pitiful, today. How is that, little Thaddiaos? Perhaps someone will feel very sorry for me and toss two coins into my bowl. We could eat two days on two coins," meaning Thaddiaos could eat two days, "and you'd no longer be hungry."

"How, Chini? How will you be especially pitiful? Will you cry, and with real tears, too?" He grinned, distracted from his hunger. From the coughing, as well. He'd never seen his sister cry, except one time when a very rich woman came by. Then she'd cried. His sister had winked at him through the door and thrown sand into her own eyes. They had immediately reddened as she gasped with the sudden sting, and tears had flowed quite freely, indeed. She'd gotten three coins from the woman, and she and her brother had feasted that night. "Will you cry for a rich woman, Chini?"

She chuckled and felt her leg twinge. When Thaddiaos shifted against her, the pain intensified, and she squeezed him tightly to make him lie still.

"Too tight, Chini. Let go!" Thaddiaos' words hissed at her in his little boy voice, but it was a weak hiss, and he couldn't fight her. The coughing had taken too much from him, that and the hunger.

"Be still, Thaddiaos." Her words were at the edge of sharpness, and he relaxed against her. She let her eyes flick along the stones that ran around the ceiling of the room, holding up the massive wooden beams that supported the stone ceiling, and she found the one she remembered from yesterday. Two rows and three more stones meant the goddess would deign to visit today. It was always the count of two rows, and after three more stones, the pain would start. No one would come near to put coins in her bowl. She'd counted the stones yesterday, and yet the hunger and the shaking of the stones had made her forget. She couldn't beg today, and yet she must, or she and Thaddiaos would be hungry again during the night.

As tears began to leak from her eyes, she had another thought that caused her even deeper pain. It was unreasonable, she knew, but it was there, nonetheless. She had no more crumbs for her three-legged friend, and if she had no food to give the animal, she was afraid it wouldn't return. She couldn't lose the friendship of one that understood what she lived every day, even though that one was only a rat. She'd be too lonely to live if she did.

PARIK TENDERLY WIPED GRAINS of dust from underneath Zekiye's sleeping eyelashes. He stoked her flat stomach, knowing what he'd given her during the night.

She would bear a son.

When the Muse took a woman, the one she possessed never became with child unless the Muse wished it. However, Parik had a power of his own, the one small power gifted from his mother's fingernail. It had been from her healing hand, and it enabled him to sense what needed to be healed within a person. If the person were willing, if the person desired it, then the touch of Parik's hand could bring healing to the essence inside of the person. That was his gift, the one he'd stolen from old Lamahätsu before she'd cursed him with immortality— and then cursed him also with his Muse. That was the gift he could share with the people around him.

Zekiye had wanted this, wanted it with all her heart. A boy child. It was growing in her flat belly even as she lay beside him, and he smiled at the idea the child would be called Parikson, the son of the son of the Goddess of Life. Poor Zekiye had no idea how true that was.

One thing had surprised him, though. She'd praised the old goddess. He hadn't thought his mother to be remembered anywhere after all this time. No one in the city recognized the truly old names: Ageless Five-Armed Goddess; the Womb of Creation; the Bringer of Life. More forgotten names were the Giver of Death and the Essence Eater. No, those names had faded with the dawn of creation.

Zekiye had known, though. Her people, pig keepers and sheepherders that they were, had somehow kept the old ways alive, and she'd known of the old goddess, Lamahätsu.

Hearing noises outside, Parik glanced up at the window slits. Shafts of light filtered through, falling on the opposite wall, and with that, he knew the day was early, yet. He hoped it would remain cool for Zekiye's sake, but he also hoped she was gone soon. This room would exist for a short time more, but it would fall, taking all within it when it did.

He stood, reaching for his vestments. He moved his blade aside and pulled his loincloth free, wrapping it around his waist and underneath his legs, tucking it in at the front. Then he slipped his leathers over his head, pulling his hair from inside. With a practiced motion, he rolled his long locks into a tail and dropped them into his catch sack, tying it up neatly at the base of his neck. He let it fall at his back before pressing the selvage edge of a cloth to his forehead and flipping it over his head.

Tucking it behind his ears, he moved toward the doorway, stopping to slip his feet into rope-topped sandals. Then, with a sure motion, he belted his blade to his side.

He paused before swinging the door wide. He'd oiled the hinges when he and the Muse had started using these rooms. However, with the shifting of the stones, he half expected it to wake the sleeping woman. He missed the old hinges of wood that simply rested in the stone. They wore more quickly, but they never needed oil, and they never cried their pain to wake everyone in the room.

Pulling the wooden door slowly, he was relieved to hear its silence. He was less relieved to find the stone lintel had shifted enough to grab the corner of the door, forcing him to yank it hard past the thick opening.

Outside, the sun was in full bloom, and the morning was already as warm as any in the city had ever been.

A wizened old man pulled a two-wheeled cart up the incline of the main street, its wheels clattering against stone paving that was freshly uneven. When the cart bounced hard on its wooden rims, a leafy vegetable fell to the pavement and skittered away to the curb. Cursing, the old man turned the cart sideways and dropped the pulling poles he'd been holding, hurrying in his hobbling way to grab the vegetable before it fell in the gutter.

Parik grinned. If the water flowing there was clean, the old man could put the vegetable back on the cart, even if it landed inside the gutter. If the water was filled with waste, he dared not retrieve the vegetable. If anyone was watching and happened to see him selling in the market, the quality of his harvest would be in doubt, and people wouldn't pay the best prices.

Parik stepped to the vegetable and stopped its roll with his foot, waiting patiently until the old man made his way to retrieve it.

"Thank you, good sir." The seller of vegetables bobbed his head repeatedly, holding up his rescued vegetable. "You are kind to an old man. Would you like a tomato from my cart? A lemon?" His voice strengthened in forced excitement. "I have four lemons, picked just this morning. Take one." He didn't offer the leafy vegetable, though, pulling it up under his arm as he stood.

When Parik didn't immediately respond, the vegetable seller paused and studied the tall man's face. He knelt and held the leafy vegetable up to the one who had rescued it. With a quaver in his voice, he murmured, "It's yours, if you wish it, the gods be praised."

Parik reached for the vegetable, and he hefted it in his hand. "The gods don't deserve your praise, my good vegetable seller. This one will bring a high price in the market. Keep it." He tossed it back at the man and smiled to see him scramble to catch it before it fell to the ground.

"A lemon, then? You'll take a lemon? Or a tomato?" The man pulled the leafy vegetable to himself again, clutching it tightly.

Parik paused in thought, and then he reached to the man and touched the vegetable. "How much will this bring at the market? Four coins?"

The man smiled, his pride showing through. "More.

Five, maybe six or more." Then he looked up at Parik, and he let a pretense of sadness fall across his face. "Or three, perhaps. People always look for bargains. They never wish to pay the true value. Two, maybe." He rubbed his hand lovingly over the leafy surface.

Parik laughed. "Two, then. This prized vegetable of yours will bring two coins, you say."

"Prized?" The man acted shocked at the word. "It's only a poor plant, and no one will want it."

"Prized." Parik chuckled. He knew it to be certain. He'd seen the wagon. This one item was clearly the best of his crop. "But worthless if it had fallen in the gutter. With the smell of the sewers on it, no one would have purchased it. You're lucky I was here to save it."

"Lucky," the man murmured. "Yes, so very lucky."

Parik motioned for the man to stand. "A lemon." The man's expression eased. "A lemon, you offered. Will it sell for one coin?"

"Or two," the man exclaimed. "The lemon is a very good choice." He made to stand, to move toward the cart.

"No," Parik called to him. "Sell your lemon. I wish you to give the coins away."

"Away?" The old man appeared puzzled.

"Away." Parik looked at him, reading his eyes. "There's a girl, a crippled beggar girl who lives up this street." He pointed beside his rooms at a series of steps that climbed one of the city's many slopes. "I see her from time to time. I'll know. Two coins. For two coins, your vegetable is yours." Parik winked, but the rest of his face was stern. "Fourth room to the left. She'll tell me."

The old man's face fell. "Two coins to the girl. I'll see her today when the market is closed." He stood. "Fourth room, you say?"

Parik nodded at him. If this seller lived far from town, he might survive. If not, the coins he received or didn't receive today were of little importance. It was vital, however, that the girl eat. Her brother, too. She didn't think Parik knew, but there had been no mistaking the protectiveness in the girl's manner. There was a brother, and today, the two of them must eat. With the seller's coins, they would, and probably for more than one day. That might be as long as they needed to worry about, and if the time was longer, Parik would face that when the moment came.

At that instant, he felt his stomach turn. This would be a strong shaking. He could feel the strong ones before they hit, and they were always strong when his rebirth was near. He braced himself against the door and looked at the seller in the street.

"Guard your cart, old man. The ground is about to shake." When the man didn't move, he growled, "Now!"

The man did move, faster once the stones underneath his feet began to shift. It was bad, too. Dust flew from between the stones of the city's walls, and somewhere off in the distance, a scream could be heard as something heavy shifted loose and fell loudly to the ground. Then, after a moment, the shaking stopped. The old man looked at Parik with fear in his eyes.

"You're the son of a god. You even know the ground, when it will shake. Four coins. I'll bring the girl four coins." He grabbed his robes and settled his crops safely onto his cart, grabbing the pulling poles with his arms.

"Two will suffice," Parik called to him, suddenly tired. He was the son of a goddess, not a god, and that hadn't helped his life. It was nothing to be proud of, nothing at all.

"Four," the man called back over his shoulder. "I'll bring her four. Four coins for the son of a god."

Parik sighed. The shaking had been bad, and when he felt it in his gut before it even happened, he knew the power that was gathering was drawing to him quickly. Two coins would be enough. The girl wouldn't live longer than that. This city wouldn't live longer than that. Parik would, though. He would live forever. His Muse would see that he didn't die, although that wasn't the blessing most men would seem to think.

Parik put aside his concerns. The crippled girl and her brother would eat today, the sun was shining, and the city hadn't fallen around its inhabitants' ears just yet. He stepped from the stoop, and as he did so, he felt a twinge in his back. The gathering power aged him quickly.

Curse you, Lamahätsu. Curse you to your own fiery hell forever and ever.

He knew his words were empty. She'd created the hells of this world, and she'd probably enjoy spending time there just fine, indeed. He was the one who was cursed, and there was nothing to be done about that.

5

THE BREATHING IN HER EAR was very shallow, and that concerned Chiarina. Little Thaddiaos had fallen back asleep, but he hadn't eaten in two days. His skin was also very hot. Sometimes she thought it would be better if he never woke, especially on days like this one, days where she hurt too much to beg, days where he hurt too much to stay awake. She shifted him to her side, biting her tongue at the pain that shot through her body.

"Sorry, small brother. You must rest alone for a time. The goddess calls to me." Has cursed me, she thought, but that was something she couldn't say aloud. She'd been cursed, though, with more than her leg: this blessing of the goddess; her brother's illness; even her parents' deaths. Yes, her parents' deaths had been a curse, although at the time she hadn't been so sure. They had been ill for so long, and before that, they had been ashamed of her, refusing to gift her with a last name. Only when they could no longer care for themselves had they allowed her to crawl across the floor of their hovel to minister to them. Only then, when all she'd wanted her entire life had been for them to approve of her. Still, even as they lay dying, they spat their vile words at her, that she should have died at birth, was an abomination, and the gods would curse this city because of her.

She was glad when they were finally gone. She then had peace, and she also had her brother, taking his surname for her own. It was comforting to whisper the words Chiarina Egidius-Lucanus in the depths of the night, even though no one else could hear.

Now, though, she knew her life was even worse. She couldn't take care of her brother, couldn't provide for him properly, and now he had her parents' cough, the cough that rarely ended in anything but death. Chiarina tried to push the knowledge of it away, but she was so frightened. She wanted to place her head on her knees and cry until the nights went away, and her parents, as cruel as they had been, were returned to her. She couldn't even do that with her withered leg. She couldn't pull it up to her chest. Her arms wouldn't wrap around it.

Now she had to stop the goddess' gift. If the pain weren't bad today, she might still be able to sit beside her door and rattle her bowl when people walked by on the wide street below. A few might step to her to drop in a coin, or maybe just a half coin. As little as a quarter coin would do. That might be enough to buy a dry piece of old bread, something to fill Thaddiaos' belly, something to ease the cough.

As she tore a piece of rag to press against the pain, she felt the rattle of the stones. The new shaking was hard, and it dislodged a small stone from high in the wall, sending it crashing to the floor near Thaddiaos' head. He didn't stir. He was too hungry and weak to notice, she guessed. When the movement finally stopped, she knew it had been bad this time, and long. Too long, and worse than before.

With her hand still pressed to the rag, forcing the pain away, she looked at the new dust floating down around her. A white film had already begun to coat her brother's skin and hair, and looking closely, there were more spaces in the stones than ever before where light could be seen forcing its way in. That unnerved her. Would the entire city fall around her ears? She'd always thought the stone buildings to be forever, and now she could no longer be sure.

At least little Thaddiaos was resting, and she didn't have to calm his fears. He needed this time to sleep. As unlike him as it was to remain still once the sun was up, she wasn't sorry to see it this time. He needed his sleep more than he could know.

THE MUSE SHIFTED IN HER bed, puzzled. The darkness around her smelled wrong. Parik had a smell, and it was one she always recognized, no matter how many lives they chased each other through. It felt wrong, too. Between her legs it felt wrong.

Then there was her inner sense of Parik. It was the fingernail. That was how she tracked him, although he didn't know. It was one of her secrets, one that she kept well hidden. At the moment, she couldn't sense the fingernail.

Without warning, the walls began to shake, and there was a loud crash nearby, with someone screaming in terror. Then, hands grabbed onto her, and a panicked voice called, "Kaius, protect me."

It was a woman's voice, and in that moment, the Muse knew. It was Parik's power that was shaking the stones. This wrongness was Parik, the drawing of the power, and it had ejected her from the woman's body she'd been in. It had thrown her—how far she didn't know—and she'd found refuge in this new body. With the stones around her still moving, she must have remained in the city, though. She felt between her legs, and she confirmed what she suspected. This was a man's body, someone, if she could trust the voice that called to her, by the name of Kaius.

"Parik!" The Muse screamed the words. "You could have warned me!" The admonition came out deep and raspy. "Keep away from that woman, Parik! She's no longer who you think she is!"

"Kaius?" The woman at the Muse's side drew back, suddenly oblivious to the dust filtering down between them. "Who's this Parik? Have you been fighting again,

Kaius?" She pushed on his arm, obviously rehashing an old disagreement. Then, as the shaking stopped, silence filled the small room, and the woman threw her arms back around the Muse.

"Kaius, hold me now. I need you. You were filled with wine last night, and you pushed me away. Now we might die, and I want to feel your arms around me. Please, Kaius. I'm so frightened. I need you."

The Muse was momentarily disgusted at the thought of being with this woman. He'd just been female and had longed for Parik's arms. However, this was a man's body, and it was designed to hold a woman. Feeling a response from his loins, one he couldn't help, he was surprised at how quickly the unknown man's body reacted to the woman's touch.

The Muse resigned himself to the inescapable physiological responses coursing through this new body. He couldn't fight the sensations any more than he could shift to another host again now that Parik's power had begun to draw itself together for his rebirth.

He reached his arms to her.

If he were far enough from Parik, he might remain in this body for a time, possibly until the city was destroyed and Parik reborn. If not, with each new shaking, the Muse would be forced to shift to another person, never knowing just where he might land. Rarely was he able to fight it, and never if he was too close to Parik.

"Your name?" The Muse questioned the woman he held in his arms.

"My name?" His companion wrapped her fingers

around the side of his neck. "Kaius, you know my name. Don't be silly."

In a sudden burst of determination, he reached to her, pushing his fingers into the woman's hair, grabbing it hard on both sides of her head, and forcing her to look at him.

"Your name, woman. I wouldn't ask if I didn't want to know."

"Rena." Her eyes flicked back and forth as she peered intently into each of his in turn. When he didn't respond, she pushed at his chest. "Kaius, it's me, Rena Gracchus. What's with you? Why are you asking these questions? I'm frightened, Kaius. The shaking. Now this. It's you, is it not, Kaius? Please say it is."

"Rena." He grinned, relaxing, reaching to brush her on the neck, the act one of supposed affection. "If I were not Kaius, who would I be, sweet Rena?"

"A wygrog, or maybe a weltie. Are you a weltie, Kaius?" Shape shifters were known to visit unwary women at night.

He laughed softly. "Of course I'm not a weltie. I'm Kaius, and I'm here with you to protect you."

"Then why did you grab me that way? You never do that."

"Because I felt it necessary. Can you understand that?" He chuckled into her ear.

"It's not like you."

"Maybe I've changed. Do you like the new me?" The Muse licked the outside of her ear as he began to hum a very old tune that had once been sung around countless campfires long before this city was built, and this was a very old city, indeed.

"I think so," she murmured. "I like that tune. Do I know it from somewhere?" She finally relaxed, and she began to move with him.

He tried to answer her, but he found the effort very distracting. "I don't think. That is possible. Sweet. Re-na."

Then the Muse could say no more. He held her in his arms, experiencing what being a man was about. Nothing else mattered, not even the stones that had shaken around them, telling them the city was about to fall.

THE RAT SNIFFED. It could tell the man had walked nearby. His scent was in the small particles of odor that he left spread along the street. It was in the air. It was where he'd stepped. It was in everything the rat sensed.

The big man hadn't walked up the series of steps towards the rat's other food source. Although the man gave better food, the girl asked less of the rat. Now the rat was out in the daylight, and it didn't like that. The daylight was dangerous. There were no hiding places in the light, and the rat always felt the need to hide.

It was the shaking that had drawn it out—that and the man. The shaking was the man. The rat knew that, could tell it with every fiber of its being. The shaking would follow the man, and while the rat didn't know why that drew it to the man, the drawing was there, nonetheless. The small creature simply had to follow him, had to sniff out the man's pheromones, be where he was. That was all the rat knew.

After all, the small furred creature was just a rat, and rats couldn't reason out the intricacies of the gods . . . or of the goddesses . . . or of their children. A rat could only do exactly what its senses told it to do.

Follow the man.

So the rat did.

DEEP WITHIN THE EARTH'S crust, forces gathered, drawing together to bring new life to Parik.

They offered immortality, of a sort.

For those who walked the face of the spinning orb that long ago had been belched from Lamahätsu's loins, immortality wasn't in the natural order of things. Many other things were, just not immortality.

Creation fell into the natural order of things. So did death. Somewhere in the middle there came life. Procreation, first. Life, afterwards. Then, the finality of death. For mortals, immortality fell into a completely different spectrum, not part of the pattern.

The gods and goddesses could supersede this pattern—for a time—and that was in the natural order of things. If people knew them—or of them—the great powers that ruled over the world were just that: great. However, when the gods and goddesses faded from racial memory, so did the power they wielded upon the face of the earth and upon the people who inhabited it. They never actually died, though. Gods couldn't die. Neither could goddesses. They just sort of faded into the background, advisors of a sort for the new generation of those who would wield power over the face of the earth.

Immortality wasn't normal, though, not human immortality, anyway. Even what the gods and goddesses had wasn't really immortality, not in the aspect of living forever. It was more like shelf life. They had a very long shelf life, but eventually being packaged and put away on a shelf was no life. The fun in living was being in with the action, and only the gods and goddesses that were currently in vogue were "in on the action," so to speak.

Parik wasn't immortal, not in the strictest sense. His body lasted no longer than that of a normal human, but his mind and his essence continued on, thanks to one very defiant Goddess of Life, otherwise known as Lamahätsu. He simply got a new body every fifty, seventy, or a hundred seasons.

He didn't die, either. The Muse took care of that. She refused to let him die. She might be flooded with desire to kill him when he loved other women, but if he died, she died, so he had to be kept alive. It was a balancing act she strove to perfect, and sometimes it almost drove her mad.

Or perhaps she was mad already.

Parik was ending a very long run in this particular life. He never contracted illnesses, and he wasn't prone to any of the symptoms of old age that normal humans had to face. After all, he fell in the direct lineage of a very powerful goddess. His rebirths hadn't hurt him any, either. Each one had fine-tuned his physiology until he was nearly perfect, superhuman, in fact. However, once the power began to attach itself to his essence, age came upon him all at once. It was painful, devastating, and totally humiliating.

Far below the city, unseen to mortal eyes, the process had begun. It was quite amazing. Water was needed. Yes, water had to gather, and from wherever it was, too. It had to collect right where Parik was. Minerals, also. Manganese. Iron. Gold. Many, many more, in addition, no matter whether they were naturally found in that location or not. Parik had to have them. Calcium, for sure. Parik had to have new bones and teeth. Electricity. Lots of electricity was needed. Human bodies run on electricity, and a very big jolt was needed to bring about life.

The final ingredient was heat, heat from the bowels of the earth. Volcanic heat. Magma. Magma that creates steam that creates pressure that creates earthquakes that create destruction that creates death. Lots of death. Lots of death and one renewed life.

Parik's.

Parik would live, and everyone else would die. The Muse would guide him, but when the power began to draw together, even the Muse was at the mercy of the power. No one was safe.

Immortality wasn't in the natural order of things.

6

A GREAT STONE HAD fallen in the street, and Parik stepped around it. He saw blood on the side, telling that someone had died. If this were the only one, it was only the first of many. There'd be scores, hundreds of scores more.

"Hey, you, man! Turn this way!"

Parik twisted to his inquisitor, surprised to see a visage that looked much like his own. A short blade hanging at the stranger's waist flashed in the sun. The man strode purposefully up to him, and with a grin on his face, he clasped him on the shoulder.

"I know your features as if they're mine!" The man

laughed and pointed to the stone. "This is quite a city, you must say. One day it's as stable as a rock, and the next it's shaking around our ears. Have you ever seen such a thing? Just moments ago, a man died right by where you're standing. I'm glad to be alive, I say. See that blood? I was nearly caught under that stone. How unlucky is that?"

"I don't think luck has much to do with the man's death." Or with all the others that would occur as the city continued to collapse with each shaking. Weak, Parik reached a hand to the stone for support.

"If not luck, then it must be the will of the gods. You would think the man who died forgot to say his prayers this morning. Do you pray, my man?" He tugged on Parik's arm, pulling him away from the stone. "I say, man, do you pray?"

"Pray?" Parik stumbled as he released the stone, his breath momentarily wrenched from him. The draining of his vitality always came as a shock each time the shaking happened. He was dismayed at how weakened he felt and the strength the gathering power had already pulled from him.

"It doesn't matter. You don't need to answer. I see you are as amazed as I am, and your words have fled you. The tavern, just there. Come in and tell me your story. I'll share my best brew with you, and we'll celebrate together." The strange man who looked so much like Parik cocked his head sideways to indicate a building just to the side.

It was with amusement that Parik noted the man was

quite as tall as he was, and broad shouldered, too, even carrying Parik's own flashing green eyes. The Muse had been generous with one of her previous hosts, it would seem, leaving the gift of a child.

"The tavern is mine, by the way. It was my father's by way of my mother, but that's another story in itself. You are my other self, and I must know about you. We surely have a connection, you and I, and I wish to learn it." The man threw an arm around Parik's shoulders, pulling him the direction of the tavern, laughing as he helped him along.

"My story? I have no story." Stumbling on a loose stone, Parik steadied himself. He had inner reservoirs he could still pull from, he knew. It simply took time to adjust.

"Bah! All men have a story. Some are just told better than others. You, I can tell, have much wisdom. I see it in your eyes. Your skin shows you to be no more than an elder brother's age. Your eyes, though. There you are the age of the earth. Your hair I cannot see." He reached to his own neck and pulled forward a catch sack much like Parik's, only his was of exotic leather. "Zebra, from Africa. I lived there once, was born there."

"Africa?" That caught Parik's attention. In this very lifetime he'd been with the Muse in Africa, but it had been many seasons ago. He'd run from her that time, smothered by her, and she'd shown up yet again, China, he remembered, finding him by some method he never intrigued. However, no one would mistake this man for a free black man. He no more stood out in this city than

Parik, himself. This man's skin was somewhat darker than Parik's olive, but it wasn't African dark.

The man released his catch sack, pulling it from his hair, and it uncurled into a thick mane of black, tumbling around his shoulders. In that motion, Parik truly saw himself. His hair was that exactly.

The man saw his expression and grabbed Parik's forearm, speaking intimately. "I see it in your eyes. You know my hair. It's familiar to you. I've met other brothers who are me, or as nearly as they can be, but you most of all. Will you expose your hair for me to see, for proof?"

Parik slapped his hand on the shoulder of the one holding his forearm. "Your mother. Was she taken by the goddess?" He remembered the Muse, still, from their time in Africa. She'd taken a princess with cinnamon skin, one most beautiful. The Muse liked that, to take beautiful women. She hated the lack of choice when Parik's impending rebirth forced her into a body she didn't wish to claim, unable to taste the person's experiences and move on. That time she'd chosen well, eventually bringing Parik into the royal household.

The man laughed. "Or crazy. I say crazy. You say taken by the goddess, whichever divine witch you may refer to, and it's all the same. What else do you know of my mother?"

Parik took a deep breath. "A princess of some great beauty, one of long limbs and a striking face, with skin the color of cinnamon ale. Her lips bore hoops of gold, and her flesh was patterned with many designs." Parik remembered many African women with the gold hoops and patterned flesh. The Muse had taken several such females, but none so beautiful as the princess. "Am I close?"

"She's your mother, too?" The tall man with the green eyes stepped to a counter and grabbed an earthenware mug. "We must share ale. I'm Umaru Afolabi Yaradua, and we are brothers." Umaru placed the jug under a wooden spigot, and with a twist of his hand, allowed a frothy liquid to fill the mug. He handed it to Parik.

"Not brothers." Parik looked at the mug Umaru held without reaching for it.

"You refuse my ale?" Umaru frowned. "Show me your hair, then. I refuse to believe we're not brothers. Each one of me I've found has proven to be a brother, even to the mole we all carry on our buttocks." He touched the side of his tunic where his own mole was discretely covered and glanced at Parik, letting a deep chuckle escape his chest.

"So," Parik began, "you and your brothers are familiar in some intimate way, to know this proof?" He kept a very serious look on his face, but he winked.

"Ahh!" Umaru caught the gibe immediately, and he slammed the mug on the counter, sloshing the contents over the top and onto his hand. Wiping his fingers on his tunic, he glared at Parik. "How can you suggest that I'm intimate with my brothers, after I've invited you into my establishment? No man has ever reached inside my tunic, and no man ever will. Curse the goddess who might suggest such a thing." He returned Parik's wink. "Now, I might see the mole on another man's buttock when we're in the public baths. That I might do, indeed." He laughed again, picking up the mug and handing it to Parik once more.

Parik smiled at last. "You don't need to see my hair. It's the same as yours. Your mother was mine for a time, and she wasn't crazy."

"No?" Umaru roared his rebuttal. "I have the scars to prove she was. She beat me to keep me from the village girls, and I chased them anyway. She never did learn."

"Does she still live?" It had been the Muse Parik had taken for a lover, but his memories of this man's mother were still strong in his mind. Not only had her skin been the creamy brown of cinnamon ale, it had tasted as spicy. He hadn't been aware the Muse had allowed a child to be conceived, though.

Umaru's face dropped. "I don't know. A raid. Many were taken. I wasn't there. I've always hoped she was treated gently." Then his face quickly brightened. "But that was over a handful of seasons ago, and I'm here now."

"Your mother, though." Parik pressed him. "You said this place came to you through your father by your mother. What did you mean?" He reached and took the mug.

"As I said, it's another story, but, as you ask, I'll tell it now." He pulled out another mug, filling it with ale for himself. "My mother may have been crazy, but she wasn't celibate. Once I was born, she took a husband, one I called my father, except we were so different, I doubted it every day. He and I were together when the raid occurred, and his share of the remains of the village wealth bought him this." He motioned to the tavern around him. "Now he's back to Africa, and it's mine."

Parik felt his stomach turn, and he hoped it was just the ale. He closed his eyes for a moment, wishing the gathering power away, and then he looked at Umaru. "Will you leave this place someday?"

"Leave?" The man's voice roared, and he waved his mug in the air. "I'll fight off all comers. This is mine." He raised a muscled arm and indicated the room around him.

Parik's stomach turned again, and he grabbed a stool, sitting. "Hold to something, Umaru. The stones are soon to shake."

"Stones? How can you know that?" Even so, Umaru removed his ale to the counter with a grin. "For safe-keeping!"

At those words, the floor moved, and stools around the room began to topple over. The barrel of ale gave leave of its stand, and it burst upon the floor. Flumes of dust billowed from the stones, and the door to the tavern swung wide, falling off its old-fashioned wooden hinges and crashing to the ground outside. After a time, the shaking stopped, and Umaru crawled from where he'd fallen to the floor.

"How could you know that, man? The stones have shaken two times and more this day, and yet you knew exactly when. How can that be?" Umaru grabbed the older man by the vestments. "Tell me, man. How can you know? You do pray. I can tell. You must to know when the stones will move even before the shaking starts."

"Pray?" Parik's energy was drained. He felt older, somehow. It was as he expected, but it was always debilitating when the shakings pulled his unnatural vitality from him. He looked up at the younger man. "I don't pray to the goddess, unless I pray that she burns in the fires of her own flaming hell. If I tell you the shaking will get worse, will you leave this city? It will get worse. Much so."

Umaru walked to the wall and slapped it. "Stone, my brother. Stone doesn't fall. It's the safest thing around. Why would I leave?" He laughed, seemingly back in good spirits now that the ground no longer shifted. He looked keenly at Parik. "I never did get your name."

"I only said I was your mother's consort."

Umaru snorted. "My mother always had consorts. She was a princess. Of course she had consorts."

"No, this is different. You're twenty-nine seasons old, correct?" Parik didn't count the seasons, but he knew each one. It had been twenty-nine.

"And you are maybe forty. What of it?"

"Ninety seasons, if you count since my most recent birth. Ninety, Umaru. I'm Parik, and I'm your father."

Umaru righted a stool and sat before Parik, laughing. "That's a good one, Parik. You're ninety as sure as I'm a pup still wet behind the ears. Why do you say this?"

"Because it's true. You'll see my seasons weigh upon me as the shakings continue. Already I'm weak, and it's only been since last night." Parik took a deep breath, wishing to somehow save this man, the son of a woman he remembered fondly. He had to try, despite the futility of the effort. "Also, you saw the fallen stone out front. This place will fall, also. You should leave now." He coughed, and he could barely speak. This man must vacate the city, if he was to live. Otherwise, his death was on Parik's head.

"How do you know this?"

"I'll tell you, Umaru, but only because you are my son, and I loved your mother very much. Also, because the ale is very good." Parik laughed, coughing again at the end, putting his hand to his mouth. During his rebirth, the damage to the city would be great. He was aging fast, and the two went hand in hand. He grasped at the words to tell something he'd told few other people in his long series of lives. "The goddess who took your mother birthed me from her womb, and then she cursed me. This around you is my curse. I can feel the shaking before it comes, and I know when it will get worse. This will get much worse." That was less than the full truth, but it would have to do.

"Much worse, you say?" Umaru looked at him askance for several moments. "I believe you're my father. You know too much to be otherwise. However, I don't believe you're the son of a goddess, except in the way that we're all sons of the goddess." The green-eyed tavern owner leaned forward suddenly. "Still, I do believe you can tell when the stones will shake before they start to move. I don't know how you do that, but I believe you. What should I do?" Then he leaned back as abruptly as he'd leaned forward, glancing around the disheveled room. "Besides abandoning my tavern. It's mine, you know. I owe no one any coin against it, and it provides me a good living."

"And a good death, if you stay," Parik whispered.

"And a good death, if I stay. I'll take that risk. How can I help you, though, Father Parik?"

"There's a woman. She's in my rooms. She was sleeping when I left. She's with child, and she must return to her people. I would ask you to take her to them, if you will." His breath was hard to catch, and he couldn't imagine how that last shaking had taken so much from him.

Umaru grinned. "And she lives far from the city?"

"I don't know. She was to be married, and she was stolen away. She must be returned to her people immediately. Today. This you can do for me, Umaru, if you will."

Umaru sighed melodramatically. "If I will. How can I refuse such a well-mannered request from a father I never knew? If I will."

He stood, shifting the blade at his side out of his way. Taking a soft cloth that still remained on the counter, he dipped it into the ale puddle on the floor. He sopped it until the cloth was full, then turned his mug right side up and wrung the cloth into it. He looked at Parik and grinned.

"I can't waste such good ale. It's my best." He

picked up the mug and downed the liquid inside.

"You'll take her? Her name is Zekiye. She's quite beautiful." Parik rubbed his old eyes. "I would do this for her, but I'm quite unable to leave the city. Someone must."

"I'll be back, falling stone or no." Umaru slammed the empty mug on the counter and laughed. "This is my home, Parik, father that I never knew. I recognized you when I saw you in the street, and I'll see you again." He clapped him on the shoulder before bending to pick up his zebra catch sack. "Which rooms? I must know at least that."

Parik pointed, giving him landmarks and directions, glad to see him walking out the door. If he could save two, that was better than saving none. That the man was his son only added a margin of satisfaction to the matter.

7

THE OLD MAN FINGERED the coins in the small pouch sewn within his robes. It had grown hot with the morning, but his crops had gone quickly, and now he could return to his home. He'd refused to remove his robes even in the heat. To do so would be to lose control over the money pouch sewn inside.

The leafy vegetable had sold for as much as he'd hoped. Six coins. The lemons had gone for two each, except for the big one. It had commanded three coins, and that had been a very good price.

He wondered if he could bypass the main road and avoid giving the beggar child any coins. He knew the girl the big man had spoken of, and he knew how badly she was crippled. He hadn't let on, though. The man also knew of the boy she watched over, and if the girl died, there might be some coins in the younger brother if he was taken to the temple. Sometimes the priests wanted small boys for their special ceremonies. If the beggar girl died, the boy would die, anyway. What did it matter if it was quickly or slowly?

Then, before he could leave the marketplace, the ground had shaken once again, and it had been strong. Small stones decorating the tops of buildings had tumbled to the ground, one nearly striking the vegetable seller. He'd been frightened, and he'd remembered how the man had predicted the shaking earlier that morning, and how he'd saved the leafy vegetable that surely would have been ruined if it had fallen into the gutter. It was nearly impossible to wash the smell of the gutter off the green leaves.

The strong shaking had convinced the seller to do as he'd promised. He wedged his cart at the edge of the road, just against the first step, not wanting it to roll off on its own, and he traveled up the stone steps to the fourth doorway. There sat the girl, half in and half out of the door. She seemed asleep. The seller glanced inside to see the boy lying on a sleeping mat. It was odd the child wasn't up, but perhaps it was time for a midday nap. The seller had never fathered children, so he didn't know just how a child's day was done.

Seeing a small bowl at the girl's side, he reached into his pouch and pulled out his two most worn coins. He held them out, considering whether to drop in both, or if anyone would know if he gave her just one. Then he remembered the big man telling him he'd ask. With a sigh of resignation, he let the coins fall, turning without waiting to see if they hit the bowl or not.

Back at the main street, he picked up the pulling poles with his hands, glad the cart was empty. It was downhill, also. That was even better. He only had to travel to just outside the city wall. He grew his vegetables there. It was safer than being inside. Inside, rocks could fall on you. Outside was only the sky, and the sky never fell. Also, his home was against the city walls. They were as sturdy as stone.

When he thought of that, the old vegetable seller actually laughed. What was he thinking? The city walls were stone. Being next to the city walls was the safest place to be if the shaking happened again.

He began to whistle as he walked through the nearly empty streets. It was a good day to be alive, even considering the two coins he'd given away.

WHISKERS TWITCHED, AND A furred nose sniffed of the fallen stone. Someone had died here. The rat could tell. The blood was fresh. However, and the rat knew this, more stones had fallen since this one. There was fresher blood in the street, but that wasn't what drew the three-legged creature.

Its small black eyes moved quickly back and forth, and its heart beat rapidly in nervousness. The sun in the sky was bright, much too bright for it to see well, especially with its poor vision, but there were odors in the air, pheromones, trails to follow. The man had been this way. The rat might not be able to see well against the brightness of the day, but its nose worked just fine.

Lifting its snout, shifting its weight to one side to accommodate a front leg that was barely there and quite unusable, the animal pointed its nostrils in one direction, then in another, pulling in the smells, sifting them, sorting out just which direction drew in the strongest sense of the man it needed to find. It was compelled, and it didn't know why. It didn't even understand compelled. However, the need was there, and finally deciding, it moved forward in its awkward three-legged scrabble, the tapping sounds of its feet on the stones unheard to any ears except its own.

At the edge of the street, the rat scurried in its awkward way underneath a fallen door, grateful for the shade that offered protection from the brutality of the sun. Turning, pressing its body against a stone stoop, the coolness of the material calming the rat's anxiety, it peered from its shadowy protection and raised its snout once again. Its whiskers twitched, and its furred nose sniffed. The man had come this way, and the pheromones were strong in the air. The rat would find him. The pheromones wouldn't let it down. It just had to sniff and wait, then sniff again. Its nose was very good.

The rat extended its snout a hair's breadth past the edge of the fallen door and sniffed once more for good measure. Then it drew its head back into the shadows. It knew it must be patient, just as it knew the pheromones would certainly lead it to the man who somehow forced the rat to follow.

The rat hunkered down, and it waited as the desperation of the city all around wailed its inhabitants' distress to the sky.

CHIARINA JERKED AWAKE WHEN the shaking started once again, her hands grasping for support at the stone door frame behind her head. A fist gripped her heart, and she looked inside her room, hers and Thaddiaos' room, glad to see he was still resting quietly. As the dust began to billow once again from between the stones, filling the room and creating a hazy murkiness in the air, she coughed.

When a stone fell and shattered on the steps at her side, she involuntarily jerked away, hitting the bowl next to her. Feeling pain shoot up through her leg and into her loins, she screamed, barely aware of the sound of the two coins as they skittered across the stone steps, lodging themselves in a rough crack that had opened just outside her doorway.

Pulling back inside the safety of her room, trusting the familiar stone surroundings to protect her, to keep her safe, she pulled her bowl in after her, pushing it into the nearest corner. When she coughed again, she looked at Thaddiaos, now aware he hadn't coughed all morning. He hadn't made a single sound. Thaddiaos always made sounds, even when he didn't feel strong. She was forced to keep him quiet when people walked by, for she was always frightened he'd be discovered and taken from her. She was always fearful of that, and now he was making no sound.

"Goddess, be merciful," she whispered as she pulled herself to him, the pain in her body forcing the tears from her eyes. "He's only a boy."

When she touched his leg, though, a keening wail drew itself from her throat. Even amidst the grinding of the city's stones, one against another, and the shattering of those stones that fell, Chiarina's high, clear voice could be heard as it carried her grief to all within earshot. Her brother, her precious Thaddiaos, lived no more.

She pulled him to her breast, his body cool but not yet cold, and she brushed the hair from his forehead. She rubbed one thumb under his opened eyes, clearing the dust that gathered even as she held him. Coughing again, she became aware of how bad the stone dust was, and she knew she must get Thaddiaos to clearer air. With great effort, she held his small body as she pulled herself back to the door, resting her back against the frame once again as the city continued to grind against itself.

Tears flowed down her face as she looked towards the main street where frightened people rushed past. One brightly robed woman huddled in the shadow of a doorway, crouched down with her hands held over her fabric-wrapped hair, obviously terrified. No one stopped to help her in her distress.

There was no justice in the world. Chiarina knew that. There was no justice. There was also no love in the world. It had all died, and she held its remnants in her arms. Even when a man passed by the end of the street, one who looked very much like a younger version of the green-eyed man who sometimes dropped a coin in her bowl, Chiarina could only watch passively. Her world had ended, and there was no longer anything for her.

There was nothing at all.

THE MUSE ROSE FROM beside the woman. He turned away, unwilling to be distracted now. The city had shaken again, although the woman at his side had been too exhausted to wake.

When the shaking had started anew, the Muse had expected to open his eyes to a different room. Yet, the scene around him hadn't changed, nor had the male appendage between his legs. For that reason, the Muse knew Parik was on the far side of the city. He was grateful. This body was one that would wear well, with strong arms and a tight waist.

Especially important to the Muse, this body was one that would fight proficiently, dying for its occupant, if necessary, and if it were killed, it was no matter. He'd use this body as he desired, and now he wished to locate Parik. He wished Parik to know the fear of mortality, to walk the knife-edge of death, and not to forget that the Muse was the one who desired him, not the fools the Muse inhabited. They were only pawns in the game.

Pulling on rough leather leggings, the Muse found a pocketed vest to slip on over his shoulders. They were wide shoulders, too, and he was glad for that. Wide shoulders meant strength, and strength meant power.

Shifting through a pile of clothing, finding rope-and-leather sandals for his feet, he made his way to a rough, wooden door. When he stepped outside was when he knew just how close Parik's rebirth was, and that it wouldn't be easy locating the man he desired to track.

A corner building had collapsed just down from the rooms this Kaius body shared with the one who called herself Rena. The blocks had tumbled out into the street on one side, and the adjoining wall had collapsed into the interior. By the efforts in progress to move the fallen stones, it was clear there had been people inside. Or perhaps it was a food storage facility, and those affected wished no more than to eat. As several men struggled to pull the fallen blocks away, yet others carried armloads of foodstuffs away from the devastation.

Then, a woman standing nearby started to wail as a bloody youth was dragged from the morass of tumbled stone. When he was freed of the wreckage and laid on a clear place in the street, she fell on him, wiping the debris from his face. It was clear he'd move no more, and the Muse turned away.

The death wasn't a concern to him. It was as it should be. All this was but the beginning of something much bigger. These people thought each shaking was the end of it, but the man who was no longer truly Kaius found that amusing. Each shaking was only the start of the next level of the game. The wailing woman? She would find her own death, perhaps before the day was out. This body the Muse inhabited, this Kaius? It would also be dead. Parik wouldn't be, though, and that was what drove the Muse.

THE RAT, WITH ITS three good legs and one withered, hunkered underneath the old wooden door, its whiskers trembling against the smells of the collapsing city. Its black eyes glistened, the light telling of danger, danger, danger.

Just inside, Parik stood, his feet moving sluggishly through the ale puddled across the tavern floor. Stepping through the doorway, he waved the dust-laden air from his face. A woman hurried by with a striped cloth held tightly across her mouth to filter the dust from her lungs. She glanced quickly at him before dropping her gaze and moving past. Her eyes glistened with tears.

Parik stepped on the tavern's fallen door, and it shifted. Underneath, the rat quivered with excitement. The pheromones were overwhelming; the man must be very near, and it could only inhale the intenseness as its saturated brain buzzed with need. Then, the door shifted again, and a pair of sandaled feet stepped into the street. The rat twitched its nose, and it knew the source of the pheromones it must follow had just moved away, was growing weaker even as it huddled in its protecting shade.

Gathering its energy into its three legs, the animal made a fateful decision. A rat in the daylight in the middle of a city street was in a place of danger. There were those who would find such an animal to be a tasty food source, indeed. Risking all, it burst forth from underneath the door, scrambling with its awkward, irregular gait, and ran after the sandaled feet, uncaring whether it was seen or not.

The creature need not have worried. Even though the feet of much larger creatures also scurried through the streets of the city, they had other things on their minds. Although the latest shaking had stopped, the occasional stones still tumbled from the tops of the buildings. Sometimes they tossed themselves harmlessly into the street, shattering on impact, and other times they found softer targets, ones of flesh and bone. Screams and then moans told where the injured could be found.

The rat no longer cared about all that. It was drawn to those feet. It was drawn to Parik, even though it didn't know just why.

FAR UNDERGROUND, THE GREAT swath of rock that the city was built on, superheated and under unimaginable stress, cracked. The fissures spiderwebbed through rock strata that had remained stable for millennia, opening up channels whose deepest reaches quickly began filling with magma. Electric charges built up as the broken rock surfaces ground against one another, ripping electrons from their atoms, shifting them from surface to surface, and capturing the power they released.

Ahead of the magma storm flashed zinc and copper, selenium and phosphorus, lacking only the all-important lubricant, water. As minerals were stripped from deposits long buried deep within the earth and channeled along the fissures, the ground far above shifted, giving way, creating pathways that had been commanded at the beginnings of time by a forgotten goddess who had desired her son for her paramour. The union wasn't to have been, though, and this destruction was his curse forever.

Yet, on the surface, the shaking had stopped once again, and the sun still shone in the sky. Birds landed once more in the green trees that dotted the countryside surrounding the lower reaches of the city, and the fear in the hearts of men settled to mere murmurs of disquiet.

After all, how many times could the ground shake? It had been half a day, from the middle of the night until noon, and the city was still standing, the vast bulk of it, anyway. The warmth of the sun brought the customary southerly breezes, and the age-old dust disturbed by the shaking was quickly carried away.

Inside those rooms left still intact, bakers stoked their fires, and moneylenders prepared their ledgers, ready once again to fuel the life of the city. In the market, tented stalls that had shifted and tumbled over were righted for the continued business of the day: fruits and vegetables for the morning; gutted meats for the afternoon. By evening, fried breads and fruit pies would fill the stalls.

Life in the city, except for those few who had already been forced to deal with the occasional and unexpected death, continued as usual. The city went on. How could it be otherwise? The walls were built of stone. It had stood for a hundred seasons plus nearly a hundred more. The shaking of a few stones wouldn't bring it down. The city was forever, and its very walls gave it an aura of safety.

It was an aura that would prove to be very misleading, indeed, as the inhabitants of the city would soon find out.

8

"RUN TO THE TEMPLE. You must tell the temple priest." The mother, simply dressed but pretty in her white and saffron smock, stood in the shadow of the age-old aqueduct that fed the city's reservoir, and she swatted her uncooperative youth on the back of the head. He might have hair newly grown between his legs, but he was still a son subject to her authority. "Go now. It's raining, and there are no clouds in the sky."

"Mother," the youth pleaded. The sun was very hot outside already, and he'd run inside to throw his tunic onto a low couch, not run an errand for his mother. "I've no coins for the temple coffers. Besides, I wish to go climb the stones of the villa that collapsed."

"Villa? Which villa?" She glanced at the cloudless sky, a new level of worry creasing her forehead. Only the ancient aqueduct thrusting its bulk overhead was visible. She was still worried about the falling rain. The summer winds were blowing, the gods were playing underneath the earth, and she'd never seen it rain from a clear sky.

"The new one, the unfinished villa at the top of the slope. You know, with the plaster ceiling that was blue? It's gone." He grinned, kicking his sandals off his feet.

"Your sandals, Æolus Cato. Return them to your feet, else you'll bring the dust from the streets into our home." Her words formed a familiar rebuke, stressed by the use of both his names, but her eyes were filled with the grit of worry.

The water gnawed at her.

"Mother! I can climb to the temple better with bare soles. Sometimes the sandals slip sideways, and I can't afford to stumble on the stones. May I stop by the fallen villa?"

"Gone? Æolus, how can it be gone?" His mother grabbed his arm. She now remembered the villa. "It isn't yet finished. There were so many stones used to build it. It must still be there."

"Come see, Mother, if you wish. The stones are strewn everywhere. I think one might have crashed through Loukas' ceiling."

"Loukanos? Your friend, Loukanos, with the missing toe?" She frowned. With a name added to the destruction, it brought matters home to her. Æolus must get to the temple, and quickly, too.

"Loukas with the severed toe, Mother. Yes, Loukas." Her son laughed. "Thank the gods they're at their estate in the wine country. Loukas might now have a severed head if they'd been home." He'd been working his way to the door, and the sunlight caught his smooth face as he stepped through, telling of the boy he still was, despite his long limbs. "After I climb the stones of the blue-ceilinged villa, I'll explore Loukas' villa. Then I can tell him all about it when he returns, how the gods threw a stone into his ceiling, bringing it tumbling down. His grandfather will probably have it repaired by the time they return, and Loukas will have missed it all, otherwise."

"He might. His grandfather once was a senator, and he has the contacts, still." Her words were said absently. She still worried about the water falling from the sky. "If you'll go by the temple on your way to explore the collapsed villa, then I'll see if arrangements can be made for you to go stay with Loukanos at their country estate." She smiled nervously. This shaking in the city felt unnatural, and she wanted her son gone.

"With Loukas? You're serious?" His eyes glistened with excitement.

"You pleaded before he left, and now's your chance. Remember the pleading?" She smiled as she teased him, but it was to hide her true feelings. "You and Loukanos always enjoy staying together in one of the workers' huts on the hillside. You'll do that again, I'm sure."

Æolus whooped and turned in a circle. With just his loincloth on, the end tucked securely at his waist, his long legs danced his anticipation.

She gave him a quick hug. "A horse-drawn supply cart is leaving for the wine country this afternoon. There might be room for you, if they don't want too many coins." They wouldn't, though. If they asked of her a hundred coins, she'd pay every one.

Æolus' eyes glowed, and a breeze ruffled the curly hair atop his head. His smile was bright, showing even, white teeth against skin the color of pale linen. She reached down and placed her hand against the side of his face.

"You are so handsome, my son. You remind me much of your father. I'll do this for you today. Be quick, though."

Then she pulled her hand away, cautious that he might feel the nervousness she could barely control.

"THANK YOU, MOTHER. I'm the wind today. I've missed my friend and shall be glad to see him again." Æolus threw his arms around her. He'd do all he'd said, and he'd visit the temple, too. To see Loukas again, he'd do all that as well as be back in time to be on the cart.

"Go, son, and remember your tunic. You must wear it to visit the temple." She pushed him away, her reminder given with the item already in her hand.

"Don't forget your promise, Mother!" His words whisked out the door after him and into the street. His youthful speed proved to be truly that of the wind, even as he slipped the short tunic over his head.

His legs flying, he passed an old man in a leather tunic with a selvage-edged cloth draped over his hair. He was followed by a three-legged rat. Laughing, Æolus turned and danced backwards for a moment, enjoying the sight of the rat as it snuffled along after the man. Then, the youth turned, his thoughts on his mission as his feet pummeled the steps of a side street that climbed the city's northern slopes. Passing by the familiar gates that opened to Loukas' villa, he paused, his feet dancing sideways, his movements more the suggestion of progress rather than actual advancement.

Through the closed gates, he could see the courtyard was dusty—as was much of the city now—but otherwise it seemed untouched. Æolus knew he'd have to climb the gates to get inside, but he also knew the loose stone in Loukas' back wall. He could shimmy it out of its place and work his way inside. Soon he'd be too big to go through the opening, but for now he still fit. Loukas had grown too muscular, already, but not Æolus. There were advantages to being small.

If you'll go by the temple . . . Æolus remembered, and as he turned to race up the street, he slammed into a pretty girl about his own age, knocking her to the ground. Her hair was draped with a cloth, and she held the hem of her sleeve to her eyes as if she'd been crying.

"Dulcia?" He stopped, reaching to help her to her feet. Her full name was Felicia Dulcia Santoro, but always, her parents had called her Dulcia. Æolus did the same, for she always smiled at him when he did. "I'm headed see the collapsed villa, the one on the top of the hill." As she stood, he noticed her eyes. "Are you crying?"

"My little ChiChi. He's run away. I can't find him." Her voice quavered with emotion.

"Not to worry." Æolus gave her a quick hug. He'd known her forever, and she was as a sister to him. "When does ChiChi not run away? He's a wild dog, and he's never been trained. No one will try to eat him, though. Don't fear. He has too much fur and not enough meat." He laughed. "Be of good spirits, Dulcia, and smile. Go see the villa with me."

"But, ChiChi. I must find him. He isn't wild, and he'll soon be hungry. Besides, his hip. It works poorly at times, and then he can't run." She did smile when Æolus called her name the second time.

"ChiChi will come back. He did last week when you cried for him, remember? Come with me. I'm off to see the villa, and then I'll show you how I get into Loukas' villa. His ceiling is crashed in." He grinned with his offering.

"Loukas? He's in the wine country. Who'll let you in?" She stepped to the filigreed gates and shook them with her hands. "It's locked. Loukas' family is very prosperous to have such a large gate." She looked at him. "I've never been inside. How will we get in?"

He grabbed her arm. "The unfinished villa, first. Then to the temple. We'll return here afterwards. Come!"

She turned, now scornful. "The temple? No one goes

to the top of the city except the temple serving women and the men who go there to plead atonement for imagined wrongs. You don't plan to visit the temple serving women there, surely. You, without doubt, can have committed no wrongs. You're but a boy. Besides, they'd desire coins of you before offering atonement."

He teased her in return, "A boy's first time is always free. A man's." He laughed and puffed up his chest, attempting to look bigger than he really was. A visit to the temple was a rite of passage, and anyone who had managed it on his own was surely a man in status, if not in fact. "Loukas visited the temple before his family went to their estate, and he said it cost him nothing. He'd spoken harshly to his tutor, and he was told to make amends." Æolus laughed loudly. "It was an excuse, I think. He said he was told he had to pay if he went back. An offering to the temple, the girl told him. I don't think he'll be back."

"Loukas' family is very rich. I'm certain his father will give him many coins. If not, then his grandfather surely will." Dulcia ran her hands over the Ricci-Moretti family crest that bridged the two halves of the villa's gates.

Æolus snickered with barking laughter. "His parents wouldn't pay, even if he asked. They'd be furious enough if they knew he's already gone for free." For children to plead atonement, parents must be in attendance. Otherwise, it was an insult against the family's standing in the city. Only one clearly matured past puberty, or an orphan, could go alone.

"They didn't take him, then?" Her fingers absently traced the raised emblems on the crest. "Poor Loukas, when they find out. I won't tell." She turned to Æolus, a smirk on her face, only to find a vestment-clad soldier in the shape of a boy, one pretending to pull a long blade from a scabbard.

"I could go, you know. I'm a man, also, but not to-day." He dropped his soldier stance, his boyish frame telling the truth of the matter. "Besides, I've done noth-ing for which I must atone. I go for my mother. She has a message for them. When I return, she has said she'll send me on the cart that leaves today for the wine coun-try. I'll stay there with Loukas until they return in the cooler season."

Dulcia looked at him, her mouth pouty, her search for her little ChiChi pushed aside by the talk of the wine country. "You're so lucky. You must have the goddess as your patron. I'll be stuck in the city with the sweat pouring down my back, and only the southern winds to keep me company. I'll never get to spend the hot season under the coolness of the grape arbors."

"Ha!" Æolus' voice rang out, not feeling sorry for her. "You always were whiny. Come on, Dulcia. Today is for the collapsed villa. It won't be collapsed forever. It may be rebuilt even by the time I return to the city. We must explore it today. Come!" He held out his hand to her.

She reached for it, giving in, and with quick steps, the two youths made their way to the construction site that had recently boasted a nearly completed grand villa with a blue-plastered ceiling. It was a stunning location for a rich man's villa, too. The southern breezes were captured by the hilltop location, and it was surprisingly cool, even in the midday heat. Also, the mountains rising behind the city protected it from the northern blasts of winter.

The entire city was spread out before them. Even the magnificent aqueduct that brought water from the distant mountains could be seen, its great archways stretching from hilltop to hilltop. It towered airily over the plain, following a rigidly straight line, leaping across the city—directly over Æolus' house at one point—bringing water to the reservoir just over the ridge against which the city nestled. It had been there for as long as anyone could remember, and it was no more than part of the countryside. With a laugh, Æolus pointed to where they could see that sure enough, a hole was right in the center of Loukas' roof. He whispered to Dulcia that Loukas would have been decapitated for sure, if his family hadn't gone to the wine country.

After the two young people had clambered among the fallen stones, admiring the carved finials that had cracked and broken as they tumbled, even chipping off pieces of the blue-painted plaster as souvenirs, they found a resting spot on the top stone of a wall that had somehow managed not to crumble.

Sitting in the sun and enjoying the southern breezes, Dulcia questioned her friend. "What message do you need to take to the temple? Does your mother need the priest to make a sacrifice? That's very expensive, you know." She broke a fragment off the piece of the blue plaster she'd picked up. Looking at it for a moment, she tossed the fragment back into the tumbled stones that had once made up the magnificent villa. "Or does she want the priest to pray for you? Before long, you'll begin to attract the girls. Perhaps your mother wishes you to remain chaste for many seasons to come." She had a sparkle in her eyes as she said it.

"It's the rain. That's the message I'm to deliver to the temple." He ran his hand through his hair, working his fingers in at the scalp, wishing it were long enough for a catch sack. Only a man could wear a catch sack. It was yet another reason to visit the temple as soon as his mother allowed.

"Rain?" Dulcia pondered that for a time, pulling her own long locks from underneath her headcloth and over her shoulder to run her fingers through them.

"Rain. That's what my mother said. I didn't understand, either." He closed his eyes against the brightness of the sun.

"I guess she wants the coolness." Dulcia laughed lightly. "It can't be that we need water. We have the aqueduct, and it brings the city all the water we need."

"No, it isn't the coolness she wants." Æolus took a deep breath, filling his lungs with the freshness of the breeze as it beat back the day's building heat. "She said it was already raining, and the priests should know." He opened his eyes and stood. "We should go. The temple next, and then we will go to Loukas'."

As he grabbed the girl's hand, the stone they were

on began to vibrate, and Dulcia screamed. Æolus stood perplexed for several seconds, and then the stone moved violently underneath them. As he was knocked off his feet, he scrambled to put a protective arm around Dulcia, and in that moment, they observed the most horrific of sights. Just where it towered over the lower city, the great aqueduct split, and water began to pour forth. Then, with an ear-piercing crack, a section lifted at one end, and with a torrent of frigid water gushing onto the buildings underneath, it shattered into a hundred separate stones, each raining down on the villas below.

Æolus gasped. "I live there, Dulcia. Right there. What should I do?"

The shaking had't stopped, though, and Æolus got no answer. His heart pounded as he grasped Dulcia's hand in his. He wanted nothing more than for the stones to stop their movement underfoot.

THE MUSE HELD TIGHTLY to the side of a building, and he watched the aqueduct shatter and tumble to the ground. He felt no real fear. His only concern was that he could no longer shift by choice, and if this body belonging to the one called Kaius were simply injured instead of killed, he might be forced to endure the pain of the injury.

It would hurt, too. The times he'd been killed by Parik, he'd discovered that. In those circumstances, the Muse had at least had the choice to remain in the body, risking death; but when the power drew itself together as now, he could only take the body that was offered, as well as when it was offered, too.

On this day, the Muse didn't want to feel pain, so he kept to sturdy stone doorways, small protecting alcoves, and open spaces, wishing to remain unharmed until he could locate Parik. The nail on the man's fourth finger would normally guide him, but it was difficult with the power drawing together under their feet. It tended to hide Parik, and at the end, it disguised him completely.

He must time his advance carefully.

A wave of dizziness hit him, and he leaned against a door recessed underneath an elaborately carved stone lintel. The closer he got to Parik, the more likely he was to be thrown into another mortal without warning. Unlike his own shifts, where the new host must be within visual contact, if the power drawing to Parik were strong enough, the Muse might find himself anywhere in the world.

"Curse you, Parik. Not now," the Muse muttered. Only distance from Parik would allow him to retain this body for a time. The queasiness said close. The man who had been Kaius blinked rapidly several times in succession, and then he was the Muse no longer.

Kaius, formerly from Gaul, now called by the name of Kaius Gallus, stumbled under the onslaught of the shaking city, unsure how he could be here on this corner when he'd just been beside Rena in their room. Then he remembered the wine from last night. He'd probably forgotten to go home, and Rena would be angry with him. She was always angry with him, angry that he drank, angry that he didn't hold her more, angry that he didn't sing to her as often as she wished.

Perhaps he wouldn't go home.

Then his eyes caught the collapsed aqueduct, and he had another thought. Perhaps he had no home to return to. That made his heart pound, and he knew Rena would be afraid. Looking around to locate familiar landmarks, he turned and began to stride insistently toward his room, determined to comfort Rena. He pushed away the black thought gathering in the back of his mind, the one that kept trying to push its way to the front.

If she's still alive. Kaius could barely think it, but there it was anyway. *If she's still alive.*

THE MUSE INHALED, and the smell of Parik was with him. They were riding in a small cart together. Then he realized it was almost Parik, more or less, but with a difference. The aroma, as intoxicating as it felt, wasn't Parik. The Muse also realized he was no longer a man. He was a woman again.

"Are you all right?" A voice, one that was Parik's and yet not, questioned her. "You seem confused."

The Muse looked at her hands. They felt very familiar, almost as if she'd lived in them before. She had no control over the shifting when the power was drawing, but she knew she rarely shifted to a previous body. First, it was uninteresting. Second, it was very difficult. The body knew the feel of the Muse's presence the second time, and it resisted her. When she tried to override the synaptic patterns of the host's brain, it would sometimes simply shut down, and the person might pass out or even die. Yet, this body was very familiar and, more surprising, very welcoming. Not all bodies the Muse took welcomed her so easily.

A big hand, a masculine one, grasped her chin and turned her face. She was taken aback to see Parik, only much younger, as he'd looked many decades ago in China, or perhaps before that, in Africa. Had something unforeseen happened? Had she skipped across the seasons, perhaps in a host that was incapacitated, possibly enduring a long sleep brought on by injury? How would she know?

However, this wasn't Parik's smell, not exactly, so she knew this couldn't be the man she was destined to pursue. To be so similar, though . . . a child of Parik's. He must be. She'd made a point to leave a few of those. She just never sought them out. It was always Parik and Parik alone who attracted her attentions, who drew her to him, who was the focus of all she did.

"Zekiye, is your child bothering you? My father said you carried, and I don't want you to travel if you're not well. We can find a place to rest."

"Zekiye?" The Muse repeated the name, looking hard at the man beside her. She remembered that name. A man had called her that the season previous when she'd taken a young girl for her host. It seemed the girl had been displaying a marriage dress to him, and the man hadn't understood why the girl had suddenly not known him. She hadn't, because she'd become the Muse. The Muse remembered the name, though. She was back in the body she'd left only the night before, the one she'd shared with Parik for a full season and a month.

"You're still Zekiye, are you not?" The man at her side laughed.

"Yes," she replied. "That's my name. You say I'm with child?" She fumed. If so, it was Parik's doing. He'd seen she was gone from the woman, and he'd given her a child. He'd known, and he'd done this for that very reason. He'd done this on purpose to spite her.

She was furious, and if she could shift again, if the man she'd just been wasn't too close to the power drawing for Parik's rebirth, she'd return to him, risk killing him, and she'd search out Parik to end his life. He preferred this wench to her, even with all she'd done for him.

"My father says so. You seem slim and beautiful to me." The man chuckled. "If this is 'with child,' I'd want a woman with child any day."

"You'd want me?" The Muse felt inspiration flood over her. She knew how to get back at Parik, if this man was who she thought he was. "You're quite handsome. May I inquire about your father?"

"No, don't give me that. You were speaking of him moments ago, and now you act as if you never heard of him. Remember your baby's name? Parikson? It seems to me that cryptic moniker would tell it all."

"Parikson. So, Parik is the father of my baby?" There was no doubt any longer. He could do this, ensure the woman took a male child. He'd eaten the fourth nail, after all. She placed a hand on her escort's arm, rubbing the skin that was so much like Parik's, a shade darker, perhaps, but very much the same. The color of this man's skin carried more cinnamon. Brown, with just a touch of cinnamon, the color of pale ale.

"So, you do remember?" He grinned. "I thought so. I'm taking you to your people. They live in the southern reaches, far from the city. Parik made me promise. I'll return soon, though. In a day, I thought at first. However, it seems the southern reaches are far, far away. I suspect this will be a very long trip."

"Take me back to the city, then." She purred her suggestion to him.

He laughed. "I can't. I gave my word."

"Supplies?" She wasn't to give up so easily. "You brought supplies for many days?"

"I didn't." He said the words with a sigh. Then he chuckled. "I'm quite a hunter, though. We won't go hungry, or at least not very hungry."

With inspiration, she grabbed his arm. "For a time, let us stop. Please. I'm very tired of riding." Her hand moved to his leg, and she felt him pause.

"For a time, yes. You must need rest." He pulled on the horse's reins.

"I don't even know your name," the Muse whispered huskily, moving her fingers against his leg.

He drew in a deep breath. "I'm called Umaru Afolabi Yaradua." He drew the horse to a standstill. "After my mother."

Afolabi. Highborn. The Muse remembered that name, and she remembered where she'd worn it, also.

She sat up and searched his face. "From Africa? You are truly African?"

"A prince, although I have no kingdom left." He looked at her with surprise at the accuracy of her guess. "My kingdom was stolen away." As her hand moved up his leg, clearly amorous and drawing his attention, he shifted positions.

"You're out of Amanishakhete Afolabi. Am I correct?" She knew this man. He was indeed hers and Parik's son, after a fashion.

He grabbed her hand. "You know my mother? She's been a slave for many seasons, if she's even alive." He released the reins as he questioned her, and the horse started slowly forward once again of its own accord.

She leaned against him. "I know of your mother, but I never knew her, not really." *I was her, Umaru. I am her, and I left her with Parik's child, you.* She twisted to touch the skin on his neck. "I would that we do as you suggest, stop by the roadside for a time of rest, for I do feel unwell."

She must do this. If she could distract him, he might yet return her to the city. Or, better yet, if they were far enough from the city, she might shift into this man, returning to the city to kill Parik. Wouldn't that be the best revenge, for Parik to be killed by his own son?

If she did this thing, though, she didn't know how she'd save Parik. She wouldn't be able to shift to another body, a female one to nurse him back from the edge of death. Perhaps, though, if she killed Parik just as the transformation started, just as the rebirth began, the powers of his curse would bring him back to life. She'd have to evaluate the risks; balance the scales. She'd die if she made a mistake and he expired at her hand before the transformation was complete. She wasn't tired of life just yet.

Umaru released her hand. "Then we'll take time from our journey. With my father's child inside of you, your care must be paramount."

"There are grasses nearby, and we could be very comfortable." She moved her hand suggestively. "I would have you rest with me, if you will."

Umaru did stop the cart once more, and the grasses were just as comfortable as the Muse suggested. She sidled up close to him, brushing her fingertips across the skin that was so much like her Parik's, as she considered how best to vent her anger upon the man she'd chased through a hundred lifetimes.

The thing that frustrated her most was her inability to undo Parik's gift of a child to this female body. He had that fourth fingernail, and when he chose to use it, it gave him a power even she couldn't untangle.

9

THE SHAKING HAD STOPPED, but the flood that belonged to the aqueduct hadn't. The sound of the falling water filled the air, and within the roar were the rising wails of people who were just now realizing the extent of the damage. Æolus jumped down from the stone wall and grabbed Dulcia's hand.

"We must go. My family. Yours, too." His voice shook, and the urgency burned in his eyes. "My mother's there. Come, Dulcia."

Her stare was blank. "It broke, Æolus. How can the aqueduct break? Will we all die?"

He pulled at her hand. "Some, maybe. The shaking's

over. We must go. What if my house is flooded? My mother, your parents, too. What if they need help?"

"ChiChi." Her face went white. "What if ChiChi's there? He might run, and his hip might fail." She flung herself down from the wall. "We must save him, Æolus. He'll be frightened."

Together they skipped down the steps, and Æolus was very glad he'd left his sandals at home. In the back of his mind, he was also aware he might have no home to return to, and that meant he'd have no sandals to wear ever again.

"Dulcia!" Æolus pulled her back as they came to the street that ran in front of Loukas' villa. "We can go no farther this way."

She tugged at his hand. "It's the shortest way. Your house lies just beyond." She pulled harder. "Let's go. Sometimes ChiChi finds himself at your door. You know he does. He might be there now. Don't stop, Æolus."

He pulled back hard on her arm. "I don't think we can. See?" He pointed to where the streetside wall that enclosed Loukas' family's villa had toppled over into the roadway. "There's another way. Follow me."

He darted down a narrow connecting street, looking once or twice to see that his friend was following, and at a street that descended once more, one that consisted mostly of a series of steps, they began their plunge into the lower parts of the city. There they would find the level streets that allowed carts and wheeled transports to travel freely.

The way wasn't really clear, though. Buildings were partially dislodged, and several times they had to climb over blocks of stone that had tumbled into their way. Some people were standing outside doors that were cracked and splintered, attempting to move the damaged wood that no longer fit into newly canted openings. Others held wounds to staunch flows of blood, and yet still more hugged lifeless loved ones in their hands. At these, Æolus and Dulcia paused, saying a quick prayer to the goddess, and sliding gingerly past on the opposite side of the street.

"I wish I could help them, Æolus." Dulcia grabbed his arm after one especially gruesome scene. "They all look so sad."

"We'll help whom we can," he whispered. "There, that one. She's an old woman." He pointed several steps down the way to a woman holding a bloody place on her head. A broken parapet stone lay at her side. "Let's help her to her rooms. If she stays on the steps, more stones may fall from the sky. She may be killed."

The woman was dazed, and she didn't want to go inside. However, her small room was intact, and it did seem stable. Æolus slipped his tunic from his shoulders, pressing it to the woman's head to staunch the flow of blood. After a few moments of reassurance, Dulcia finally managed to convince her it was safer than being outdoors.

"There," Dulcia pointed when they were finished, indicating another needy person. "There's a girl. She's holding an injured child. Maybe she needs help."

Æolus looked to where his friend pointed. "I see no blood, and the main street is just past. Should we not go to see about our families? I'm sure she has family to help her."

"What would the goddess say if we didn't take a moment to assist? My father, also, would wish for us to help those along the way, and I'm sure your mother would say the same." She tugged his arm.

Æolus knew she was right. His mother was either well, or she wasn't. These people were right in front of him. He'd take the time to help whom he could. His mother would expect that, or at least he thought she would.

"Let's go to her." Æolus started forward, his sense of purpose solidified.

He had to step carefully. Much stone had broken here, and he had only his bare soles to walk with. When he reached the girl, he squatted at her side, reaching to stroke the head of the small boy she held. As he did, he realized there was no life in the child. He glanced up at Dulcia with a question on his face, unsure what to do. His eyes burned with emotion.

"I know this girl," Dulcia whispered, kneeling beside him. "She begs with a small container." There were two worn coins on the step, and she picked them up for the girl. "Her leg's crippled. This must be her brother. He looks like her. How sad that she still holds him, yet he no longer breathes."

"Do you think she still lives?" When Dulcia shrugged, Æolus reached his hand to the crippled girl.

He touched her shoulder, and her eyes jerked open. She drew in a sudden breath.

"Goddess, am I dead?" Her voice was the raw whisper of disbelief, of one who had faced more than she dared, of one who could face no more.

"I'm Dulcia, and this is Æolus. I know you. I've seen you, rather, but I don't know your name. Will you tell us?"

"Chiarina." Her voice was flat, and her eyes were dull, as if she resided far away. "Chiarina Egidius-Lucanus, for neither my father nor my mother wanted me."

"Is this your brother?" Dulcia reached to him, brushing hair out of one eye.

Chiarina nodded blankly.

"Did he die in the shaking?"

"He coughed until he could cough no more. Then he died, and I didn't even know." Tears began to drop from Chiarina's chin. "I thought he was sleeping, and I didn't know he was dead."

Æolus and Dulcia paused for a few moments to let that sink in, and Dulcia spoke first. "We can't leave her here, Æolus. See her leg? She can't walk. We must take her to the temple. The temple serving women will watch over her. It's the best we can do."

He looked at his loincloth and at Dulcia, aware he must be fully clothed if he visited the temple. He wished he hadn't given away his tunic. Coins, also! His mother had forgotten to give him coins for the temple coffers. After a moment, he nodded. The loincloth and the coins were problems for the temple steps, and they could be dealt with at that time.

"You're right, Dulcia." He leaned to Chiarina and touched her chin to get her to look at him. "I'll carry you to the temple. You'll be safe there. May I cover your brother for now? Someone will have to come for him later. The city is injured, and people will be very busy for a time, I think. He'll be safe here." He was relieved when she nodded in agreement.

"There's a mat inside. It has a cloth. Cover him with that. It will be familiar to him."

Chiarina sat lifeless while Æolus lifted Thaddiaos from her arms. After he covered him on the mat, he returned and squatted by her once again. "I wish to pick you up now. I see you're crippled and don't wish to hurt you."

"His name was Thaddiaos, and he carried the surname of Egidius-Lucanus, gifting it to me once our parents died. He and I were one." With those words, the crippled girl's face shifted, hardened, and she reached her arms to the stones at her side to help Æolus lift her. "You won't hurt me, no more than I've been hurt today. You're very kind." Something passed across her face, and for a moment she was very pretty. "Both of you are so very kind."

When Æolus stood with Chiarina in his arms, he whispered to her, "Lay your head on my shoulder. I'll walk gently."

"Thank you," she replied, her words barely reaching his ear.

Dulcia followed. She carried the coins she'd picked up from the steps. They belonged to the girl, and it would be only right to leave them with the temple serving women.

PARIK LEANED AGAINST THE wall with his eyes closed, glad the most recent shaking was done. The aqueduct had fallen this time. Cold water now flooded around his feet, and it was refreshing. Of course, this meant the piping in the city would soon run dry, and as that thought crossed his mind, he laughed sourly. The city would soon be destroyed. What was the need of water?

Looked around, he was surprised to find everyone was ignoring him, even as he laughed during all this destruction. In this city that was taking blow after blow, why didn't these people leave? They could survive if they just walked away, but as always, each time the shaking stopped, the people were convinced it was over for good.

Glancing down, Parik was surprised to see a waterlogged rat desperately swimming against the current. He grinned when he realized it was aimed right for his feet. Leaning down, he wrapped his hand around its body and held it up to his face. That was when he noticed the withered front leg.

"Why, little friend. You came and found me, and I didn't even leave you any food." He stroked the rat's snout, brushing tender fingers along the quivering whiskers. "Are you ready, yet? You must want healing for me to give it to you." He brushed his fourth finger along the rat's furred head, and he stopped just behind its ear. "Yes? You are ready?"

This was what made it bearable, the enduring of the destruction, the sudden old age, and the endless numbers of deaths. This was the only thing that made it tolerable, the helping of those who couldn't help themselves. Parik knew even the rat would die. He couldn't force it to leave its territory, any more than he could force the people of the city to leave their homes. However, if it wanted, and wanted it badly enough, it could have a short time of wholeness. It could enjoy that.

Parik's fingernail glowed, and he felt it burn with warmth. The rat's snout quivered with excitement. It flicked its tail, and then, closing its eyes, it held very still as if mesmerized. Once or twice its nostrils twitched, and almost unnoticed, the leg it had lived with for a lifetime began to change. The leg that was once a puny thing to get in the rat's way quivered and elongated. Nails that had been mere suggestions lengthened, and muscles that had never formed took on bulk and firmness.

Then, the man moved his finger, and the rat opened its eyes. It flicked its tail again and shook its head, and its whiskers shivered in the sun. Its fur was dry, and it squirmed.

Parik laughed.

"We must find you a dry place to enjoy your new leg, my friend. I called to you, and you finally gave in. You're healed. You simply had to want it, to be willing to give in to it. Now, you are whole."

Turning to a side street, Parik walked to a step that was out of the water, and he knelt more carefully and slowly than he would have a day before. He whispered to the rat, "Go to the temple, little friend. They'll treat you as a godlet there. In addition, it's sturdy, and the ground will have to shake many times before it falls. They have grain, also, lots and lots of it. It needs to be eaten and soon. When the destruction comes, it will all be lost, anyway."

He chuckled, wondering how much the creature understood. Not much, he guessed. He could summon the creatures in the most limited of ways, the injured ones, anyway. It was the fingernail that enabled him to do so. The nail was behind the healing, also. However, they did have to want it. The healing couldn't be forced.

He set the rat down, and it turned to look at him with gleaming black eyes.

"Go, friend." He reached down and flicked the creature's tail. "To the temple. Make friends and eat well."

As if it really did understand him, the rat twitched its whiskers twice and turned, scampering up the steps toward the temple in a surprisingly even scramble. Several steps up it turned to look at Parik once more, and then it was gone.

Parik stood. "One good deed. It doesn't balance out the evil you've done, Lamahätsu, but it's the best I can do."

It was, too, and he was very tired. Old age never fit well on anyone, and on Parik least of all. After all, he was very old, indeed, and despite the seasons he'd begun to show, he knew those around him had no idea.

THE GRASSES WERE RUMPLED, and sun glistened on moist skin. Two times the Muse and Umaru had held each other, and yet she was determined to force herself on him yet again. His interest was satiated already, but she needed him utterly exhausted. With the drawing of Parik's power, she wasn't sure whether she could shift to Umaru this close to the city, but this was something she had to do. If he were weak, it would make the shift easier, and she was willing to do whatever it took to avenge the child Parik had placed in this woman's body.

"Zekiye, I can't give myself to you again." Umaru groaned at the woman's advances. "We must return to the cart. However, I can certainly see why my father desired you so."

"You can see my allure, can you?" She brushed her hand along the side of the face that was so familiar to her, yet not the man she knew. "One last time, Umaru. Then we'll continue our journey. Will you give me that? Perhaps I'll have twins, just for you." She might be able to do just that, she realized. She hadn't been able to undo what Parik had done, but she might be able to add to it. It would be easier if she were in this body when it happened. Then she could quickly shift to the man in his moment of exhaustion. That would work. Then this body would carry one child of the father's and one of the son's. How deliciously wonderful that would be!

As the Muse pulled Umaru to her, tempting him, encouraging him with soft words in his ears and soft pressure elsewhere, the Muse did as she intended, bringing another egg in the woman to fruition, and offering it to the man's seed as he released it into her body. Then, in a final moment of inspiration, she reached to the egg and twisted it inside. She made it male to match the first child, and she made it something else, also. It was all so very easy, and then as the man she held in her arms relaxed with exhaustion, she closed her eyes and shifted.

It was with relief that the Muse opened his eyes to see himself lying at the woman's side. The Muse had no need to determine if he were now the man. He knew this feeling. He was this man—Umaru—now, and he instantly knew every nuance and exhausted muscle in this male body.

He also knew there was no magic word to reenergize his new form. The heat from their exertions must be allowed to fade until the exhaustion passed. It would pass, too, and then he'd head back to the city. The Muse had an offense to right, and the only way to do it was for someone to die.

Humming the same ancient tune he'd let Rena enjoy just that morning, the Muse allowed his energy to rebuild. Finally, finding the strength to sit, he looked at the woman at his side. She returned his look with some confusion, but there was no fear. He had no interest in her, now, though. She was to be left to fend for herself.

"You're Parik, are you not?" She was Zekiye again, and her eyes were filled with uncertainty.

The Muse turned, annoyed. "What do you think?"

"You look younger. Your hair, there's no age in it. Yes, now it comes to me. You're Umaru, I seem to remember."

The Muse stood and looked at her, ignoring her queries. "Your items are in the cart. I'll leave them for you. You may walk the rest of the way. You now carry twins, one from the father, and the other its companion. You may name the second as you wish."

"Are both boys?"

He paused and glanced at her with distraction. He was no longer concerned with the matter of her unborn children. However, he knew the answer to the question she asked. It was a small concession to reassure her, even though his answer wasn't forthcoming with all the details of what he'd done.

"Yes. You have two male children."

"Praise the Goddess of Life." Zekiye looked at the Muse and seemed strangely pleased.

He walked to the cart and murmured ruefully, "You have no idea how true your statement is." Then, reaching inside, he flipped her clothing and sandals her way. "That direction." He pointed. "There's your home."

Sorting through the other items, he turned up his nose at wearing the disgusting zebra catch sack. He pulled the tunic over his head and threw the sandals he found on the ground, slipping his feet inside. He stepped into the cart, and pushing a knife and scabbard aside, sat, pulling on the horse's reins to turn it around. Without a backwards glance, and with his hair wild in the breeze, he headed back to the city.

There was a new line of thoughts plodding through the Muse's mind. *So, this is what it feels like to be Parik.* Then he laughed very long and very loudly. It was a joke that only he could know, and it was a very funny one, indeed.

10

ÆOLUS LAID THE CRIPPLED girl on the temple steps. He knelt and touched his head to the stone and whispered absolutions learned many seasons ago. He knew he profaned the holy stones by wearing only his loincloth, but what could he do? The crippled girl had to have care, and he and Dulcia couldn't give her what she needed.

"Child, what's this you bring us?"

Æolus looked up to see one of the temple serving women, and a very old one at that, wearing the white temple robe with the red stripe across the loins that told of her status. He hoped Loukas hadn't been forced to plead his absolutions with this one. Then he dropped his head, ashamed of his critical thought. He was here only to deliver the girl. Relief flooded his chest when Dulcia stepped to his rescue.

"Kind lady, this girl is named Chiarina. The city is falling. Her brother is dead, and she nearly was."

Æolus knew Dulcia was fudging the facts, making it sound as if the shaking had been the cause. His heart pounded with the near untruth, but he didn't correct her. Help was what the girl needed, no matter the cause.

Dulcia went on, "We brought her to you. She can't run from the falling stones, and the temple is high above the city. No stones can fall on her while she's here. Will the goddess take her?"

The temple serving woman knelt at Chiarina's side with a smile. "I know this one, and I know her brother. She took her brother's name when her parents were gone. He's dead, you say?"

Æolus stepped back nervously, tightening his loin-cloth for fear it would come loose on the temple steps. Feeling the need to make the truth clear, he forced his voice to be strong.

"From the cough, she said. He was very thin. I laid him on his pallet, and he lies there still." He bowed, frowning, making sure to hold the front of his loincloth. Small children could run in public with their bodies exposed, but he couldn't. He was no longer a child, and he was on the temple steps improperly dressed. All he wanted was to get away.

The temple serving woman touched his chin, lifting

it to look into his eyes. "What's your name, youth? I don't recognize your face. Have you petitioned one of us yet, my child?"

Æolus' face burned at the very notion. Not that he didn't want to become a man—be seen as a man, anyway—but to have such an old one ask so very intimate a question mortified him. She smiled, and he was certain it was at the fire raging across his face. His obvious humiliation only made his embarrassment worse.

"Your name?"

"Æolus." He coughed once. "My friend, Loukas, came, but I haven't."

The old woman paused for a moment, and then her expression brightened. "Loukas! Is he tall with strong muscles and a scar about here?" She reached and touched Æolus' stomach just below his navel. "It seemed there was something with a toe, also."

Æolus felt his face grow even hotter, remembering that to receive a first absolution meant a ritual washing by the serving women. He hadn't known the washing was so complete.

Dulcia chuckled and poked her friend. "Tell her, Æolus. It's an easy question."

"It's there; I've seen the scar. The toe, in addition."

The old woman reached and patted his hand. "The temple girls were pleased with him. Your friend was properly contrite and is now fully considered a man. If you come back with your friend, I can promise neither will have to pay, no matter what he was told." She smiled. "Now, as far as this girl. She's at this instant my problem, and you can rest easy that you've done a good deed. The goddess will keep and protect her."

"Bless you, kind lady." Æolus backed down one step, fumbling with his loincloth. He refused to look up, fearing the color of his face would give away his inner turmoil. His mother always said she could tell. The thought of his mother forced a hard place into his throat. He felt his eyes burn, and he wanted to be away.

"I see you're filled with contriteness because you're not properly dressed." The temple serving woman called to Æolus, even as she smiled behind one hand. "Boy, you needn't worry about your loincloth. I'll have the priest sanctify the temple steps before the next feast day." She snapped her fingers, and several similarly dressed women—although much younger—darted from the interior of the temple to gently pick up the crippled girl and carry her into the darkness of the citadel's interior reaches.

Dulcia called to the old woman in her red stripe as she stood to return to the temple. "Her brother. What should we do?"

The old woman paused and then smiled. "There'll be plenty of injured and as many dead. I suspect he'll be as well situated in his own rooms as anywhere else. The city fathers will send someone for him when he starts to stink. You've done all you could." With no more words, she moved toward the doorway and was gone.

Dulcia poked Æolus in the ribs. "So, what was that about Loukas' scar? You got really red there, Æolus. How do you know about Loukas' scar?" When he just slipped his hands up under his armpits and dropped his head, she grabbed an ear and pinched it. "Why, even your ears are embarrassed. I think this must be good. When Loukas gets back, I'll have to ask him."

She laughed when a large gray rat pranced purposefully past them up the temple steps, running inside, and she pointed it out to Æolus. Then, leaving the temple, the two turned a corner to a panoramic view of the city. The teasing had been a welcome break from the tensions of the day, but theirs was still a city in turmoil. The water from the aqueduct poured down on the section of the city where Æolus' home was located, and little ChiChi was still missing. He might have fallen into a deep hole and would be lost forever.

Drawing her hand from her clothing, Dulcia dropped her eyes to her fist. There were the two coins that belonged to the crippled girl. She looked at Æolus.

"I have the girl's coins. I must take these back to the temple. I can't keep them. The goddess will know."

This time it was Æolus' turn not to answer. The occasion with Loukas' scar was forgotten, and even the coins seemed unimportant. From the temple entrance, for the first time, he could truly take it all in, and yet he couldn't take it in.

Without further warning, the ground chose to shake once again, and Dulcia grabbed Æolus to hold on. All he could do was return her grasp. He was quickly learning that when the stones underneath their feet moved, there was nothing to do, nothing except wait until it stopped; and then it was time to pick up the pieces that were left over—if there were any remaining.

FAR OFF A DOG barked, low-pitched and rapid, the bark of an animal that had lost its sense of its surroundings and was very frightened. Of course, with a dog, very frightened could also be interpreted as very aggressive, but the sound was far away, and Parik wasn't worried. He could only help the animal if it wished to be helped; otherwise, it would simply vent its fears on him just as it would any other human being.

It was the woman in front of him that was of more concern. In the last violent shaking, she'd run from her home, fearful of it falling in upon her. Her home still stood. However, the building across the narrow street had been a tall one, two stories, and it hadn't fared as well. When the stones had given up their hold on the determined order in which they had long ago been assembled, acquiescing to the ragtail shaking that was wresting the city from its foundations, one great block had tumbled directly onto the woman's lower torso, crushing her firmly into the pavement below. Her lifeblood spilling from underneath was evidence of the extent of her injuries.

"Please, good sir," she gasped. Her breathing was rapid but shallow, and the color had fled from her face. Her grasp on Parik's hand was firm, though, telling of a desperate pain no one should have to endure. She looked at him with pleading. "Help me die. I'm crushed, and no one can see how badly. I can feel it, though. Death is better than this."

"I wish that I could give you your wish," he murmured. That was one thing he couldn't give. She would die, though, and not from the final devastation the city would endure. Her death was much more imminent, and she might consider herself lucky in that way. He thought she wouldn't, though.

He might help in another way, if she wished it. With his free hand, he touched the side of her face, brushing the hair from her temple. He stroked the skin for a moment, smoothing a tear that had gathered at the corner of her eye.

"The stone . . ." She weakly pushed at it, and her body shivered. "I'm so cold."

"Peace. I can give you that." Parik's hand pushed forward, working his fingers into her hair, his fourth finger pressing gently against her scalp. He felt no release of power, though. He could give it, but she must want it. He'd know when she did. "I can't help you live or die, but I can ease your path to your destination. Will you have that of me?"

Her blood now pooled underneath his sandals, and he dared not move suddenly. To slip would be to jar her injured body, and she could take no additional pain. He watched the muscles in her face twitch, one eye slowly closing before coming open fully once again.

"I wanted only to be safe." She tried to smile at him, the effect more gruesome than pleasant. "My daughter, you see, is traveling to see me. I have a new grandchild. I was preparing her room. The dust from the stones has made it hard." Her words were weak by the time she was finished, and she let her face relax, her eyes looking away to the sky above. Thin, white clouds had begun to gather, but the heavens were still blue, and the day was brilliant. A large bird could be seen flying far overhead. The woman took in none of it.

"Do you wish to be free of your pain?" Parik so wanted to do this. It was the one thing he could do in all this. "Let me help."

Her eyes turned to him, unfocused, and she whispered, "Make it go away. I can stand no more."

Parik took a deep breath as he felt his fourth finger warm, the nail really, then it turned hot, as the healing force flowed from him. Her life would soon leave her, but she would have at least these final few moments of peace. Her crushed body he could do nothing about. If the stone were removed, perhaps, but it was very large, impossible to shift without levers and many men. What he gave was all he had to offer. He smiled as the woman's face took on a tranquil expression.

"Your grandchild. Male or female?"

When she turned, the woman's eyes saw him now. "I've seen her once. I traveled to the Eastern Lands where spices grow as the grasses in the fields. Five days travel, it was, and she was yet to be born." She smiled at the memory, and tears of joy ran down her face. "When she came, her fingers were so tiny, and her eyes were green, the color of yours." She chuckled at her remembrances, and it caused her to cough, bringing blood to her lips. "She's three seasons, now. It will be my second time to see her. My husband went to fetch them to the city." She gave Parik's hand a quick squeeze. "You'll be glad to meet them."

"Your grandchild's name?" Parik patted the blood from her mouth with the sleeve of her tunic.

"Eileithyia. My daughter calls her Eile." The woman's voice tapered off, and her hand released its grip on Parik's. Slowly, her head rolled to the side, her eyes wide and unseeing.

A sudden odor of urine filled the air, and Parik knew. This grandmother was dead, her essence released to whatever gods she worshipped. She would never see her Eile again, and if the grandchild was lucky, she and her protectors were still far from the city and wouldn't arrive for some time. Only that might save them. Parik couldn't. He couldn't even stop this nightmare he drew unto this people. He'd benefit from it, if benefit was a word he could use to describe his hellish immortality.

With resignation, he released the woman's hand and stood. He had at least done two good deeds, the first with the rat and the second with the woman lying here beside him. Three if he counted the woman during the night. She had her child, and she was on her way out of the city.

Parik stepped from the tumbled stone and moved down into the main thoroughfare. The road was very wide here, and it parted in the center to pass on either side of a fountain. The water still flowed into the cascade, drawn in by piping from the reservoir outside the city walls. The top of the fountain had shaken loose, and the water gurgled forth rather than doing its usual dance in the air.

Parik stepped to the reflecting pool at the base of the fountain and sat on the low surrounding wall. Leaning over, he reached to splash water on his face, and in a glimpse, he saw what others saw. The shakings had truly taken any semblance of youth from him. Below the selvage of his headcloth, lines were gouged deeply into his skin, and dark circles had sprouted under his eyes.

He knew the damage ran deeper. Beneath his skin, he was tired, filled with the exhaustion of old age. It would get worse, too, with each shaking the city endured.

Breaking the water with his hand, he splashed it across his face, not caring if his headcloth or vestments were moistened as well. Rubbing the liquid over his arms, he was relieved to see the dust of the city disperse from his skin. In all his centuries, he hadn't learned to enjoy being filthy, and this small refreshing was one he didn't hesitate to indulge.

A noise caught his attention. It was the barking of a dog. Parik looked up, knowing this sound had no relation to the earlier frightened yelping in the distance. This was high-pitched and moving very quickly, a barking that was insistent and self-righteous.

From a side street, one that ran with steps up to the highest reaches of the city, a small bit of fluff darted out, its four little legs barely visible underneath its coat of downy fur. Parik smiled. The source of all the noise had made itself known.

Then, as the animal darted from person to person,

occasionally stumbling, telling everyone it could find to pay attention, two youths dashed from the same side street, a male, tall and slender, wearing only a loincloth, and a girl, about the same age and very pretty. They stopped, apparently taken aback by the confusion in the street, the youth's chest heaving with his exertion, and the girl pulling her clothing away from her body in an effort to cool off. Sighting the dog, the youth burst into a scrambling pursuit followed by the girl.

Parik cupped his hands in the fountain, bringing out water. Holding it at street level, he waited. The animal must be thirsty, and if so, it would perhaps pause to take a drink. Sure enough, when the dog approached Parik to bark its message to him in hopes he'd understand, the water caught its attention, and it did exactly as Parik expected. In one quick motion, the big man dropped the water and wrapped his hands around the creature. Then his eyes saw the youth's bare feet slide to a stop right in front of him.

"Thank you, kind sir." The youth's shoulders heaved as he dropped his hands to rest them on his knees in exhaustion. The sheen on his skin was evidence of his recent run down the obstructed city street in his efforts to catch the dog. "ChiChi—" he raised one hand to point to the dog, gasping, "—belongs to my friend." The youth turned to point to the girl, only to have her bump into him, grabbing one of his bare arms for support.

"ChiChi!" She released her young companion's arm and held her hands out. "You bad little thing! Come to Dulcia!"

Parik wagged a finger to tell her to wait. Holding the dog securely, he lowered it to the surface of the pool and was pleased to see it continue to drink. When it was finished, he lifted it up to hold it in his lap, running his hand over the animal's body, hoping to find why it had stumbled in its run across the street.

"Your name, youth?" Parik continued to run his hand over the dog's head as he looked at the boy. "This is ChiChi, and your friend is obviously Dulcia. That's clear." He chuckled when he saw her pull the corner of her headcloth over the bottom of her face. His eyes turned back to the youth. "Your name I don't know, and I can only identify such a nameless one as Loincloth. Do you have a different name, one you would prefer to be called? Or will Loincloth suit you well?"

Flushing brightly around the neck, Æolus choked out an answer. "Not Loincloth, please, sir." He glanced at Dulcia to find a grin not quite hidden behind the corner of her headcloth. Self-consciously, he reached to tighten his wrappings, pulling the top loose and tucking it more tightly to ensure his modesty.

"Well?" Parik chuckled, finding the boy's shyness refreshing.

"Æolus, if you please," the embarrassed young man mumbled.

Parik laughed. "Louder, youth." He was enjoying this. These children were still involved in life, concerned about small things such as a fluff of a dog, modesty, and Loincloth, while death and destruction rained down all around them. He pressed the youth once again, "Your name, Loincloth?"

"Æolus," the answer was repeated, but stronger this time. "My name is Æolus, good friend of Loukas who has been to see the temple serving women." Æolus stood tall at that pronouncement.

"And you haven't, I presume. By the way you boast, I assume you could. Have you nothing to confess?"

"I've been invited. Just now on the temple steps, by one of the temple serving women." He glanced at Dulcia for corroboration and turned red when he saw her laughing.

"So, Æolus, also known as Loincloth. You've been on the temple steps. I didn't know one had to have an invitation to visit the temple serving women. They're simply there for your supplication, as long as you drop coins in the coffer box. Is there more to this story? Was this a practice trip, just in case the city walls begin to fall? You do want to make sure to visit the temple serving women to beg the gods' forgiveness before you die, after all." Of what the boy needed forgiveness, Parik was sure there was nothing. After all, this boy was no more than a child just entering the first stages of manhood.

"Please, sir, don't call the name of Loincloth, even in jest. Others might overhear." The boy's eyes pleaded, as did his hands, pressing together to form a small prayer temple.

"Not Loincloth, then." With a not-quite-concealed grin, Parik turned his eyes to the dog, brushing its fur with his hand, finding the weak spot in its hip joint. He could help this animal before it died. These children would also die, but they were not dead, yet. They were very full of life, and Parik needed to see life around him.

"Sir, my friend's dog? He belongs to Dulcia, and we would take him and go, leaving you in peace." When Parik didn't reply, Æolus tried again. "You've family you need to attend to, I'm sure. Please, sir, may I have ChiChi?"

"I've no one." Parik's voice was soft as he looked up at Æolus, and he paused as he felt the warmth flow from his finger. "I also don't wish to be left in peace. If you weren't at the temple for absolution from the serving women, why did you brag to me about it? You were there for some reason, or you weren't there. Your city is falling around you. Were you there to pray? I see no coinsack at your waist to carry the coins the priests would require for a prayer mighty enough to save your city."

"I had no coins. My mother forgot to hand them to me." He dropped his head in shame.

"Good sir." Dulcia broke in. "There was a crippled girl, and her brother had died. We took her to the temple serving women for care. Æolus carried her all the way." She smiled at that, reaching to gently touch her friend's arm.

Parik lifted his hand to his headcloth and pulled it from his hair. At the same time, he slipped his catch sack free, shaking his head to let his locks loosen in the breeze. Then, he bit one corner of the headcloth, and with one hand, he stripped the selvage edge from the fabric in one long tear. Deftly, he tied it around the dog's neck and formed the loose end into a loop. Letting the dog to the ground, he handed the loop to the girl.

"Now, he won't run away. You must protect your little ChiChi." Almost as if an afterthought, he questioned, "The girl's name. Was it Chiarina?"

Dulcia looked at Æolus and then to Parik. She knelt to pick up her pet as she asked, "Does she know you? Her brother, he's still there. Æolus placed him on the mat and covered him. There was nothing we could do."

"Not by name, she doesn't. I had thought to help her, but she wasn't ready—"

"ChiChi." Excitement flooded Dulcia's voice, as well as disbelief, also. "His hip no longer shifts. How?" She looked at Æolus for a time, and then she turned to Parik. "You did something, didn't you, when you held him?"

She placed the dog on the ground, letting it run at the end of the makeshift leash. "See, Æolus, he no longer stumbles." Her eyes glowed as she scooped the small animal back into her arms.

"You did this?" Æolus looked at Parik. "It was you I saw earlier. I thought so when I saw you here. A rat was following you, one with three legs. Then I saw a rat enter the temple."

"It made it, then." Parik smiled.

Æolus turned to Dulcia with a grin. "Remember, the rat you pointed out on the temple steps? It had four legs. Let me see ChiChi." He held the dog and felt of its hindquarters through its fur. Then he grinned broadly, looking at Parik. "It was the same rat, wasn't it?"

Kneeling in front of Parik, Dulcia touched him on the knee. "Are you from the goddess? You've healed my ChiChi. Æolus thinks you healed a rat. Did you?"

"He did, Dulcia." Æolus sat on the wall by Parik, excitement running fingers of color over his skin, the flush quickly crawling into his neck and face. His loincloth and the teasing were clearly forgotten, as were the absent coins. "You don't have to ask, Dulcia, for I'm convinced the healings are true."

He turned to the man at his side and spoke with enthusiastic vigor. "We're attempting to reach our homes. Everything's gotten in our way. The aqueduct—" The youth's voice, only weeks into its deepened register, cracked. At the mention of where their homes were located, his body drooped. "My home's just there. I live with my mother. She said it was raining, and no clouds were in the sky."

"The goddess will help us. Surely. What's your name, sir?" Dulcia reached to kiss her dog on the tip of its nose, but her eyes stayed on the man who had helped them. "Are you a servant of the goddess, here to save us?"

"Parik is how I'm called." He wished he were here to save this city. Instead, he was the one destroying it. He couldn't tell this girl that, though. It would rob her, as well as the boy, of hope, and hope was now all the mortals in the city had to cling to.

As he paused, Parik felt the familiar lurching in his body that told of what was to come. He grabbed the arms of the youths with him and hissed, "The stones are about to shake, and hard. Stand not near a building nor anything tall. Be safe."

Dulcia frowned. "When, sir?" She looked up at the slender wisps of clouds stringing across the blue sky, squinting at the sun as its warmth brushed her face. The destruction around her was severe, but the air was pleasant, if a bit too warm. Here by the fountain it was cool, though, and for a moment, the horrors she and Æolus had seen had been pushed away.

"Now, child." He pulled them away from the fountain, crouching with them in the street, his arms over their shoulders. "Prepare. Many will die this time."

As if on cue, the world around them began to heave, and the screams and the crashing of stone told the devastation. Before the shaking was done, it seemed as if not one stone could be left stacked upon another. The final affront was when even the arches holding the remaining spans of the compromised aqueduct shifted on their foundations and came crashing to the ground.

Many did die, and there was nothing Parik could do.

Nothing at all.

11

THE HORSE STOOD CONTENTEDLY munching grass. The Muse was less contented. He curled in the back of the cart, his skin covered with the stink of sweat, and his eyes frantic under closed lids.

Despite the Muse's problems, the ground was still, and the sky was clear. Field birds chattered and hopped among their nests. The city could be seen rising against the foothills in the distance, with the mists of the mountain's highest reaches swelling farther behind.

The Muse was in excruciating pain. He was too close to the city, and Parik was pulling much power. While still in the city proper, he'd managed to hold to a body despite Parik's shaking of the stones. To have the man's changes affect him this far away, the time of his rebirth must be very near, with the energy drawing around him exponentially. Still, the Muse mustn't lose this body, and the holding on was tearing him apart. Never had Parik been so cruel. If only Parik hadn't given that wench a child, the Muse could have run from the city's destruction, free for a time.

This body was a good one, though, and the Muse didn't intend to give it up, not willingly, anyway. He wanted to see the shock in Parik's face when his own son pierced him with a blade. The son would curse the father for his lack of affection, and just before Parik died, the Muse would reveal who he really was. The justice would be supreme.

Now, though? The Muse groaned in torment, and the horse lifted its head to look at him. The day was beautiful, despite the Muse's noises, and the animal had no cause for concern. For that reason, it dropped its head and began to eat once again.

"THADDIAOS WAS GONE." The words were soft, and only one set of ears was close enough to hear. "He was gone, and I didn't know. I was glad he was sleeping."

"Shush, my dear. Your brother is in the final sleep, and nothing can hurt him now. Rest." The old temple serving woman who had congratulated this girl on her immunity from joining the temple was sorrowful to see her here now. The demands of temple protocol drew much from the women, especially ones who were newly entered into service, and if the duty of absolution—the carrying of water basins and the washing of the defiled; the many steps to be climbed to the High Altar—caused the girl discomfort, some petitioners would enjoy it so much the better.

Yet, what choices did the girl have? She couldn't earn a living outside of the temple, and to beg was to die. Her brother was proof of that. There were herbs, though. Many of the temple serving women took them to endure the onslaught of petitioners during feast days when there was no charge for the use of the temple facilities, especially the baser petitions for those who wished the use of the most secluded chambers. On those days, the serving women not chosen for more carnal duties would stand swinging the incense braziers for hours on end, often until their joints hurt.

Thank the goddess those times only happened on the solstice days. Even she'd been forced to hear the petitions the last feast day, willing those in attendance not to comment on her extreme age, or the shaking in her voice as she read the prescribed questions. Then there had been the ritual washing of the petitioners and the many trips up the steps carrying the heavy basins. Afterwards, she was relieved she was too old to be desired for the more carnal duties anymore. Several of the younger women had been forced to endure multiple private observances, and they had walked gingerly for days.

She looked down as a rat scampered across her foot. She'd seen it earlier, and it seemed to have an affinity for this girl. Rats that resided in the temple were considered holy by all, and they did sometimes attach themselves to certain individuals.

This wasn't an animal she recognized, however, and she wondered if it had come in with the cripple. If so, the old temple serving woman would have proof beyond a doubt that this girl was blessed by the goddess, and the child would have a special place in the temple forever. She might never have to join the others on the temple floor.

Suddenly feeling dizzy, as if the world were moving around her, the old woman realized the stones were indeed shaking once again. As dust filtered down on her head, she reached to cover Chiarina's face with a cloth. From outside the temple walls, screaming could be heard, and she knew it must be very bad this time.

Then she noticed a movement under Chiarina's thin blanket, and after a short time, a long snout with whiskers and two dark eyes peeked out. Despite the dust falling all around her, the old temple serving woman smiled. The two young people had been right to bring the child to the temple. If the rat had followed her here and befriended her, this crippled child was indeed blessed of the goddess, perhaps even one of her daughters, no matter who the child's earthly parents had been.

Somehow that made it worth all the alms the old temple serving woman had given the child the past few seasons. The other women had laughed at her for doing so, and now she was justified to have followed the goddess' leading, just as she'd always claimed to the critics around her. Vindication felt very good, and once the shaking was stopped and the city was put back into order, she'd make sure everyone knew.

"YOU MAY RISE, CHILDREN." Parik released his arms from their shoulders and stood.

"Is it over?" Dulcia wrinkled her nose as she pulled ChiChi close. "ChiChi, don't be afraid. I know you are. I can smell it on you. Just be glad this man was with us to warn us." She turned to Æolus. "Æolus, it's over, isn't it?"

"I hope so." His words shook.

When his eyes joined hers, and they looked about them, they found a city severely injured. The fountain they had sat at still burbled water, but the central structure had fallen just where they'd been sitting. It had broken the low wall, and water was leaking onto the paving of the street.

"Look," she said, pointing to where the aqueduct had once arched over the lower city. "It's gone."

Parik motioned to his new wards. "Up, children. There's nothing to be done here. We must find your families."

"Nothing?" Æolus called out, his voice cracking with emotion. "Listen. Do you hear the people moaning? More walls have fallen. There's much to be done."

Parik searched the boy's face. The remains of the aqueduct had tumbled onto the city and its inhabitants, and what would be found when the young man returned to the street of his home? Yet, the boy desired to help others. His face showed his earnestness—or desperation—and for that, Parik was pleased.

"You're right, my friend, Æolus." He reached and placed a newly parchment-layered hand on the youth's shoulder. "How could someone who is concerned about others not be a friend of mine? Now, what should we do for them? Let's decide that."

Centuries before, Parik had wanted to help everyone, just as this youth did now. However, those same centuries had taught him much. It was impossible for one man to help all, and so one man simply had to do what he could, even if that wasn't much. It had taken lifetimes for Parik to learn that truth. This youth wouldn't have the one lifetime he deserved.

Æolus danced around and pointed. "There, those stones need to be moved, and up the steps, a house has collapsed. We should check for people inside. Water. We have water still here at the fountain. We can take them water." He turned to Dulcia, who stood in silence holding her small companion. "Dulcia, tell him."

Her voice was small. "I want to go home, Æolus." Tears began to run from her eyes, and ChiChi squirmed in her grasp.

"Æolus." Parik's pressure on the boy's shoulder was gentle. "You have a family, and I'm sure your friend does, also. Do you think they might be looking for you?"

"I'm right here, wanting to help." He threw his shoulders back, making himself tall. "I'm safe. My mother shouldn't worry."

"Does she know that?" Parik's hand still rested on the boy's skin, taming his impulsive drive to help undo the damage that had been done. It couldn't be undone. Parik knew that, and he also knew the youth's enthusiasm would wane once the hard work started. He needed to find his family. That was all that was important. Those who now lay around them dying? No matter how much help the youth gave the injured, these people would be dead in a day.

"Please, Æolus." Dulcia touched his arm, and in that motion, ChiChi saw the perfect chance to jump to the ground to drink from the spreading puddle, pulling the newly made leash from Dulcia's hand.

"Dulcia! The cord!" Æolus called and pointed. "Grab it quickly."

"ChiChi! No!" The girl called in a panic-stricken voice. "Come back, ChiChi!"

Parik stepped on the makeshift leash with his sandal, and he reached to pick up the loop he'd contrived. Handing it to the girl, he turned to the youth. "Home, first? For your friend?"

"Please, Æolus." Dulcia knelt to pick up her pet.

"Let him walk, girl." Parik motioned, waiting until she stood without him. "That's what the leash is for."

Æolus' shoulders drooping, he gave in. "I'll go with you, Parik, sir, if you think you can help us find our way. We tried earlier, but my friend, Loukas, his house's wall fell into the street, and we had to go around. Then there was the girl who had to be taken to the temple." He paused, wiping the backs of his hands against his face, creating smears in the gathered dust. Then, without warning, his true feelings poured forth. "What if my mother is injured, or even . . ." He could speak no more as the water in his eyes flooded down.

"Æolus." Parik called his name, watching him for a moment until the youth's eyes slowed and he looked up. "We'll go look. We'll all be together, and we'll find what we find. That's all I can offer." Parik looked at Dulcia. "Are you with us?" When she nodded, he took her arm and started them the right direction, asking the two young people directions as necessary.

As they progressed farther into the lower city, the press of the displaced populace became more disconcerting. At one point, rounding a corner to a disruptive scene, Parik pulled the two youths into a doorway without explanation, wrapping his arms around them and drawing their heads to his chest. He turned his eyes, refusing to look at the events in progress in the street just past the doorway.

He'd seen it before in other lives and in other cities, and he wondered if men would ever outgrow the moral depravities that convenient opportunity offered them. Partially clothed, bloodied children were being dragged down the pavement, none older than the two he held at his side. They may well have been orphaned in the shakings that had begun to pull the city apart, or perhaps not. Even so, these children would be dead by these men's doings within a handsbreadth of time, Parik had no doubt. It was cruel, even if they would soon die with everyone else in the city, no matter what.

When ChiChi grew tired of being trapped, the dog's sudden, rapid barking finally chided Æolus into breaking free of Parik's hold.

"What are you hiding from us, Parik? I know what you're doing. I'm not a child."

"Back, boy. There are things no eyes should see, whether boy or man."

By then Æolus had leaned out through the doorway, and his face grew pale as a scream from across the way pierced the air. Turning to look at Parik, he blanched even more.

"Æolus!" Dulcia reached for her friend's arm. "What did you see?" She made to move forward, but Parik put his arm out to bar her way.

"No, young Dulcia. I suspect I know, and you don't need to see. Æolus," he reached for the youth's arm, "stand back with us. The scene will pass, and then we'll move on."

"One is my tutor, Thanatos. He comes to Loukas' villa to tutor the two of us." Æolus' voice was dazed, and newfound shock was in his eyes. "He . . . he was a soldier once. I knew that, but he never gave us a reason to fear. Now, he beats my friend Zakkhaios with a stout beam. What can I do?"

"Shush. Hold, boy. Don't say more." Parik pushed him back and stepped to the door. What he saw was morbidly horrific as a bulky, older man wearing a red tunic hit a smooth-skinned youth about Æolus' size over and over. The boy's hands clawed the wall, and his panicked face was pressed to the side. His clothing was torn and hung loosely from one shoulder. It was clear that the man was demanding the boy do something, steal for him, perhaps answer to him as a slave to a master, or, heaven forbid, something worse.

"The older man in red, heavyset, is your tutor?" When Æolus nodded, Parik asked a second question. "The youth with him? He's the one you call a friend?"

"Zakkhaios. He's my father's godson, from when my father still lived, and he's one whom I call a true friend. He tutors with Loukas and me when his own tutor is ill." Æolus' eyes showed tears of desperation. "Our tutor always favored him of the three of us."

Parik thought he understood why. He whipped his blade from its sheath. He'd still make this body do as he commanded, even as his vitality was taken from him, and he'd help this friend of a friend. He pointed at the two he protected.

"Stay, no matter what happens. We won't abandon a friend. We can't help everyone, but this one will benefit from my blade this day." He paused, and with a sudden reach of his hand, he touched the headcloth Dulcia still wore. "The boy may need bandages, if I'm able to return with him alive. Will you share if need be? This, just to wrap his wounds?"

Without waiting for a reply, Parik leaped into the street, and despite the rapid draining of his strength, he pulled from his aging body remnants of the soldier's quickness he'd garnered over many lifetimes of experience. His tight-fitting sandals slapping the paving stones, he leaped over one child who had been dropped already, eyes wide, obviously dead, and dodged a hysterical woman, keeping his eyes trained on the youth he intended to rescue. The child might be dead by sunrise even without this tutor's assault, but no boy deserved to endure this torture.

Parik grabbed the old tutor's shoulder roughly and barked his demand to him. "Leave this boy be. He isn't yours to take."

"What's it to you?" The old tutor, perspiring and obviously exhausted by his beating of the youth, breathed his responses heavily. Without looking, he raised the board once again, yelling to the boy, "Will you do as I say?"

Parik brandished his blade, and grabbing at what Æolus had said, lied. "This boy is Zakkhaios, my godson."

"You're a fool, if you think I believe that." The tutor's hands gripped the boy's shoulders, pulling his half-naked, bloody body to him, holding him tightly in the way one holds an intended lover. "This one will be my slave, or he will die. Get your own boy. This one is mine." The man turned from Parik, lifting his arm once again to bury the massive beam in the youth's hair. The boy yelled in fear, reaching one bloodied hand ineffectually to ward off the blow.

Parik placed the point of his blade against the man's back, and he burned his words into his ears. "This one *is* my boy!" Then, with the heel of his palm on the butt of the blade, he drove it upwards with all his strength.

The man staggered and collapsed, and in the falling, he took his youthful victim to the ground with him. Parik pulled his blade free and wiped it on the fallen man's tunic. Then, with a look of compassion, he reached down and took the youth's hand.

"Zakkhaios. Your friend, Æolus, asked me to help. He waits for us. Come, now." He pulled hard, bringing the youth to a standing position. Throwing his arm around him, he ran with him to the doorway where Parik's other two wards waited. Reaching them, Dulcia already had her headcloth prepared, and the blood from Zakkhaios' wounds was soon sopped with the fabric.

Æolus wiped his eyes and gave his friend a quick hug. "You're safe, Zakkhaios. I saw old Thanatos at you, and I was afraid."

The new youth turned his eyes to catch Parik's as he hugged Æolus back. "I was, too, Æole. I was afraid, too."

It was the gratefulness in his look that caught at Parik's heart. This rebirth was certain to be very hard. He now had three charges, he knew they would all die, and he was finding he cared about them very much. For the first time in many lives, he felt moisture at his eyes, knowing full well the price of his immortality. It was a price he wished these three youths wouldn't be required to pay.

12

IN THE MOST ANCIENT of days, the beds of coals that had erupted from the bowels of creation still burned hot, and only Lamahätsu dared walk near. This night she strode the edges of the fires that licked from the coals, her mind heavy in thought. She'd thrown her Stones of Divination, and they had given her unusual visions. Her Fifth Arm of Death toyed with her hair, sometimes pulling too hard, at which times she stopped and growled her annoyance.

This youth she'd birthed, this man, wasn't yet ripe, and her patience was stretched. He had three seasons more to mature, three turns of this world around the axis of its sun, and he'd be ready. Already, though, he was tall, and his arms were strong. She watched him at night, coming to him in his dreams, and she knew he was mature in his longings, as well. He dreamed of things that told her so. Yet, she wouldn't pluck him too soon, despite her need.

He must be ready.

Still, the Stones, and what they had said. Could tonight be the night?

Pausing, she heard the faintest of sounds. It was Parikshit, and he called for her. Her heart leaped, or perhaps it was her loins that leaped, for there was a surge of vitality that raged through Lamahätsu's ancient body, a longing that she couldn't contain, and she wanted nothing else than to be by Parikshit's side.

She clapped her Two Hands of Life, and a great wind arose, shearing the flames from the superheated beds of coals at her back. It swirled around her with a violence that no mortal could have survived. Her Fifth Arm of Death hovering over her head fluttered randomly, not liking this emotion, this arousal, this lust. Yet, Lamahätsu didn't care. She was the Goddess of Life, the Mother Goddess, and the Eater of Essences. She could do as she pleased, and as long as none forgot her, she'd wield her powers long upon the earth. The very forces of nature were at her command, and none could deprive her of her every wish.

Except satisfaction.

That was the one wish she'd long been deprived of. Since the birthing of the world, the time when the very essence of life had surreptitiously dumped itself from her womb, she'd known no satisfaction, and that's why she'd birthed Parikshit.

Now he called her.

The wind became a maelstrom, and raising her Two Hands of Healing, Lamahätsu clapped them sharply together. With a flash of lightning, Lamahätsu was the wind, and she rushed to find Parik. Within moments, she was flinging herself over vast oceans, leaving violently turbulent seas in her wake. Then, approaching land, she pulled the waters ashore with her in a deadly tidal wave. As she swept over snow-covered mountaintops, the moisture she carried with her was flung into the highest reaches of the atmosphere. Freezing into crystals of ice and snow, the remains of the seawater layered blizzards down the leeward sides. It was only when she reached the forest that she slowed her progress, made herself into a gentle breeze, and became the accommodating goddess men desired to worship.

Searching the trees, stroking each bough tenderly, she questioned them, "Have you seen a handsome youth, one with dark hair and fiery green eyes? His is the skin of the palest olive, and his voice is the flutter of an eagle's wing. Laugh with me, trees, because he's here among you."

They did laugh with the great Goddess Lamahätsu. They hardly dared not do so. However, they did love her son, and they would have laughed anyway, for he was everything she said, and kindhearted as well.

That didn't keep him from the maidens, though, as

Lamahätsu would find out this night.

Pointing with their boughs, she was directed to an old stone hut, one with a massive thatched roof, weathered gray with age. Outside the hut, a great fire raged in an opening in the ground, one that was ringed with a double row of standing stones. People crowded around great boards spread with food, and the mood was festive.

As the wind that was Lamahätsu settled to the ground, the flames from the fire flickered, drawing the crowd's attention, all except for one dark-haired, green-eyed youth. He knew what the disturbance was, for he'd called.

As the wind calmed, out of a flash of light appeared his mother, the Womb of Creation, the Bringer of Life. She kept her Two Arms of Healing tucked neatly into her robes, and in her wild disarray of hair, her Fifth Arm of Death was practically invisible.

Parikshit, as he was known then, called to those gathered with him. "All, you must come. It's as I promised. My mother has come to my celebration." He raised an earthen mug, and as he did, he turned in a great circle, making sure none ignored his call. He stopped to find his mother's arm at his side, and as she ran her First Hand of Life up his back, letting it touch the bare skin at his neck, a surge of energy flowed from her, one that invigorated the furthest parts of his body.

"What celebration, precious son of mine? I wasn't aware." Her voice shimmered softly as she spoke, beating with the wings of gathering butterflies.

He turned, surprise spilling across his face. "I'm fifteen, Mother. Have you forgotten?" He smiled at her. "You should come out of your lair more often. The world is changing, and you'll be left behind."

"Changing, and I'll be left behind? What custom is this celebration of which you speak?" The butterflies' wings blurred faster, harder, the words carrying an edge, as if the beautiful creatures feared for their lives. Lamahätsu's First Hand of Life traced sensuously down Parik's back. The leathers of his rugged clothing kept his skin from her direct contact, though, and it was just a touch.

"It's a wonderful custom, Mother, and you know quite well the feel of my back. Hands off, today." Parik laughed and pushed her hand away, his earlier invigoration softened with the absence of his mother's hand against his neck. "Come. Join in the merriment. I've invited you to celebrate my entrance into manhood, and I've someone special for you to meet." He reached to take her hand, the Second Hand of Life, the one that was safe to touch. With this hand, no wooden mugs would grow roots or doors sprout leaves; no flowers would spring forth overnight; or ewes become with lamb.

"Ah." Lamahätsu felt his hesitancy. "So, in what way do we celebrate this special day?" As she spoke, her voice keened as a blade of grass held between the fingers and blown upon. It indicated her disappointment with his skittering answers. Yet, she was here for Parik. She'd rather he'd called her for a time spent alone, but he hadn't, and any time spent with him was better than time spent in her own company. He'd be hers, eventually. She must be patient.

"Eat and drink, Mother." Parik motioned with his hand to the crowd. "Visit. Tell an amusing story." He paused and turned to her with a pleading look. "I make one request of you, though. Only touch with this, your Second Hand. No one would understand if you blessed them with your First. Be good, Mother. I've anticipated your attendance today. You're my only parent, and I treasure you greatly."

"For that I'm grateful, Parikshit." The gathering butterflies once again whispered her words in his ear, speaking with their beating wings. She reached with her First Hand and touched his collarbone, running it alongside his neck against the engorged blood vessel that ran just there, smiling sweetly, knowing full well what she was doing to him.

He sighed and pushed her hand away.

"Mother, I can manage that quite well on my own. I'm fifteen. I need no help there." He stepped away, turning to motion once again to all that was spread out before them. "Enjoy, Mother, and remember, later you have someone to meet."

"Parikshit!" A distant clap of thunder called his name, causing everyone to turn.

"Sweetly, Mother." Parik's rebuke was softly spoken. "These are my friends. Please." He held his finger to his lips and smiled.

"Where's this person I'm to meet? I wish to know." A bird's sweet voice sang Lamahätsu's words, the sounds tinkling softly across the clearing, for she harbored her irritation. The bird was her change in approach, and her peace offering was its song.

He stepped to her and took her Second Hand with a wide smile. He pulled it to his mouth to kiss it. "Inside, Mother. She's preparing."

"For what, dear son?" The bird's song hardened, becoming the caw of a crow. She'd thrown the Stones of Divination, reading from them what she could, and the Stones had whispered of the fulfillment of Parikshit's most intimate dreams. She heard the gender word he used, and she didn't like it. This youth was to be hers and hers alone. It was why she'd birthed him.

However, divinations were rarely clear, for they whispered of possibilities only, and they could be misleading. She must know, and Parik must tell her.

"For me, Mother. Of course, she's preparing for me." With those words, Parik laughed and darted off, his green eyes sparkling with his words, and his black hair blowing in the wind.

Lamahätsu's heart twisted in her ancient body, and it twisted for two reasons. She lusted after that laughing youth, the one she called her son, and she lusted strongly, too. Also, she no longer needed divinations to know that the person in that hut did, too, and if that was what played out here this day, Lamahätsu would be very displeased, indeed.

THE SHADOWS HAD GROWN long, and still Lamahätsu hadn't seen this special person from within the thatch-roofed stone hut. She'd done and been everything Parik had asked of her, though. Her words had been the flutter of fairy wings, and her laughter had tinkled like summer showers dancing upon still water. Her Two Arms of Healing had stayed inside her cloak, and her Fifth Arm of Death hadn't moved. Only her Second Hand of Life, the hand that gave the energy of existence, the extended strength to keep the celebration flowing for many handbreadths of time, had been allowed to touch any of Parik's friends. She'd charmed everyone, and she knew it. Parik did, too, and in the cooling evening, as those around gathered close to the warming flames, he stepped to his mother and kissed her on the cheek.

"It's time, Mother." He beamed his smile. "She's ready, and you'll meet her now." He grasped his mother's Second Hand and pulled her to stand in a place of honor just outside the hut's rough door. He stood beside her, and he motioned with one hand to a young maid who seemed barely older than Parik, his face grinning stupidly as the maid reached to open the door.

When the door swung wide, out stepped a vision of mortal loveliness. Her hair was the color of the winter snows, and it was piled high atop her head. Tendrils loosely wrapped in vines and small flowers cascaded along her forehead and down the back of her neck. She wore a simple white shift adorned with berries and small blossoms. Her lips were the red of the rose, and when she looked up, the green foam of the sea was in her eyes.

The crowd sighed with anticipation while Lamahätsu silently fumed. She knew confirmation, then. This was no simple mortal gathering to celebrate her son's seasons. This was to be a bonding with this girl.

Even as she smiled, Lamahätsu smoldered with the knowledge that Parik, her son, was to be wasted on this child who could clearly take any mortal she wanted. It was unfair of the fledgling to steal Lamahätsu's son for herself. It was cruel to do such a thing.

As the girl approached, Lamahätsu smiled sweetly, and her words were soft. The goddess admired her hair and commented favorably on the choice of berries on her dress. She brushed her face with her Second Hand, admiring the beautiful texture of her skin. Then, as she reached to kiss the girl's cheek, gently and carefully so Parik didn't see, Lamahätsu softly touched the girl's side with her First Hand. The girl gave a quick frown as if her stomach was suddenly queasy, and then she forcibly brightened once more, returning a kiss of her own to Lamahätsu's left cheek.

Lamahätsu's mood lightened considerably. She knew that by morning the girl would have all the early signs of carrying a child, and the queasiness in the girl's stomach would quite spoil Parik's admirations the rest of the evening.

After the pair disappeared into the hut, Lamahätsu decided her joy in the evening wasn't quite complete. She made the rounds of Parik's friends once again, but with a different intent in mind.

"The flowers you've managed to work into your hair, dear . . ." The whisper was heard in the colors of the setting sun, and their vibrancy made clear the sincerity of Lamahätsu's compliment. "Are they wild, or have you managed to tame them yourself?" She reached with her First Hand, giving just a touch. The young woman pressed against her stomach as if something disagreed with her.

Next, Lamahätsu turned to the young man at her side. They were obviously a pair, and it wouldn't do for the woman to receive such a wonderful gift without offering her young man the pleasure that went along with it. She reached and cupped his chin in her First Hand.

"So handsome." She paused, watching the surprise on his face. When he could no longer look her in the eyes, his own glazing with the intensity of pleasure coursing through his body, Lamahätsu patted his face. Then, she leaned to him, whispering, "No woman will ever again match my touch."

Lamahätsu did make the rounds that evening, leaving a string of queasy young women and sheepish boymen, most no more than the age of her son. Her only disappointment was a serving boy who seemed barely into manhood, if that. He was the second male she'd blessed. He followed Lamahätsu the rest of the evening with a hopeful smile on his face, and just before she clapped her hands for the winds to carry her away, Lamahätsu took pity on him, reaching to his shoulder one more time. To experience her touch twice in one day, well, now he'd indeed be spoiled forever. Each of the males who was touched by Lamahätsu's First Hand of Life was. No mortal woman would ever be able to compare.

"MOTHER!" PARIK STORMED THROUGH the clearing. The stones still stood tall and straight, but the ashes in the pit were three weeks old. It was his first time back since, and he was certain what Lamahätsu had done.

He strode angrily to the hut and threw back the door. The bedding was as they had left it. The girl had been so ill that they had done nothing at all, and now she was clearly with child. It wasn't Parik's child, though, and the girl claimed she'd been with no one else before or after. Parik, for one, believed her. That left only his insanely jealous mother.

Then the wind in the trees made Parik look up. He could tell she'd heard, and he scowled expectantly. He hoped she was contrite. If not, he'd endure her anger. It wouldn't matter to him. Lightning, thunder, even hail. None could be worse than what he'd already experienced.

"I love you, Parikshit. I await, and yet you've failed to come to me."

The leaves rustled, but Parik understood every word.

"The women are with child, Mother. Every single one. Why did you do it?" He knew, though, or at least he thought he did. She was insanely jealous. He didn't quite understand her grand plan, though. Not yet, anyway.

The leaves rustled louder, and the sound was the laughter in her words. "It was a celebration, my son. Why must it be me?"

"Because, Mother dear," he yelled the words, "half the females there that day have never taken a partner. They're chaste. Do you know that word, Mother, or is it just another series of sounds strung together for you to mutilate? Now they carry children, and they're still chaste." The sky had darkened, but Parik didn't care. The more he talked, the angrier he became. "Of the males, I've no proof, but I suspect they received your touch, also. I wish I had never let you know of my celebration. What you did was wrong."

"Wrong?" The sky had blackened to deepest ink as Parik spoke, and now the color shifted to become a twisting vortex of obsidian shards. Thunder threw Lamahätsu's words at him. "Wrong? I am the ageless Five-Armed Goddess, the Womb of Creation, the Bringer of Life." Rain began to pound the ground, and mixed in was hail. "I carry the Fifth Arm of Death. My Two Arms of Life are my constant companions, as are my Two Arms of Healing. I birthed the world from my womb, and you have the audacity to call me wrong? I birthed you, Parikshit, and I decide what's right and wrong. I'm the Goddess of Life who walks the beds of coals that erupted from the bowels of creation. Don't lecture me, my son."

Parik withstood the onslaught as long as he could, but when the hail began to tear his skin, he ran for the stone hut. Once inside he pushed the wooden door shut, and he sat on the bed where he'd never gotten to celebrate the night he turned fifteen. The hail on the roof was muffled, but he could still understand his mother's ranting words. She wasn't being kind. He lay back on the cold bedding and looked at the ceiling.

"You didn't hear a word I said, did you, Mother? I

see, now, how it is, how you intend it to be. You're pleasant and comforting when it suits you, but only when it suits you." Parik whispered his next words. "Tell me, Mother, why are you so tolerant of me? What do I have that you want?"

He was surprised when the hail and rain immediately ceased. Even as well as he knew his mother, he hadn't expected that. Sitting up, he looked to the door, not knowing just what to expect. In the barest of voices, he whispered the ice buried in his heart, still thoroughly irritated and very much fifteen seasons old, and not understanding when to leave well enough alone.

"Whatever it is, Mother, you can't have it."

Just then a rapid series of lightning strikes hit immediately outside the hut, and the reverberating thunder made Parik curl up on the bed with his arms around his head. When he looked up, the door had blown open, and several of the stones had cracked and were lying on the ground. Parik knew better than to speak aloud this time. His words were only in his head.

You could have just told me, Mother. You didn't have to get angry.

Truly afraid now, he refused even to get up to close the door. He simply pulled the bedding over his body and drew his legs to his chest underneath, wishing his mother hadn't spoiled the night that should have been his and his alone.

Well, he allowed, and the girl's, too, but mostly his.

13

THE SUN STILL BLAZED overhead, and the sheerest of clouds graced the horizon. The horse flicked its ears, driving a fly away, before leaning down to tear a clump of grass at its feet.

The Muse groaned and rolled to his side, the rough wood of the cart pressing into his skin. His body hurt this time. He'd never fought so hard against Parik's gathering power. With a sudden, overwhelming need to be certain, he reached between his legs, relieved to find he was still the man he'd worked so hard to remain.

Grasping the side of the cart with Umaru's big hand, the Muse pulled himself up to look around. He chuckled when he saw the horse with its head to the ground, eating, oblivious to the unseen battle that had just been won.

"You're lucky, animal." The Muse forced himself to a squat, one hand still on the floor of the cart. When the conveyance shifted with his movements, the horse raised its head to look at him. The Muse called to it, "We have work to do, you brute. You've rested long enough, and I've vengeance to mete out."

The horse flicked an ear at him and returned to its grassy meal, from time to time pulling an additional clump from the dirt to nibble the undergrowth.

Putting his pains aside and jumping down to gather the reins, the Muse placed his hand on the animal's neck, patting it roughly, and he reached to gather some of what the creature found so tempting. Wrapping his hand around a clump and forcefully pulling it from the ground, he smelled of it, and then he smiled. Twiggleroot. The mild stimulant had once been smoked as an aphrodisiac by those familiar with its properties.

With a practiced eye, the Muse glanced around, realizing they'd stopped in an infestation. The plant was considered an invasive weed whose more interesting properties had been, for all intents, forgotten in the past half-dozen centuries or so. As nothing else would grow in a field of twiggleroot, it was systematically routed from the soil, but to benefit the Muse, nothing else needed to grow here. This alone should give the animal the increased speed required to pull the cart to the city before Parik's power shook the stones once again.

The Muse collected several dozen clumps and tossed them into the rear of the wooden conveyance. He could feed the addictive roots to the horse each time it slowed. It would wear at the animal's health, but that was as it should be. The creature would be required to give the Muse all it had to give, and then it would die in the city along with all the inhabitants therein.

Moving to wrap an arm around the animal's muscular neck, the Muse whispered into its ear, suggesting that the animal had eaten enough. With a jerk, the horse raised its head, its eyes suddenly wide, and with a snort, its nostrils flared. The Muse smiled. While he no longer had his previous level of powers, there were a few tricks he could still perform, if the victim were impressionable.

"Easy, brute." The Muse stroked its neck until the animal calmed down. "I've need of your services for a handsbreadth of time or two. Easy, now. Keep your head up. We need to move ahead. The city and Parik await."

Grinning, the Muse glanced to the horizon, looking for the city rising against the landscape. It was as he expected. High clouds had started to thicken overhead, and although they didn't obscure the sun just yet, they would. The power, when it broke free, would fall from the sky to greet that now rising in the earth. Everything in between would be decimated. Everything except Parik, of course. Parik would come out a new man, full of vigor and youth. The thought made the Muse burn with desire. It was the desire that had been upon him since the beginnings of time.

Only, first Parik had a lesson to learn. The Muse

placed a hand on the blade lying within the cart, Umaru's blade, and slapping the horse hard on the withers, he grabbed the reins and threw himself onto the conveyance. The doomed city awaited, and the Muse intended to be there to see it die.

"Gi-ayah!" His strong voice called to the horse, and it responded by jerking the cart forward. The twiggleroot was working, and it was working well, coupled with the suggestion the Muse had whispered in its ear. They would make the return trip in record time. Parik had offended the Muse, and for that, he'd pay.

KAIUS THREW HIS SHOULDER into the stone that blocked the doorway into his and Rena's room. It was very heavy, but it would move. It had to. If he must break it in two, it would move.

"Rena, you are there?" He paused in his exertions, waiting. There was wailing from all over the city, and still the stones fell, even though the shaking had since stopped.

"Kaius, you're really you?"

The voice was weak, but it was Rena, and Kaius sagged against the offensive stone with an exhausted laugh, relieved.

"It's I, my love. Why do you ask such a question? Don't you know my voice?" She always was a strange one with strange ideas and even stranger requests. However, he cared very much for her, and he'd worried that the stones had taken her life.

"It doesn't matter. You must come get me free. A

stone from the ceiling, it rests over me, and I can't move."

"Are you in pain?" Rising panic squeezed him, taking his breath away, and he stood, attempting to see over the intruder blocking his way. "Rena, answer me!"

"There's no pain. I'm trapped and afraid, though. Perhaps from the roof. You can come through there, I think."

"Oh, you're so observant, Rena. I'll do as you say. Be alive when I reach you. I can't live without you." His heart felt as if his emotions would explode in his chest, and he knew he spoke the truth. Without his Rena, he couldn't survive.

"Don't be afraid, for I live." Her voice took on a new, forced energy. "I'm uninjured, I think. I need you to pull me free, please."

"Hold still. I'm climbing to the roof, and I'll come in to get you. Then we'll leave this city and be safe."

She laughed, and her words filtered through the blockage. "Be safe? The shaking's stopped, my Kaius. We'll replace the stone in the ceiling, and our roof will be good as new. The city is safe. After all, it's built of stone, and there's nothing stronger in the world."

Kaius had a bad feeling, though, as he climbed the tumbled blocks and heavy wooden beams lying against the outside wall of his and Rena's room. She didn't know how bad this was, and he was certain of one thing. The stones that made up the city didn't make them safe. Not at all.

A SMALL, FURRED SHOULDER snuggled against the warmth of a broken girl's body. The diminutive creature felt secure in its cocoon of warmth, but it also felt a knot of hunger in its body. Without food, it couldn't remain still much longer.

Creeping forward, the animal exposed its nose, searching for the odors that would tell it whether it was safe to proceed out of its haven of safety. Only smelling the safe aroma of the girl and the dustiness of the ancient temple stones, the rat pressed ahead, exposing its coal black eyes.

Its snout quivering, it picked up the faintest odor of grain, and with a quick burst of motion, it was soon out of the girl's bed and onto the hardness of the floor. It was very pleased to see a small pile of seeds off to the side, and in the dimness of the temple's interior, it scrambled forward to sample its meal.

Off the opposite direction, another set of eyes watched, and the old temple serving woman smiled to see her gift to the rat taken with no question. If the rat had refused the offering, it would have been a rebuke beyond measure. However, all was as it should be, and the old woman was vindicated once again.

"YOU CAN MANAGE, I do hope." Parik looked his new charge, Zakkhaios, in the face. The boy had injuries, but they were no longer bleeding. "Will you be able to walk with us?"

"Manage? To walk?" Dulcia knew Zakkhaios from her circle of friends, also, and she teased him. "He has two legs. Of course, he can walk. He won't let Æolus best him. Also, why were you with Æolus' tutor, Zakkhaios? It's the middle of the day."

The youth's eyes reddened, and his chin began to quiver. He dropped his eyes.

"Dulcia!" Æolus was sharp, and with good reason. He'd seen what the girl hadn't. "Leave him be. Be glad you didn't watch the events on the street. Thanatos is dead, isn't he, Parik?"

"He forced my hand. He wouldn't quit beating my godson." Parik nodded. Rarely did he enjoy taking a man's life, but this man's life had deserved to be taken. In any case, Parik had given the man a chance to relinquish the boy willingly. When he refused, he'd written his own death warrant.

Zakkhaios' voice shook as he found the words to speak. "I'd only come out to see the city shake, and then our villa collapsed. No one screamed inside, and there were no answers to my calls, so I knew they were dead." He reached his hand to wipe his eyes. "I saw Thanatos and thought he might help. He was always especially cordial and helpful to me at Loukas' when I went there for tutoring. Then he began to beat me, telling me I must be his slave." He took a ragged breath, and the tears began again.

"Was that when your tunic got torn?" Dulcia reached to tug it over his chest, only to have it fall away again. She whispered, although not as quietly as she might, "You're no longer a little boy to run the city unclothed."

Although Parik wasn't of the city, not for more than

the past season, he understood her words as she meant them. The boy's tunic was so torn as to be nonexistent. He was approaching real manhood, and city etiquette said he couldn't remain unclothed without good reason. From his proud bearing, Parik thought the boy was also too well-mannered.

He made to give her a gentle rebuke, having seen the boy being mistreated, but her friend took that away from him, and Parik smiled as he listened.

"Dulcia," Æolus hissed, jabbing her in the side with his elbow. "Leave him be. You didn't see what I did."

"Thanatos ripped it from me. I didn't know why at first, until he said he wanted to . . ." He choked, and his eyes became a fountain of unwelcome memories.

"It's all right." Æolus put his arm across his friend's shoulder.

"Let him get it out, Æolus." Parik held his finger to his lips for the youth to be silent.

"I didn't ask him to do that. I belong to no one except my parents, and they no longer live." Zakkhaios' breath came in ragged jerks.

"You did nothing amiss," Parik reassured him.

"He asked me if my parents still lived." Zakkhaios' words tumbled from him. "I was desperate, and I told him I heard no one, but they'd all been inside. I asked him to come help, and instead, he grabbed me, laughing. I didn't understand.

"Then there were other men dragging other boys— girls, too—pulling them into empty rooms, and there were screams as we passed. I tried to beat at Thanatos' arms, but he was once a soldier. He got angry and tore my tunic, and then he hit me, telling me he'd beat me in the street where everyone could see, not in the empty rooms where we'd be hidden. Then he'd give me to others to do with as they will." He put his arms over his face. "He said he'd kill me if I didn't serve him. I was afraid of what he'd do to me, and I didn't want to go in the rooms with him. The sounds I heard as I passed—" His voice cracked, and his words failed him.

Parik whispered to him very quietly, "I suspect he'd have killed you in any case. Your friend, Æolus, saved you. Be grateful. Now, my question again. Can you travel? You're sore, I'm sure, but we must go for Æolus' mother. Dulcia's parents, too."

Zakkhaios looked up and nodded, his eyes red, and his chest still heaving. "I'll walk, and run if need be." He smiled and looked at Parik. "I'm at your service, whatever help you may need. I'm certain my family is gone, and if so—"

Æolus grabbed him again, stopping his words. "If so, then I'm your family. We're your family. Right, Dulcia?"

"I feel I must interrupt. More shaking will come, and soon." Parik stepped to peer through the doorway. "The way seems safer now. We must go."

"Sir?" Zakkhaios grabbed his arm. "More shaking? How can you know? With each one, my father said it was over, and the city would still stand."

"My name is Parik, boy. You may call me that." He looked the youth in the face. It was a pretty face, and even though Parik had no interest in such things, he could see what must have attracted the old soldier to such a handsome child.

"Thank you, sir. I will." Zakkhaios' question still hovered in his eyes. "The shaking, sir? How can you know?"

"Was your father correct in his words?" When no answer came, Parik prompted him once again, "Did the shaking stop, Zakkhaios?"

"My parents are dead. The shaking got worse."

"And it will continue to do so. Believe me, Zakkhaios, when I say there'll be more, and even worse. I've seen this before."

"Then some will live?" Dulcia hugged ChiChi to her chest, and her voice quavered with the need for hope. "What I ask is only this: If you've seen this before, and you still live, then some must survive."

"Some." Parik looked away, hating his lie. "Don't give up hope, sweet Dulcia. You have a friend that depends on you." He pointed to the pet she held. "The animal will need you to be strong."

"ChiChi?" She brushed the dog's fur with her hand as she looked down at it. "I can do that; I'll be strong for him. He must live. Otherwise, you wouldn't have healed his hip, would you?" She smiled brightly at Parik.

He knew the truth, though. The animal would die. He simply smiled at her and reached to pat the small dog on the head. Then it was time to move. "Zakkhaios? Æolus? Ready?" Parik motioned with his hand, pulling them to the door. "Our direction, Æolus? Left, still?"

Once outside, Parik saw Zakkhaios' eyes turn to the old tutor lying dead on the ground, and the boy's face twisted with obvious distress. He put his hand on the youth's neck. "Do you hate him, boy?" Parik could do nothing for hate.

"I don't want to. I don't know why he did what he did to me. I thought he cared for me. I want to feel sorry that he's dead." He sniffled with emotion.

"I can help you let it go. Do you want that?" When Parik saw the youth nod, he squeezed with his hand, and he felt his fourth finger warm. With satisfaction, he watched the youth's features soften as several darkening bruises faded, and a wound on his forehead began to close.

Dulcia stepped to Zakkhaios' side and grinned. "Did Parik heal you, too? I saw how he touched you. He's here to save us. I know. He healed a rat, and ChiChi, too. ChiChi no longer stumbles when he runs, does he, Æolus?" She turned to her friend, only to find he was already headed down the street, anxious to be in motion.

Zakkhaios looked at Parik with his eyes wide. "I do feel well, in my feelings as well as my body. Is Dulcia correct? Are you here to save our city?"

Parik smiled at him, wishing he could answer the youth with the words he so needed to hear. Instead, he clutched his arm and pulled him forward.

"I only do as much as I can, and sometimes that isn't very much." He reached with his free hand to push his newly age-streaked hair over his shoulder. "I only ask that you do the same."

It wasn't the answer the youth needed, he knew, but it was the best he had to give.

"COULD IT BE TRUE?" The sky was blue, the sun was bright, and Zekiye lay all alone by the side of the road. She spoke her thoughts aloud as she felt of her belly. It was as flat as it had been yesterday, and yet two men had each promised her she would have a child. She rolled over in the grass, amused at the blades that tickled her arms. If she could believe the promises, she had two children inside of her womb.

She had no doubt of one thing. She'd been taken by the goddess twice. She'd awakened beside a strange man in the stone city far from her home, and then, without having gotten out of the cart, she'd been here on the grass with another man at her side. For that very reason, she believed the words they'd spoken to her.

Her first baby would be called Parikson. She rolled to her back once again. There'd be a twin, or close to a twin, anyway. Both babies would grow inside her at the same time, and she'd call them twins. Twins blessed from the goddess. She was twice blessed. No one in her village had ever received anything better, and Zekiye wasn't displeased.

Sitting up, she looked for what she'd seen the man throw from the cart. Umaru had been his name. It was he who had lain beside her this day. The goddess had come over her once again, and Umaruson would be the name she'd give the second child. Her people would be very pleased.

Gathering her items, she pulled her long tunic over her head and worked her feet into her rope-topped sandals, It was a very long way to the home of her people, she was certain. The city was surely closer. Her decision wasn't difficult. She really wanted to go home. Her people would understand what the goddess had done for her. No one would doubt the words of the two-times-great-granddaughter, and besides, she missed her mother.

Stepping along the grassy ruts, Zekiye began to whistle softly. The sun was shining, the birds were singing, and she was headed home. Twice-blessed Zekiye was traveling to her family's abode where her mother would kiss her cheek, her father would throw his arms around her neck, and everyone she knew would treat her sons like the gifts from the goddess they were.

Oddly enough, the tune she whistled was one that hadn't been heard in many hundreds of seasons, or at least not since earlier that morning. She only vaguely remembered hearing Umaru whistle it, but it had somehow stuck in her thoughts. Now, she couldn't get rid of it.

With determination, she decided both her babies would learn the melody. It seemed the right thing to do, something of their fathers, so to speak. It would remind each one of the parent he would never know.

14

"SHE BRINGS TROUBLE TO the temple." Several of the temple serving women had come to the most high priest to complain.

The Moica Priest in his gold and red tunic stepped to a stone platform that allowed him to view the city. There was no higher authority to be found inside the city walls, and he made the supreme decisions. The markings inscribed into his skin indicated as such.

On the surface, those decisions were made during his consultations with the sky gods that flew overhead each night, if the supplicants followed the newer religions, or with the Goddess Lamahätsu, if the petitioners were of the old ways. By strict adherence to the temple rules, the Moica Priest must rely on the gods for his decisions. Otherwise, the wrath of the gods—or of the goddess—would bring calamity upon the people.

However, the priest knew there was never anyone in the divination room except him, plus perhaps, on occasion, one of the new male acolytes, if any pleased the priest. On those occasions his consultations, his divinations, would take place with the help of the youth, as the Moica Priest perused the various orifices though which the gods might speak to him.

This day he groaned as he was forced to consider this matter from the temple serving women. They were a sorry lot, even the best of them, and he wished beyond wish that he could rid the temple of each and every one of them. He would, too, if the people would bring their alms any other way. However, the temple coffers needed filling, and the ministrations of the temple serving women swelled the boxes far quicker than the cost of their upkeep drained the coins away. He must placate them.

"How does this small crippled girl bring trouble to the temple?" The priest turned, keeping his hands behind his back. He knew he presented quite a dramatic figure, and he often used his appearance to his best advantage to cow the weak of mind. People were easier to handle when they were intimidated.

"It's as you've seen." The unidentified serving woman who spoke was sharp in her tone. It seemed the priest's dramatic figure wouldn't sway these women so easily.

"What have I seen, good woman?" His question was aimed at the speaker, but the final two words suggested a slur of a broader scope. These women were not good at all. Many had started as illegal thieves in the city, filching funds from the temple by entertaining men in private quarters. Then, a number of them had to be chained to the temple binding rings until their spirits were broken, to keep them from desecrating the city and its populace with their untoward actions. After all, what better place to crush such an ignoble profession than in a place where the women could be as close to the gods as possible?

"The shaking," several shouted out as one.

The priest held up his hand for silence, and he pointed to one fresh-faced girl. He knew this one. She'd come to them just months ago, new from her leap into womanhood. Many men clamored for her to hear their absolutions. It was the very reason her parents had brought her to the temple in the first place. She'd claimed the blessing of the gods, and men had clamored for her down in the city, even with the exorbitant fees she asked to absolve them of their errant deeds. Her parents hadn't been able to stomach the influx of "suitors" to her room at all times of the day.

Only a week at the chains, and the girl had been more than willing to bare her most private charms on the next feast day, so that she might help line the temple coffers. Now, rarely after feast days did her coffer turn up unfilled.

"You, girl. Voice this complaint to me." The Moica Priest stepped to her to take her hand. It was warm and moist, and he was reminded of the acolyte he'd invited to divine with him the previous evening. The youth had been capable, but he'd need time to recover before he received a second invitation.

"The temple shakes, Holy One—"

"As does our city," he bit back at her. When he saw her cringe, he knew his response was too harsh. After all, he'd asked, and she was very tender. "I'm sorry, my dear. Please continue."

"We are frightened—"

As is everyone in the city, but he didn't throw that at her.

"—and we're certain it's because of the crippled girl."

"Thank you, dear." Her voice was the same as all the rest. He waved her back to the others and walked to the platform once again. Fires could be seen, and the city's water was now sluicing from the remains of the aqueduct into the countryside, creating a new river where there had been none before. Soon the reservoir would run low, and the people would be reduced to paying merchants to retrieve the water from the flooded fields. There was a minor bright spot in all the devastation. He'd seen cities made of wood, and he was glad this one couldn't burn. The few plumes of smoke would soon quench themselves, as stone burns with great difficulty, indeed.

However, a great many buildings had toppled walls, and some of the most beautiful villas in the city were crushed under the collapsed aqueduct. The priest sighed, thinking that no matter what he did, they'd remain underneath the aqueduct, along with many of the city's wealthier inhabitants.

The marauding crowds he could occasionally catch glimpses of had him concerned even more greatly than the collapsed villas. He'd already received reports of brutality against children, mostly those youths barely out of childhood, both boys and girls. He couldn't command much sympathy for the boys and girls, but he didn't want the people to revolt over such brutalities.

Then there was the matter of the temple. It must stand inviolate at any cost, whether the price demanded was a crippled girl, a new temple serving woman just into the arts, or the unwary youths who were learning invaluable lessons in the streets of the city.

He turned to the temple serving women, making sure his profile was silhouetted beautifully against the sky. The gathering clouds made for a powerful backdrop to his planned words.

"So, we must abandon the crippled girl, or our city will fall. Is that our decision?" At the expressions of hope on the women's faces, he knew it was. "Who will be the one to carry the girl to the city gates?" Several of the women started to lift their hands, dropping them again when others didn't follow suit.

He didn't like this, but he was only one man, and in his heart, he knew there was no goddess on this earth or gods in the lights that circled the heavens. His position of power was maintained by juggling his constituents' wishes with the practical matters of managing a good-sized city. The girl had nothing to do with the events shaking the buildings all around them. However, if he removed her and the shaking stopped—as the priest was certain it would—then he was a demigod. If he kept the girl in the temple, and the shaking stopped, he had discredited the temple serving women, and they would see that the coffers remained emptier than ever before.

One hand at the back of the group of petitioners, belonging to a very old temple serving woman, lifted tentatively, and the priest pointed.

"You. You wish to volunteer?" The old serving woman was incredibly lined, and it was difficult for the priest to believe she'd ever been attractive enough for a man to desire her for his absolutions. However, she did wear the white tunic with the red stripe.

She stood stiffly. "There's something you don't know, Holy One."

"Hush, woman!" One middle-aged temple serving woman grabbed at her robe.

"He's agreed to our demands. Don't spoil this." Another swatted her arm.

Several additional voices tried to silence her, but the old temple serving woman wouldn't back down. The location of the red stripe told of her position of authority in the temple, and that she must be allowed to exercise her right to speak.

"Yes, old woman?" The priest motioned for her to feel free to speak. "Your cronies seem to wish your words to be left unspoken. I would hear them before we abandon this girl to the wild rats." He chuckled with the image. Tame rats were highly sought after, and they carried the blessing of the gods—or the goddess, depending on a particular supplicant's beliefs. Wild rodents were an affront to the temple and all it stood for.

His eyes opened with surprise as she began to speak of one.

"A rat, one that followed the crippled girl to the temple, has bedded with her."

"And you have someone who can verify this?" The priest tried to appear indifferent, and he looked over the city as he spoke.

"An acolyte was at my side, the one known as Rufus—"

"With the red hair?" The priest turned to her, interrupting sharply, as memories of the youth flooded his thoughts. It *would* be him. The boy was a goad in his side. Not two seasons previously, the old woman had been there to ready the room when this one had divined with the Moica Priest. The red hair had been a most unusual characteristic, and the priest had so looked forward to his time alone with the youth. Then, things had gone awry when the priest had become overzealous in his probe for new truths from the gods.

"Yes, your grace. He aids me in my work."

"Ah. What else can you tell us?" He could barely keep the bitterness from his voice. The boy had fought back at a most inopportune time, and the divination had been a dismal failure. The priest had received injuries, although he hadn't spoken of them to the old woman. His failure to complete his divination was an affront to his position of supremacy in the temple complex, and he'd felt humiliated.

"I've left it grain, and it has eaten of it. I fear that if we remove the girl, we will lose the rat, also. I've seen it in a dream. If the rat leaves the temple, the city falls." She pulled her headcloth tightly around her neck and bowed her head respectfully.

"A rat in the temple and bedding with the girl. That tells the matter differently." The Moica Priest was pleased with the old woman's revelation. The girl wouldn't be cast outside the walls today. The rat would help him postpone this decision—as well as present him an opportunity for an additional and much needed session with a fresh acolyte new to the temple.

He turned to look out over the city once more as if in deep thought. Then he returned his attention to the women. "I shall have to summon an acolyte, one new to the temple with uncluttered thoughts, to join me in the divination chambers. Only with a word from the gods . . . er, from the goddess, shall I know the right path to pursue. I shall go now to select the acolyte of my choice."

With a quick step, he absented himself from the chamber. Things had gone much better than he could have planned if he'd thought it out ahead of time. He had a whole day to put off the decision, and soon an acolyte would divine with him in the chambers. He was certain an answer would be found to the problem, if not in the food and drink he would order to the divination chambers, then in the intensely pleasurable divinations the acolyte would participate in afterward.

"IN HERE!" KAIUS CALLED to the voices he heard in the street. They entreated those who wished aid. "I must have help. Rena, my woman, is trapped underneath a fallen stone."

"Does she live?" The response was sharp and concise but very pertinent. No time could be spent on pulling the dead from underneath fallen stones. The living must be the rescuers' focus.

"Yes," Kaius called. "She's uninjured, also. However, I can't lift the stone without help. You must come through the ceiling."

He reached through a small opening to touch Rena's hand. It seemed as if the floor had dropped a small distance, just where she lay, giving her a small amount of space in which to stay alive. It frightened him that he could hear water running underneath. There was no piping from the reservoir beneath their room.

A face appeared in the ceiling and as quickly disappeared. "Rope!" The face reappeared. "We carry that to pull the stones free, and I see we may need it. Where may we climb without injuring anyone?"

"Anywhere." Kaius motioned with his hand. "The stone has collapsed to the floor. All is stable."

"To the floor?" The man crawled through, and he carried with him a strong back and legs like tree trunks. "How does your woman breathe?" He leaned in to peer past a splintered support column and down the opening as two other strong men clambered in after him.

Kaius shrugged, perplexed. "The floor dropped. I

hear water running underneath the stones."

The man looked at his companions. "Xerxes, here, too. The reservoir will make the floors in this part of the city fall soon."

"Fall?" Kaius grabbed his benefactor's arm, newly afraid for Rena's safety all over again.

The man gently clapped Kaius' shoulder to steady him. "Not to worry. We'll move this stone long before that happens."

"Kaius?" Rena called from the opening. Her voice was high-pitched and shook with fright. "What do they say about the reservoir? It's on the other side of the hill. How can it make the floors in the city fall?"

As he dropped the rope down around the corner of the stone that held Rena captive, another of the rescuers gave the answer she sought.

"The shaking has cracked the land far below the city's foundations. The level of the reservoir has fallen by a quarter, and it drops more every handsbreadth of time. It leaks directly under the city and has already collapsed a section of the lower wall. Drak heard your calls, and we'll get you out."

"Perhaps it was the shaking that brought down the wall. When the stones shook last, other buildings just fell. I saw them." Kaius frowned, unable to accept that the reservoir now bled its life underneath the city.

The first man laughed as he looped the end of the rope into a sturdy knot. "You should see the water washing up from under the wall's fallen stones. You wouldn't think so, then." The others with him nodded in silent agreement.

"Ready." The first man called to the other two, and they quickly crawled back out the ceiling, carrying the loose end of the rope with them.

"Where are they going?" Kaius grabbed the first man's arm. "Rena is still under the stone."

"Kaius, don't let them leave me." Rena's high-pitched voice was clearly panicked, and it cracked as she spoke.

The man at Kaius' side called to her through the opening, "We are readying to pull the stone. Be quick to climb out, if you can. We can't hold it for long." He clapped Kaius on the shoulder and pointed to the corner of the stone with the rope wrapped around it. "It'll lift here. Pull her out quickly, and then tug here to release the rope. When the rope is free, we'll pull you through the opening in the ceiling and then go quickly to help someone else." He stood and looked in Kaius' eyes. "Do you understand?"

Kaius nodded, and the man leaped for the opening. The rope tightened, and he called down to his woman, "Be ready, Rena. The stone is about to lift."

At that moment, it moved, and Kaius reached for her outstretched arm. As space was made, he pulled her frantically, forcing her body through the opening as it widened. As she fell onto him, free and unharmed, the rope slipped off the stone of its own volition, crashing the behemoth back to the floor. Kaius was horrified to see the collapsed place in the floor where Rena had lain drop away into a rushing torrent of water. Only the block from the ceiling protected them from its depths. Then, as he and Rena scrambled for the hands that appeared through the opening in the ceiling, the block that had kept Rena penned also fell through the floor with a loud, watery reverberation, leaving a darkened pit just where she'd lain.

Pulling them through the roof, the three men slapped Kaius and Rena on the back. They grinned with the excitement of it all, as they laughed at their success. "We got you out, just barely."

One of the men, Kaius was no longer sure just which, reached to plant a kiss on Rena's beautiful face.

"Go," another encouraged. "Find a safer part of the city. You see how dangerous it is." Then, in a quick scrabble of feet, the men and their rope were gone, off to help someone else.

"I thought you were lost, my dear Rena. And I didn't even come to you last night. I'm so ashamed." Kaius hugged her and pressed his face in her hair, uncaring of the stone dust covering her body.

"But—" Rena frowned for a moment, returning his hug hesitantly at first, then with growing enthusiasm. "You did come to me, Kaius."

"You've forgiven me already. I could find no better woman to remain at my side." Kaius began to kiss the dust from her face, laughing when she started to kiss him back.

It had been the Muse at Rena's side, but who would ever be able to understand that?

THE GREAT CITY FALTERED more with each shaking, its facade of enduring stone gradually becoming no more than a memory of glories from long ago.

With the earliest movements of the ground that morning, a fault running directly under the city had sheared far back into the mountain, causing a small gap in the reservoir's rocky bed. A steady river of water rushed to penetrate the bands of soil snaking beneath the city streets, moistening much of the substrate upon which the city was rooted. Then, with subsequent shakings, the cracks in the reservoir's bed had widened, and the dampened earth underneath the city turned into slurry. Eventually, the flowing water scoured new underground channels. Once the supporting soil was removed, the city rested on no more than a flooded honeycomb of fragile rock. It was now a city held in place by two centuries of continued existence, as well as the enormous pressure of well-placed stones wedged next to well-placed stones. It was a city holding itself up—barely—while teetering on unsure foundations, and few people inside its walls knew the extent of the truth.

Deeper within the earth, white-hot magma welcomed the inrush of the city's reservoir. In fact, before half the day was expired, it would have the great body of water drained dry, accepting the moisture as fuel for equalizing the ferocity of the molten rock rising to meet it. By the time that happened, there'd be no support left underneath the city, except a great warren of previously unknown natural catacombs, ones ripe to serve as steam chambers when the magma finally reached the water flooding down to greet it.

BLOOD OOZED FROM SLASHES on the horse's back.

The Muse pulled the reins roughly, and the wild-eyed beast skidded to a stop, its nostrils flaring and foam oozing from its mouth. Before he'd taken to whipping the animal, the Muse had already been furious with Parik for the child given to the woman. He'd been determined to make him pay and make him pay sorely. Now, other things made him angry, and he seemed to be helpless against them, taking out his frustrations on the animal pulling the cart in which he rode.

The twiggleroot had served its purpose, that of getting back to the city before Parik had the gall to force the Muse to shift again, but it hadn't stopped the flies and the gnats that had assaulted and angered the Muse as he neared the city. The flies had attacked his skin, biting him in places he didn't know this mortal body possessed, and the gnats had flooded his eyes and ears with their thirst for moisture.

To relieve the frustrations was why the horse had been forced to suffer, why the Muse had beaten the poor animal with the raw end of the reins, yelling for it to run faster, faster, faster. It had finally done as he commanded, and yet the Muse now found the city wasn't accessible. Water had flooded from underneath the city walls, was still doing so, it seemed, and if the Muse could judge from the crumbled walls at the lowest reaches, it had undermined the foundations severely. It had also flooded the fields surrounding the city, and the small horse and lightweight cart could go no farther.

The flooding might have made sense to the Muse if the aqueduct were still gushing its flow of snowmelt into the city streets, but that particular water source now flooded the fields far outside of the city, creating a new river of its own down the path of lowest elevation. Who knew the source of this latest affront? It seemed the only way back inside the city was to slog his way through.

The Muse stopped his deliberations and let out an anguished yell. Still, the cursed gnats wouldn't leave him alone! He wished they'd go back to the swamps and waterways from which the shaking of the earth had disturbed them.

In the distance, he saw a man walking beside a giant draft horse and pulling a loaded cart of his own, one much larger than the Muse's, and it was slowly making its way through the flooded fields and away from the crumbling city. The Muse jumped from his small cart, and he slapped the flank of the wild-eyed animal that had served him so well, yelling the last of his frustrations at it.

"Go, bcast! Break loose from your cart, and consume the twiggleroot still in the back. Enjoy the measure of time you have left. You might yet survive if you run—if you still can!" The Muse let an unkind laugh rumble from his gut as he walked away from the animal.

He must secure the larger animal and cart, one with more draft and bulkier wheels to dig through the mud, although he could manage with just the horse, if he could convince the man to part with it. If not, then the man might live no longer than he took to refuse the Muse's request.

It was when the Muse reached for the weapon he'd carried with him in the cart that he realized his stupidity. The knife was in its scabbard, the scabbard was in the small wagon, and the wagon was attached to the horse. The Muse had no armament with which to battle for the massive animal.

The Muse cursed aloud, and then he stopped. There were other ways. If the man were so inclined, the Muse could suggest. Many a suggestion had become deed in the untold seasons of the Muse's life.

"Hail!" The Muse called to the man as he pulled off his sandals, flinging them to the side, aware they would simply bog him down in the mud. "May I join you to the city?"

"City?" The man's voice was faint, coming to the Muse over the flooding water, but his response was clear. He waved the Muse away as he continued to slog beside his horse, fighting against the muck slowly but successfully. "T'will be no city by nightfall. Stay away, if you ask me."

The Muse snorted to himself. The man's prediction was a certainty. Still, he called loudly, "I do ask, but I ask for a ride."

The man stood ankle deep in the mud, having pulled nearly free from the morass, and as the Muse approached, he pointed the opposite direction. "The wine country. I go with supplies. I don't get paid until I deliver. I was waiting on a youth, and he never showed. I think he's maybe dead by now. I won't go back to the city, and you're a crazy one, if you do. Pah!" He waved the Muse away and yanked on the rough bridle around the horse's head. The massive animal leaned forward, and with a groan of tortured wood, the great wheels on the cart started to follow.

Looking to the city and the watery chaos blocking his way, the Muse drew a deep breath and wriggled his toes in the deepening mud, stoking his determination. He'd get there, with the man's help or without. He had a driving, escapable reason. Being male, he was coerced by his hatred of Parik; he was driven passionately, desperately, to end his paramour's life.

It was inescapable.

Each man the Muse inhabited always had the same drive, to kill Parik. Quite a few had succeeded, although to say such a thing wasn't entirely accurate. Each of the men had succeeded in delivering a killing blow—or a deadly push off a high cliff; perhaps mixing poison into Parik's food. Yet, the Muse always stepped in to ensure things didn't go too wrong. While he did want Parik to die, truly wanted him to die, the feeling was driven by jealously. What the Muse really wanted was for Parik to appreciate him for who he'd become: Parik's rescuer from the knife-edge of death. It was only when Parik's life hung in the balance, and death's door had been opened—if only for a glimpse of what lay beyond—that he could truly appreciate just how fortunate he was to have the Muse at his side.

To reach that end, Parik had to die, and it had to be today.

THERE WAS ONE OTHER difficulty with killing Parik. For some reason, in all the centuries they'd spent together, the Muse never understood one thing invested with a substantial level of significance. That fingernail. It healed those who desired its touch. Who could say it mightn't save just a bit of that healing for the one who wore it? Lamahätsu had been gone from the face of the earth for countless centuries, and she was the only one who could have said for sure.

But then, she might not have known the answer to that herself.

15

"SEE THERE." PARIK POINTED, not liking what he saw. "The street's flooded just in front. We must go around." The water was rising, too, slipping up from between the paving stones as they watched. "What direction do we go, youths? You're more familiar with this section of the city."

"Perhaps we can make it across." Æolus ran forward, the silt-filled water quickly rising above his ankles. He stopped and turned, looking back at his three companions. "It's cold, very cold. Yet, it isn't from the aqueduct. Where could it be coming from?"

"I don't know, Æolus, but I feel it isn't good." Parik

motioned him out of the brown effluent.

"We saw the aqueduct fall. It was flooding the city earlier. Remember, Æolus?" Dulcia's face was pale. "Maybe it hasn't all drained away." She looked at Parik and pointed to a street that branched off in the distance, its entrance already underwater. "My home's just there. I walk up seventeen steps to my door. Please don't make us go around."

Parik could see the entrance to the street she indicated. He might have the strength to try it on his own, but with the drawing of the energy stealing the remains of his youth, he couldn't do so and help these children across at the same time, and especially not if it was as cold as Æolus said.

"See, Parik?" Æolus pointed. "People are crossing. Zakkhaios and I will go, and you'll see how to do it." He seemed excited at his unexpected chance to show off to this man who had already done so much for them. However, even as he stood there, the level of the water had already risen to his knees. He took two steps backwards to keep his loincloth dry. "One is my friend's uncle."

Indeed, not far from them, there were people moving along the street, and several of them carried possessions wrapped in cloth balanced on the tops of their heads. The water swirled nearly to their armpits, and without any sort of warning, one suddenly disappeared below the surface, leaving the bundle he was carrying bobbing on the surface. As they watched, it slowly sank, also. The man beside him looked around, surprised his companion was nowhere to be seen, and then he wobbled, and too, was gone.

"Æolus, I don't think we'll trust the water. It seems to be hungry for the people who walk its depths." Parik put his arms out to back up the other two at his side. Finally, he stepped forward, wetting his sandals, and he grabbed Æolus' shoulder. "Æolus, now."

Æolus turned, red tingeing his eyes. "I saw Nigellus' uncle disappear. How can he be gone when he was just here? It's only water."

Parik pulled him back. "It isn't only water, boy. Please stand behind me with your friend. We'll find another way."

"But my house." Æolus stood as if in shock. "It's on the lowest level of the city. It'll be in the water, too. Nigellus' uncle just fell." His eyes turned first to Parik, and then to Dulcia, and next to Zakkhaios. They returned to Parik. "What if my house sank, just as Nigellus' uncle did? My mother—" Not for the first time this day, tears began to flood down his face.

"Cry, boy. There's no shame." Parik motioned to Zakkhaios. "He's your friend, young Zakkhaios. Treat him as such. Æolus was your rescuer from earlier. He insisted I save you. Now he needs your arm on his shoulder."

He looked to Dulcia to speak other words to her. "Be strong, girl. Think. How else do we get to where you live?" He smiled and reached to stroke the dog she held, touching it gently with his fingers. "Which street will take us the shortest way?"

She pointed across the water. "That's the shortest

way." She took several very shallow breaths before she could speak again, and then she turned to a street just behind where they stood. "If we go up there, a narrow alley will cut across. No gate blocked the way the last time I chased ChiChi there."

"That's our plan." He turned to the youths. "Zakkhaios, is Æolus ready?"

"Ready." Zakkhaios had one arm around Æolus' neck, and he gave it a quick jerk of a squeeze. "Æole, it will be all right. We're all together. We're friends. Compé?" The word carried a very intimate inflection when spoken person to person, indicating the speaker was a true friend.

"Yes, I understand." Æolus licked his lips, the sheen of nervousness tightly controlled on his face.

"Æole, the water still rises." Zakkhaios tugged him forward.

"He's right, boy." Parik began to move. "Let Dulcia lead the way." When he motioned to her, the girl stepped ahead.

Parik knew she still held out hope that her family might live. Zakkhaios accepted his were dead, and Æolus was learning to deal with the loss of his hope, also. However, it was no more than Parik had known all along, and he knew one more thing they didn't. The worst of the day's events hadn't started, yet. No matter the death and destruction already around them, it would get much, much worse, and by the time it was over, those left alive in the city would pray to die. He wouldn't be able to help more than a few of them, and none would remain alive.

OVERHEAD THE SKIES HAD finally begun to darken. From the city streets, the ones that weren't underwater and collapsing under the inhabitants' feet, it seemed as if a thunderstorm must be brewing. It *would* have thunder, and it *would* shower lightning on the city. However, it was no normal thunderstorm. In the first place, it was directly over the city and nowhere else. In addition, it contained no moisture, at least not any that would fall as rain. This cloud was the opposite field to that gathering underneath the city's bowels, and there was a cloud gathering there, a cloud full of ominous electricity and levels of energy that no living man on Earth had ever experienced and survived . . . well, none except Parik, of course.

THREE KERNELS OF GRAIN were strewn together on the floor, and after a distance, there were three more. The pattern continued in a straight line for the length of the space, and at the end, it turned down a sloping corridor. The old temple serving woman knew those who had gone to see the priest with her, and she also knew they wouldn't bide their time while the city shook apart around them. Both the rat and the girl had to be saved. It was the only way to rescue the city, and the old woman couldn't see why no one else could understand that. Their salvation was paramount, and she'd see them protected no matter what.

She set her oil lamp aside and clicked her teeth, relieved to hear the gentle start and stop of the rat's nails on the surface of the stone. That meant it was pausing at each cache of grain, and it also meant it was following her as she'd planned. She'd placed a sizeable bag of grain in a small room down this old corridor, and a bowl of water, too. In all her seasons in the temple, this had been the one place she'd been able to come for solitude. It seemed to descend into the flank of the mountain against which the city rested.

Many years previously, an ancient temple serving woman who'd been old when the old woman was still a youth fresh to the temple had said a small chamber off the room once housed a well. The story dated to a time before the reservoir was built. Of course, as it was never visited, even by the priests, it was very dusty, especially the roughly matched stones that filled in the lower portion. There was a series of steps that wound around the small chamber just off the room, rising into unseen darkness, but the old temple serving woman had never climbed them. If they'd once gone down, the rough stones had long since closed that way.

It was the perfect hiding place.

The chamber provided safety where the rat could live without harm until the Moica Priest made his final determination. Perhaps it would take two nights in the divination chambers, and as sorry as she sometimes felt for the freshly arrived acolytes—having attended the injuries of a few of the youths afterward, and having no illusions about the special favors the old priest expected from the newest attendants—the old woman might even suggest just that. She knew how much the Moica Priest enjoyed his sessions, attended exclusively by his hand-picked divination attendants.

She knelt, dropping three additional kernels of grain, thinking, an acolyte for the girl and the rat. The trade seemed cruel, but it was the way of things.

Not for the first time, she felt sympathy for the acolytes who came to the temple to serve the gods, either willingly or unwillingly, as some were wont to do.

FISTS OF COLD WATER dragged at the Muse's tunic.

Although he was tempted, he refused to take the simple clothing off. He'd need vestments of some sort to wear when he entered the city, and he wouldn't be able to take time to search. The soil oozed around his legs with each step, and the rushing water pulled the tunic behind him even more, slowing him down.

At least this body he'd managed to retain was strong. Parik had sired a son who was certainly worthy of him. Occupying a weaker body, he'd have been forced to give up long ago.

As his feet fought for solid footing, he began to despair of reaching the city in one piece. It seemed as if the reservoir behind the city was empting the snowmelt of the mountains directly underneath its foundations.

With a curse, the Muse felt his feet swept from underneath him, and he struggled as a massive flush of water tore his hold away. Sinking, scrambling for fresh purchase, he understood this body might actually die here, shifting him into goddess knew what mortal.

Fighting for breath, the Muse felt objects pummel his body in the outrush of fluid being flushed from underneath the city. The tunic he wore hindered his attempts to find the surface, and he struggled to remove it, concluding that life over modesty might be an acceptable trade. He was relieved when some unknown object snagged the sodden fabric, pulling it until it tore at the shoulders, ripping it from his body. It became immensely easier to maneuver in the onslaught, and he broke the surface, moving sideways with a swimming motion. Unable to see clearly, he felt something hit the water at his side.

"You! Grab hold!"

Looking up, he saw three sturdy men of a youthful age standing on a portion of the city wall. One held the end of a thick rope. The other end was very near to where he struggled. He threw his arm at it, but the surging water took it another direction.

"Hold on," a different one of the three cried. "We'll toss it again."

Quickly the line was pulled up in great loops and flung to the Muse once more. This time the aim was perfect, and expecting it, the Muse grabbed it with his hand, wrapping it in several loops around his forearm.

"Pull," the Muse flung coarsely at the men. "I have it firmly. It won't come loose from my grasp." If they couldn't drag him in, his arm would be separated from his body before he'd give up this rope.

As the rope tightened, it felt a relief not to fight with his feet constantly to keep his head above water. While they reeled him in, the Muse was pleased to see they used wisdom, walking him along the city's wall toward where solid ground could be seen just along the base. He'd also have to convince them to pull him up the wall with the rope, but he thought that would be a simple matter. They wanted to help, and that meant they would be susceptible to his suggestions.

As he finally reached firm footing, the Muse struggled to stand, becoming entangled in thick mud more than once, yet keeping the rope fully twisted around his forearm. Looking to the top of the wall, he yelled his wishes to his rescuers: "I can climb if you'll pull the rope. Will you help me in that way?" He held out his arm and showed them the rope still twisted there.

"Your waist!" The third man leaned far over and yelled to him, making a circling motion with his hand. "Tie it around your waist. We wouldn't lose you after having pulled you from the flood. We need all hands possible to save others in the city. Do you know a knot that won't slip?"

The Muse waved his assent, and he twirled his arm several times to release the rope. Then, with the skill of many lifetimes of knowledge learned, he put the roughly textured line around his waist, and he quickly made it firm against the layer of mud coating his body.

"Pull," he yelled to the men. "I'm ready."

The rope tightened, and from its grasp on his skin, the Muse knew he'd done a good job with his knot. His hand clambering for holds and his toes finding purchase, sometimes from sheer determination, he fought a path up the wall until other hands firmly grasped his own. It was when he was pulled on top of the wide fortification that his rescuers exclaimed their astonishment. The Muse— or at least the body inhabited by the Muse—was well known to them.

"Umaru!" One of the men reached and wiped mud from the Muse's face, pushing his matted hair from his forehead, and then he called to the other two. "Come look at the friend we pulled from the mud. It's Umaru, and we never knew."

The Muse knew that name from the woman, but he didn't know these men, even if this one seemed to recognize him. He smiled briefly and looked down to release the rope from his waist.

"Umar!" One of the men slapped him on the shoulder, calling him by a familiar, shortened name. Then, he turned to the other two. "The water's knocked him senseless. He doesn't know us."

"Is this true?" Another stepped to him as he wound the rope around his arm. "It's I, Drakon. I was at your tavern a fortnight ago. Look in my face. Tell me you don't know me. We shared the absolutions of a serving woman in the temple afterwards. She pronounced all our dark deeds banished in the eyes of the gods, as she cleansed our bodies with holy water from her basin." The man laughed as he turned away, and he spoke loudly to the other two. "It's Umaru, for sure, even if he's senseless. His clothes have been torn from him, unless he was at the baths when the floor dropped him into the water. He has the mole we've all come to know."

Another man, not Drakon, also slapped the Muse on his shoulder, and he laughed, too. "Is this true, Umaru? You left your bathing companions under the flow and swam to safety? How unkind!" The third man nodded sagely. "Not all our rescues have gone well, and to have found an old friend and pulled him to safety is invigorating."

"If you've truly forgotten, I'm Xerxes, and that's Paulus. You'll understand why when you stand beside him." He grinned as the one he called Paulus turned his head, an irritated look on his face. The name indicated something diminutive, and using it derisively apparently voiced a subtle, although friendly insult.

The Muse quickly perceived the men might be able to help him, and over the centuries, he'd learned how to pretend to know people.

"Drakon?" The Muse smiled. "Xerxes?" He'd seen the look on the face of the one called Paulus, and he assumed this was a name the man normally accepted, since he hadn't corrected Drakon's use of it. He spoke to the man warmly, "Paulus, you must forgive these two brutes. They don't realize excellence is in the skill of a man's arms, not the height of his head. With more experience, they may become as desired of the army commanders as yourself." He saw the man's face ease, although Xerxes' snicker was unmistakable.

"Skill? He has no skill." The razzing was Xerxes', and the slap to the back of Xerxes' head was Drakon's.

"Close the mouth, Xerxes. Umaru is righter than you know. The training attendants do yelp with excitement when he shows up for target practice."

"Or with disappointment." He shut up quickly, when another slap connected with the back of his head.

"I'm looking for someone," the Muse ventured, glad to see the good-natured banter among the men. If he could mimic it, he might get their assistance. "In the melee, I've lost my father."

"The goddess is great and good," Paulus cried, jumping forward, grabbing the Muse's hand, and laughing. "To have lost him, well, that means you've finally found him after all this time. Did he bring you the remaining fortunes of your African kingdom?"

The Muse frowned, momentarily thrown off by the reference. Then, deciding on how best to get his request for help across, he laid it all out, skirting the connection to Africa entirely. "Parik is my father, and I never knew. You'll know him, as he's as like me as the sun today and the sun tomorrow. My father is growing old, though, and I fear for him in these newest dangers coming upon the city. Will you help me locate him?" The Muse was relieved to see interest spark on the men's faces.

"Where should we start? We all know your tavern, and we could go there. Your father knows your tavern, also, Umaru?" Drakon tossed the rope down on the top of the wall before walking to the Muse and grabbing both of his shoulders roughly. "We're with you in this, Umar, my friend. What a joy to find a father even as the city falls around us! As Paulus says, the goddess is truly good to us today."

The Muse laughed inwardly at the man's comment.

The goodness of the goddess was certainly debatable, especially as the goddess had brought all these troubles upon the city, but the help of these men was welcome, and for that, the Muse wouldn't argue the point.

"A tunic, first, friend Umaru." Xerxes put his arm across the Muse's muddy shoulders. "We'll wash you in the water running in the city's streets, and then we'll find you a tunic to cover yourself. Perhaps a loincloth, also."

"You're good friends to me." The Muse thought he could do without the loincloth, but he nodded, not willing to dispute the help he'd been offered. "Thank you for pulling me from the water and mud. How do we get down the wall?"

"This way." Paulus laughed and picked up the rope, motioning to the Muse. "We've climbed these steps together since before kneeling at our first temple serving women's feet as grown men. You, also, Umaru, since you came from Africa to our city. I see now that your head is truly fogged from your swim. We'll watch over you, though. Trust your friends, and all will be well."

As the four men started down the steps, Drakon put his hand on the Muse's shoulder and questioned him. "How do we first guess your father's location? Where did you last see him?"

The Muse smiled. He could help there. "My father, Parik, has a healing touch. He'll be wandering the city, and people will tell of his interventions. If we follow their stories, we'll find my father." *And kill him.* The Muse didn't say that part aloud, however. It didn't seem appropriate. These three mortals would find out soon enough, just as quickly as they helped him find Parik.

16

CHICHI RECOGNIZED THE ALLEY, and it was the way home. With a busy scramble of the dog's short legs, it burst barking from its mistress' arms, and with the makeshift collar flailing behind, the animal flew along the narrow path.

"No, ChiChi!" Dulcia threw her hands to her mouth. "Æolus, you must stop him."

"Now?" Æolus had stopped to adjust his loincloth. It had gotten wet in the flooded street and was partially undone.

Zakkhaios grinned, slapping his friend on the shoulder. "I can run fast, Æole. Stay, fix your cloth, and I'll bring the fur ball back safely." He waved to Dulcia as his feet began to move, his own flapping loincloth barely providing any modesty.

No one noticed Zakkhaios' lack of modesty, though, because right in front of them, the alley began to disappear. Just behind the pounding of each of Zakkhaios' leaping feet, the ground dropped away after him, sinkholes eating the dirt as he ran, a monster snapping its hungry jaws in its efforts to consume the tempting morsel of smooth and tender flesh. Dulcia screamed as she watched one after another form.

The rumbling sounds of rushing water could be heard underneath.

Parik looked up the hill to the temple at the very top. From this angle, the side of the hill that retained the reservoir couldn't be seen, but it was clear to him just what was happening. He grabbed Æolus' forearm, and he pressed him hard with his words.

"The city's foundations are crumbling. The water we hear is the reservoir flooding underneath our feet. We must stay on pavement and hope it holds. What's another way we can get across?" He pointed to where Zakkhaios had now captured his quarry and was standing with a panicked look on his face, staring at the holes in the ground where he'd just run.

Æolus looked at the buildings around him, and swiftly stuffing the loose end of his loincloth securely into the wrappings that covered his youthful body, grabbed a low wall attached to a small house.

"The roofs here run to the other side just where

Zakkhaios stands. Loukas and I used to run down them when we were boys. The roof tiles cause the feet to slip, though, and it can be dangerous. We no longer ran the roofs when Loukas grew, because with his size, the tiles sometimes shook under his feet."

Parik nodded his understanding.

"Zakkhaios is there, and we must join him. I'll be safe, as will you and Dulcia." He turned to her. "Come, my pretty girl. I'll help you up."

She looked at Æolus and winked as Parik took her hand. "Pretty girl," she said, as she stepped past Æolus and up to the roofs.

"Pretty stupid," Æolus sniped back. "Hold the leash next time."

"Hush," Parik reprimanded. "If we had walked across, we would have all gone inside the holes." *And I might have finally met an end from which the Muse couldn't save me.* He kept that thought to himself, pushing it aside. No amount of longing would grant that wish, and right at this moment, these children needed his help. In this instant, he must focus on nothing else.

"Up, Æolus. You next. Watch your feet and be safe." He reached for the youth's hand, expecting the occasional braggart he'd seen in the boy to push his help aside. The youth grabbed Parik in a firm grip, holding on for a moment longer than necessary until Parik looked in his face.

"You may call me Æole. I'd like that. My father . . . is no more. You saved Zakkhaios, and I'd like you to call me Æole." The youth glanced away, his eyes red.

His final word was whispered. "Compé?"

Although Parik had grown up in a culture far removed from this one, and the words that spoke to his heart most sweetly were unknown to this youth, the word Æolus had used to form his question was one that Parik did know. It was used only when the emotions ran deep, and once offered, to refuse it was to cut a person at the knees. He wouldn't do that to this youth, even though Æolus would be dead before the day was out. The drawing of the power had grown too strong for it to wait any longer for the final events of Lamahätsu's curse to manifest themselves in all the atrocities they would bring.

Parik squeezed the youth's hand, waiting until Æolus turned back to him. "Compé, Æole. Please follow Dulcia, and hurry. Your friend, Zakkhaios, awaits."

Before he let go of Parik's hand, a smile ghosted the youth's reddened features, and Æolus spoke his heart. "You are my friend." Then he was gone across the rooftops in a wild scramble.

It was a moment before Parik moved. He wasn't able, couldn't rescue Æolus from the death his own resurrection would lash across the city before night fell. The transition from life to life was never easy, but it was far less painful when he didn't care intimately about those who would die. This day he cared, and he cared far more than was good for his heart.

Æolus called to him from the other side, and heavily, Parik grasped the wall at his side to heave his weary frame to the roof. The tiles were slippery, just as Æolus had suggested, but when Parik reached the places that were the worst, a hand was there for him. It was Æolus, returning along the tiles to lend his support, and he steadied the old man that Parik had become as he walked the final few paces.

"Thank you, Æole." Parik's emotion-ravaged heart made his words quiver as though the exertion had strained him. It was true that it did, but the feelings were the reason.

Still holding his hand, the youth pulled the old man close, throwing his free hand around his neck, and whispering into his ear. "You are welcome, pater-amicus."

Æolus had claimed him as a father-friend. There was no closer bond between two unrelated males. Then, with a quick tightening of his arm, he released the man, turning to his two friends. "We'll be safe, now. Parik won't let harm come to us."

Parik's heart knew the bruising anguish of Lamahätsu's curse once again. He understood the term that had been spoken to him in confidence, and he only wished the youth's words could be true. With his whole being, he wished they could be true.

"YOU'VE HIDDEN IT from us."

The crowd of temple serving women was frightened. However, the old woman didn't intend to give in to them.

"Hidden? I don't know what you mean." She reached to brush a cool rag against the crippled girl's brow. "This child needs my care. You can see she hasn't awakened since being brought to us. She may die, yet, and it will be on you." She didn't need to point as she said her words. Her verbal finger was aimed directly at them. The gathered women knew just who she was referring to. They wouldn't like her suggestion, and she was unconcerned.

"You!" One especially heavy-featured woman pushed through the others. "The rat has been secreted away, and you're refusing to tell. It must be taken to the priests. Only they can tell if it's truly of the goddess. Where have you hidden it?" She spat her disgruntlement to the stone that made up the temple paving, both indoors and out.

Another leaned her face in, her white robe pulled close to her neck. "If the temple falls, how will we earn our meals? We must eat, you know. Will this girl fill your stomach? She has one leg, and one only."

The old temple serving woman knew she'd been right to hide the rat, and she hissed her reply at them. "What do you know of earning meals? You earn nothing. Night after night, you stand on the temple floor, and the men bring their coins. The most work you do is open your scrolls, reading your questions of absolution, and yet you expect to have meals brought to you each day. How many of you even carry your own basins of water? This child has lain in the street begging, not knowing if she'd eat each evening. When not enough coins came, she fed her small brother instead. Then there were still not enough coins, and the brother went hungry. Just this morning, the boy breathed his last, and even still he lies in his own bed with no one to care for his final needs. You suffer? Nah, I think not. This child has suffered, and it's right that she should suffer no more."

One voice in the back, unfazed and unrepentant, cried shrilly, "Then let her die, and her troubles will be over."

The old temple serving woman rebuked her. "Then let you die, and all your troubles will be over. Leave us, and don't return. The Moica Priest will decide the girl's fate; it isn't up to you."

"It isn't up to a too-young acolyte, either," one of the women hissed. "That's the only reason the priest gave you a day. In the pretense of divining a reply, he wishes to have the youth quench his desires with stewed meats and fresh fruits while we dine on hard bread."

"And perhaps quench other desires, too," a peevish voice called from the crowd.

"Shush," another quieted her. "Such things should not be spoken. The acolytes have been dedicated to the temple, and they're the priest's to do with as he wills, the goddess be praised."

"The youths should run," the first woman hissed. "If they would all run away, the goddess would no longer shake our city, and the Moica Priest would come to us for his divinations." Several of the more naive women had repeatedly asked to serve in the divination sessions, hoping to enjoy tidbits of the sumptuous foods the priest consumed, and each had been refused. They considered it an insult beyond measure.

The old temple serving woman laughed, no longer

caring about the argument brought to her by these women. They couldn't even decide amongst themselves why the city was suffering this devastation.

"So," and she stood. "Which is it to be? Is the girl causing the devastation, or is it the Moica Priest's base desires, serviced by the youngest of the acolytes? You can't have it both ways. The priest has been using the acolytes since before many of you were born. The girl? She's been here but a short measure of time, not arriving until after the shaking started. Find a way to blame that on her."

"But the temple walls may fall. We can't remove the priest from the city."

The old woman laughed. "I don't ask you to. I suspect it would do no good in any case. Just wait, as the priest has suggested. True, his time with the acolyte may be just what you suggest—" She knew it was. She'd cared for many of the acolytes' injuries after the divination sessions. "—but the old man may still give you sound advice. He's been Moica Priest for many seasons, and he's served the city well."

"So, we should just wait?" Their rantings had stilled, finally giving heed to the old woman's words.

"Wait one day." She knelt back at the girl's side. "That's all the priest requested." She still hoped for two, if she could arrange for a fresh acolyte to grace the divination chambers on the second day. She did feel sorry for the acolytes who attended the Moica Priest, but she felt more so for the girl.

"You'll surrender the rat, if he declares it must be

banished?" The words were spoken hopefully.

"And the girl?" Yet another temple serving woman, making the deal complete.

"Of course. I'll do whatever it takes." She whispered the words to the child, knowing the women would take their meaning in their own fashion. She didn't care. No matter what the old priest decided, whether today, in two days, or in two seasons, this girl would have the old woman's protection, and she'd fight for her if she had to.

No one else would, after all.

"TELL ME AGAIN WHAT this man did." The Muse seized the old woman's arm, and he pulled her to his face. "I must know."

The four men had spoken to several people who had talked of mysterious occurrences involving an unfamiliar sage, a wise man and healer. The Muse had eventually proclaimed each as having to do with his father. None had given them direction as to his location, though.

"It was only a rat." Her aged voice quavered. "I don't see the importance of a rat."

"I understand it was only a rat. I wish to hear your tale again." This might be the one, if this old woman could get her facts straight.

Drakon restrained the Muse's arm. "Umaru, she's suffered much today. Don't make it worse for her. She's very old." He motioned for the other two to help him calm their old friend. This wasn't the first time Umaru had been overly harsh with someone.

"Yes, Umaru. Let me have a try. Perhaps I can persuade her to retell her story. I was with my old great gran in her final days, and she was much like this." Xerxes pulled the man's hand away, and he knelt in front of the old woman.

"I'm frightened, sir," she began, tears running down her lined cheeks. "I've a home no longer, and when I run, I find great stone blocks in my way. The beams that support our ceilings split with each shaking. Will the city really fall?" Whimpers, like mists, escaped her throat.

Xerxes took one of her weathered old hands in his, and he stroked it gently. "For a hundred seasons and nearly as many more before that, this city has stood. Do you think it will fall today?" He looked reassuringly into her eyes, and he did it well, despite the water he'd seen flowing underneath the city.

"Not today." She smiled tentatively, reassured, just as he'd intended.

"Where was the man with the rat?" Xerxes looked around, as if he could help her locate it.

"There." She pointed, and her finger indicated the fallen door from the tavern.

"Your door, Umaru." Paulus grinned. "From your tavern."

The Muse quieted him with a hand motion. He didn't know the tavern, and it didn't concern him. He wanted to know of the rat. This sounded just like something Parik would do.

Xerxes looked at Umaru for a moment, and when there was no response, he turned back to draw more of the story from the old woman. "The rat chased this man, you say?"

Nodding vigorously, the woman pointed to the door again. "Rats are holy. It was waiting just there under the door, in the shadows. When the man stepped out, the rat followed, like *that*." She snapped two weathered fingers together. "On three legs. I saw that. Three legs."

The Muse interrupted, "What did he look like?"

"Gray." Trepidation clouded her eyes once again.

"The man, woman! His hair, his face!"

"I couldn't see—" Her hand shook in front of her mouth. "His face—" She blinked rapidly, looking away.

Xerxes held up his hand. "Patience, friend. I'll get your story. I know this skill." He turned back to her and patted her hand once again. "Why couldn't you see him, old mother? Was he far away?"

"Headcloth." Her hands shook as she reached her fingers to her forehead and drew a line just where the selvage edge had creased his skin. "He had on a headcloth, good sir, and a long catch sack at his back. No one could see his hair." She smacked her lips, and she chuckled. "He was big, though. Very big. Much like that one." As she pointed to the Muse, her head nodded reassurances to the other three men, telling them that her eyes hadn't misled her.

Xerxes glanced at his friend before he turned and stroked her hand again. "The rat. You were telling us of the rat."

"The rat." Her eyes opened wide, and she suddenly seemed cognizant of what Xerxes wanted from her. "It had only three legs. I thought that very suspicious, so I followed it. It was right on the heels of the man, and then the water came up in the streets. The aqueduct came down, you know. Water filled the streets." She motioned all around them, making sure they knew just how bad it had been.

"Yes, water everywhere," Xerxes agreed. "What about the rat?" He glanced at the Muse, the man he knew as Umaru, to find a frown on his face. His eyes were fixed on the old woman. Turning back to her, Xerxes whispered, "Go on."

"It swam. All rats can, you know. This one swam with just three legs, and right to the man, too." The old woman leaned in close to Xerxes and closed one eye. "I tell you, it was following him from the start. I know. I watched it. It was a holy rat." She sat back, a look of satisfaction on her face.

The Muse slapped Xerxes on the shoulder. "More quickly," he hissed.

Drakon placed his hand on his shoulder. "Umaru, be patient. She's talking, and there's no real hurry. The city has stopped shaking, and we'll find this father who's finally come to you. Have no concern."

The Muse bit his tongue. There was a real hurry, if he wanted to remain in this body. He obviously couldn't force this along, though, and Parik would remain hidden if he didn't learn this woman's story. The person she was speaking of might be a false coin that only appeared to be of the finest gold, and to chase after her story without proof was to hold an empty money sack.

"Thank you, Drakon." The Muse did his best not to

look chagrined. "I'll hold my tongue. Your reminder is appreciated."

Drakon nodded, and he motioned for Xerxes to continue.

"Next?" Xerxes prompted the woman.

"Next?" Her face perked up. "Why, he picked up that rat like it was a good friend and spoke to it, just like to you and me. He did. Then, when he put that rat down, it scampered away on four good legs. Four, I tell you, just as real as the cracks in the stone I sit on, and straight up to the temple, too." Her hand slapped the stone slab at her side, barely missing the places where it had split when it fell from the topmost section of the adjoining building. "It was the power of the goddess," the old woman admonished. "The old one, the Goddess of Life."

"Lamahätsu?" The Muse interjected his question with a condescending smile. The time of the goddess had been a very long time ago, and he was surprised to hear her mentioned so specifically.

"Lamb hot soup? You say you want hot lamb soup? Say it like you mean to say it, boy." The old woman's hands fluttered at her chin as she suddenly looked around, her expression going slack. "My cookware is all smashed. Nothing left. Nothing left."

She began to mumble, and the Muse knew they would get nothing else from her. He turned away, deep in thought.

"Is it he, Umar?" Drakon looked his friend in the eyes. "Did the old woman describe your father, the one named Parik?"

"Was it he, Umaru?" Xerxes smiled, his anticipation lighting his expression. "The old woman's story hardly seems believable, but I'll trust you, if you claim her words to be fact."

The Muse grinned. "It's my father. This is something he'd do."

Paulus laughed. "Heal a three-legged rat? He'd use a healing power to do that?"

"Without question. We must go find this man. He will be the one I seek."

"Then the temple is where we must head next." Drakon laughed as his feet started the direction of the temple, the others following in his wake.

17

PARIK AND HIS SMALL troupe had stopped for a short rest. The day had grown hot, and Æolus had pulled several lemons from a fallen tree. Now they feasted, although the yellow fruits were bitter, and they had brought a strong thirst to their throats.

Now the boy had found a new thing to interest him, the footings from the fallen aqueduct. It was a man-made mountain of hand-cut stone, flat on top and geometric, but a mountain nonetheless. It towered over Æolus. He'd begged permission to scramble to the top to view the scene below.

Parik suspected he wished to look for his home. He

also suspected he wouldn't find good news. Even so, preventing him from this wouldn't change the events that had transpired around them. For that reason, he consented.

"You may climb the mountain." Parik nodded. He motioned to Æolus as he rested on a fallen stone. "Tell me what you find, as we must still locate a way through the city."

With sure fingers, and toes that found opportunities for hold, Æolus scrambled to the top. Looking out over the city, he called out, "Many piles of stone are fallen everywhere."

"I suspected as much. They're the remains of homes and villas decimated by the collapse of the aqueduct's towers. What else, my young friend?"

"Much as we've already seen." The words carried a measure of despair.

Such didn't surprise Parik. Rather, the opposite. If the boy hadn't despaired, that would be of concern. Where he and his friends were, all had come down. Trees from small gardens were on their sides, with their root balls extending into the air. Household furnishings were strewn about. Only one wall of a two-story villa next to the footing still stood.

The dying city was a shock beyond all understanding, unless one had seen such devastation before. Parik had. The inhabitants of this city hadn't.

"There!" Æolus pointed to where a group of walls were nearly drowned in the murky soup spewed across the city by the rising water. Massive logs, support columns for the thick stone walls, were splintered like kindling. "My house!" he cried, his voice rising in pitch.

"Where, Æole? Is it standing, still?" Zakkhaios scrambled up, joining him on the stones. He called to Dulcia, "Come see. Æole has found his family."

"I must go check on my mother!" Æolus moved quickly to climb down from the stone footing. He jumped, and as he hit, his foot sank into a soft spot in the soil. To steady him, Parik grasped his arm. When the youth tried to pull away, the big man held him tightly.

"Æolus." Parik had seen the water also, and he knew what it meant. He was certain the youth had seen the other thing in addition, the floating thing, the one in the shape of a woman with long hair. He spoke to the boy a second time with the more familiar name of a friend. "Æole, you mustn't go."

"Pater-amicus, I must. It's my home. My mother was there when I left, and she'd wait for me. She knows I would return."

Parik spoke to the youth in a whisper, naming the boy as his son-friend. "Please, Æole, filius-amicus, you mustn't."

"Pater-amicus." Æolus looked into Parik's eyes with pleading, until tears flooded into his own.

Then the tall man pulled the youth to rest his head against his leather vestments; and as the young mortal in his arms was racked with sobs, the man who would live forever whispered into his hair, "You're my filius-amicus, Æole. So long as you live, you are filius-amicus to me."

He meant it, too, no matter how few handbreadths of time the youth had left to live.

"THERE, TAKE THAT. IT'S of no use to anyone, anyway." The Muse grabbed a long loaf of bread from a dead man's hand and thrust it at Paulus. "You'll eat and be satisfied, and we'll still get to the temple."

The street they'd started out on was supposed to lead directly to the temple. However, with the damage the city had taken, the direct way seemed not to be the best way. Now, the three men traveling with the Muse implored him to stop and locate food. They'd been helping people since the morning, and their stomachs were knots of pain.

"Umaru, you can't mean that, to eat a dead man's food. Why, it was in his hand when he died." Drakon had ceased calling the man by Umar, the shortened name of familiarity, grumbling to his friends that the name seemed to belong to someone else.

"It'll just go to waste." The Muse stopped and frowned at him. "Would you have it ruin? Eat what's available." He grabbed the bread from Paulus' hand and broke off a large section. "I'm hungry, myself. The bread hasn't spoiled, and the baker was clearly very skilled. You should eat. You'll find it fills your stomachs nicely." He offered the rest of his section to the three men with him, holding it out generously and with the pretense of a smile.

"It's the baker, indeed, who lies there," Xerxes whispered. "His bakery is collapsed. All the walls are down." He'd looked inside to see several dogs tearing at the remains of the baker's wife. One had growled at him when he'd called to it to go away.

The Muse dropped the bread when no one would take it, and he looked up the hill. There were several small trees planted along the street they were climbing, and their leaves blocked much of the view of the temple. He pointed out several large, missing stones in the pavement.

"Go check, Xerxes," the Muse directed. He'd begun ordering the men about. Their names had confused him at first, but he knew this was the weak one. He'd follow what anyone else told him. Drakon was the leader of the group, and the Muse had to approach him more carefully, reasoning with him rather than making demands. Drakon hadn't refused a direct request yet, though. He just questioned too much. The Muse wouldn't need additional help after reaching the temple, not if Parik was there. Otherwise . . . and that was why he couldn't abandon these men just yet.

"The ground's gone." Xerxes peered into the hole and looked up with astonishment. "Water runs here, also."

"Here?" Drakon ran up the steps to stand beside him, looking down into the abyss. The sound of the water was strong. "Umaru, Paulus, it seems the entire city will soon collapse."

With a grinding sound, the block they were on shifted beneath their feet, dropping on one side. A small tree fell just behind them, entangling them in its branches.

Before anyone could cry out, a further grinding this time vibrated the entire street, shaking them to the core.

"Stay back, Paulus, Umaru." Drakon caught the dire sense of the situation, and the look on his face told of his intent. "We'll be safe, as you must be." Fighting free from the branches, grabbing Xerxes as he did so, and seeing no escape backwards, he leapt with him past the hole and onto yet a higher step. Landing roughly against a partially collapsed wall, all was silent for a moment. Then, the stone they'd been standing on disappeared without warning, and the empty place was double the size it was before.

"We must be wise," the Muse encouraged, non-plussed, as he stepped over the trunk of the tree, pushing branches aside, and skirting the missing stones. "This must be happening all over the city. Come, Paulus," he called, seeing he was the only one who hadn't made it across the damaged place in the street. The Muse groaned when he saw the look of terror on the man's face. Paulus was the timid one. However, if he couldn't walk past the hole, the Muse wouldn't wait on him.

When the Muse looked commandingly at the other two men with him and made to continue, Paulus' voice called him back.

"Wait! I have the rope. I'll throw you one end, and you can hold it while I cross." He pulled it from his shoulder and held it in front of him.

"Just come around." The Muse motioned impatiently. The man would die, anyway, and for that reason, the Muse had no patience at his timidity. "We're all safe.

You will be, also. Just stay to the side."

"Please, Drak, Xerxes. It'll only take a moment to throw the rope." His voice trembled, and he didn't call to Umaru. "What if more stones fall? Remember the woman we helped earlier? We raised the block, and when it fell, the entire floor of the room dropped into the underground river. We barely saved her and her man. Here, take the rope." He'd coiled the end while talking, and without waiting, he tossed it directly to Drakon.

"I have it, Paulus. Walk past the hole, now." Drakon waved to him to go along the wall.

"Wrap it, Drak." Paulus showed him, wrapping it around his own wrist. "For me, please. It's an easy thing to do, and I'll feel better."

"For you, small frightened kitten." Drakon laughed overloudly, holding the rope in a loose loop.

"Wrap it, Drak." Paulus called to him again, holding his own wrapped forearm high in the air. He relaxed and smiled to see his friend finally take the loose loop and wrap his own arm.

"Now?" The Muse felt his patience stretched to the breaking point. "Can you do this now, Paulus?" He turned to Drakon. "Pull him across if you have to. I'm moving up the steps. Join me when you're finished." He pointed to Xerxes. "Come on, friend. You're with me."

Drakon frowned, but he nodded, coiling the extra rope around his arm to take up the slack. "Now, Paulus," he called. "I'm ready."

As Paulus sidled past the hole, unable to look away, Drakon coiled the slack into a pile. Then, just as Paulus' feet reached the step upon which Drakon and Xerxes had fallen, the stones underneath Paulus began to cant. The vibration of their movement shook the leaves on the fallen tree.

"Paulus, come quickly!" Drakon wrapped his forearm again at the new place in the rope, and he scrambled farther up the steps, keeping the line as taut as possible. His feet catching on a cracked step, he fell backwards, yanking Paulus hard as he went down.

His eyes went wide as the entire width of street dropped into nothingness. Then, the wall of a building alongside the sinkhole also gave way.

When the falling stones were once again quiet, Paulus lay on a steeply canted stone with one arm outstretched, still attached to the rope. His legs extended over a gaping maw that was many times larger than it had been when they first saw it.

When his friend didn't tighten the rope, Paulus yelled to Drakon, "Gi-ayah, you lazy mule. I'm hanging over the hole. I'm close enough to death, and I'd like to breathe for a few more handbreadths of time."

With a great surge of clambering motion, Drakon pulled his friend away from the hole. "There'll be no coming back down this street," he laughed.

"How can you laugh?" Xerxes ran to him and slapped him on the back of the head. "It isn't funny. Paulus nearly died."

"Ow!" Drakon hit him back, hissing, "I know he did, and I saved him. It scared me, and that's why I laughed."

"Look!" Paulus ran to them, coiling the rope that

Drakon had dropped to his feet, and he pointed. "Umaru's leaving us. We must hurry."

The Muse was already far up the street. He really needed to find Parik, and the warning feeling in his stomach had begun to grow. The ground would shake again very soon, and this time it would move the city as never before.

ZAKKHAIOS STOOD ATOP THE stone pylon, unaware that a great calamity was about to take place directly underneath his feet. Long ago, when the city was fresh with newness, the foundations for the aqueduct's many footings had been dug far into the earth, plunging deep into the ground to ensure absolute stability. Its builders had thought they built upon solid rock, and so they had, leveling the footings' underpinnings far beneath the soil's surface with gravel and crushed stone dust.

However, even bedrock must rest upon something, and the great footings of stone had two strikes that were now against them. The repeated shaking had cracked the rock ledge that had held the aqueduct stable for the better part of two centuries, and the waters flooding from the reservoir had washed out the compacted gravel upon which the footings once rested.

As the city wallowed in the throes of death, it had already begun to collapse in upon itself. For the next course in this gluttonous meal of destruction, the evil released millennia before by a jealous goddess cried to the massive stone footings to give in and return to the ground from which they had been hewn. And so it happened that at this exact time, this one particular monolith succumbed to the entreaties of the dying city.

The soft soil where Æolus had so recently slipped began to slide underneath the footing, its sands disappearing into an hourglass whose time had run out, and the great stones on which Zakkhaios stood began to tilt. ChiChi's yipping was the first signal that something was sorely amiss.

"Zakkhaios," Dulcia cried. "Get down. The stones are moving."

Despite Dulcia's warning, or perhaps because of it, Zakkhaios froze. Then, with the dust of age-old joints now in motion rising into the air, he was thrown from his feet. His hands grasped at rough places in the stone.

"Zakkhaios," Æolus cried. "Come off. You must jump, for the ground's hungry for you."

Parik stumbled in his efforts to aid the boy, falling roughly against the stone. Painfully, he pulled himself to his feet to reach out to him. "My hand, boy. Take it—"

"Parik." Dulcia's voice broke into the elder man's entreaty. "The wall of the villa. It's moving, also!"

As the great footing slipped into the soil, the back side dislodged the foundations of the house that had once stood against it. The wall towered overhead, blocking the sky, and a wave of dust flushed from between its newly-moving stones. A thick parapet decoration from the very top slipped loose and sailed down, and it hit near Zakkhaios' head, shattering into hundreds of small, sharp fragments.

"Zakkhaios, you must jump," Æolus called with enthusiasm.

Unable to do more than just watch all that was occurring around him, Zakkhaios' face revealed his terror and incomprehension.

"Jump to me, boy!" Parik held his arms to the youth.

"Æolus," Dulcia screamed. "You must pull him off! He'll die!"

In a rush of youthful energy, Æolus vaulted onto the stone, sliding next to his friend and shoving him into Parik's waiting arms. Then, exhaling a whoop of joy, he stood erect on the canted surface. With the sweaty sheen on his skin shimmering in the afternoon heat, he pumped a fist into the air.

"Wa-hoo!"

His excitement in his rescue was palpable, but very short lived. For at that exact moment, the rock ledge far underneath the footing fully gave way, and the remaining stones, ones that had stood stalwartly for nearly two centuries, slipped with little sound into the ground.

The falling wall of the house wasn't noiseless, however. The stones tore themselves apart with a roaring commotion, and as one, they followed the stone footing directly into the hole where Æolus had just disappeared.

THE CLOUDS IN THE sky roiled; the city was taking on an unusual measure of darkness, although it was still the middle of the afternoon. Much had happened that day, however, and the measures of time had seemed long. For that reason, it felt to most of those still alive that the evening surely must have arrived.

For those who looked up, the blackened clouds appeared to flicker along the edges, and the shifting light was a sickly green. Occasionally, a strange crackling reverberated hollowly, as green flashes within the clouds revealed layers upon layers in the growing heaviness.

Lower down, nearer the ground, sparks, fireflies of light, seemed to jump when hands touched one another or fabric drew too close to the ground. Looking closely, those who paid attention to such things saw the same sickly green color in the sparks as the clouds flashed along their edges.

What was visible to no one was the green electricity surging through the cracks in the bedrock that had been shattered by the repeated shaking of the ground, for the damage that had been done to the city above was only the smallest fraction of the devastation that extended far below its foundations. The great fist of power that was building to crush the life from the city and bring one solitary diamond from the carbonized residue was about to drive itself through the city's paving stones, and when it did, there'd be no place to run, no redoubt to be considered safe, and no one who could survive.

Even farther below, rising magma churned the fractured rock into liquefied propellant, exploding pressurized plant and animal remains, while rising faster and faster to the surface. The water from the reservoir had slowed in its descent, the great man-made lake now emptied, but it remained, captured in deep subterranean caverns, waiting still, and soon it would react strongly to the magma rising to meet it, bursting into torrential billows of steam.

The labyrinth of catacombs directly beneath the city was mostly void for the time being. Rivers of water flowed there no longer, leaving the remains of the reservoir's deluge to slowly drain from the lower reaches of the city into the underground chambers far below its foundations. That which couldn't escape quickly enough continued to surge into the fields beyond the city walls. Where for a time the city streets had reverberated with thunderous watery explosions each time a stone gave way, now only echoing silence could be heard.

The silence was ominous, and it screamed its message: Run. Abandon your homes, the streets of your childhood, the rooms that belonged to your fathers' fathers. Run to the hills, the plains, or the great wine country villas; just run.

Nevertheless, with each shaking, once it was over, the city's stalwart populace stamped the paving and hit the walls that had stood for nearly two centuries. Then, with the fortitude of ten generations, shoulders were braced against those blocks that must be moved today, hands marked those blocks that could wait until tomorrow, and businessmen made plans to get on with life.

After all, stone lasts forever, and there's nothing safer in the world.

THE STONE MOUNTAIN WAS gone, and dust swirled from the opening. Parik coughed as he waved one hand in front of his face.

"Æolus!" Dulcia's scream split the air, and ChiChi

leaped from her hands to run to the edge of the pit, barking sharply in the sudden stillness. "Æolus," Dulcia screamed again. "He's gone!"

"I'll rescue him," Zakkhaios called, but the older man restrained his arm. Already the soil under Parik and Zakkhaios' feet had begun to give way, and they separated and scrambled back from the edge of the pit, leaving the small fluff of frantic fur to battle the depths alone.

Parik's chest heaved with the extended age upon him. It was surely time for all this to end. Yet, it wasn't over for these youths who had turned to him for protection, and for that reason he couldn't simply find a place of solitude and insulate himself from the destruction until it was complete.

"Wait, boy. One may be lost, but that doesn't mean two need be." Parik listened. Except for ChiChi's frustrated yipping, the only sounds were those that had been there before the great stones had sunk into the bowels of the earth. Parik pushed the youth's shoulder gently. "Get the dog. Take the loop and pull him away from the hole. Remember the alley? The dog may stand securely, yet we may fall. No one else must join our friend in the pit."

"Chi, come to me." Zakkhaios called to the animal, crawling slowly along the ground.

"Good, boy. Move gently, and test the ground continually." Parik felt Dulcia's hand on his arm, and he turned to her.

"I'm frightened, Parik. Will we all die?" Her eyes were red, and without asking, she slipped her hand into his. "I'm afraid, for all the city is suffering."

"We're all afraid, sweet Dulcia." He brought her hand to his lips and kissed it.

"Is Æolus dead?" Her voice cracked, and she pulled her hand from Parik's to put it to her mouth, biting on the knuckles. "He fell, and the wall . . . he couldn't have survived."

"Hope, Dulcia. You must retain hope, or all is already lost." He put his arm around her shoulders, torn with his words. He felt no reassurance in his heart, not for this city or its people, and especially not for himself. Always, his own hope was hard to find and even harder to hold, for he had no way to escape the curse his mother had placed upon him. How could he offer hope to another?

"Got you!" Zakkhaios' voice rang out, and ChiChi gave a short high bark as the loop around the animal's neck tightened and jerked it away from the hole. Grabbing the dog in his hands, the youth scrambled back to Parik, shoving the wayward creature into Dulcia's arms.

"Chi," she crooned, even as tears rolled down her cheeks. She held him to her face, and his small tongue lapped at her skin.

"It's like a stair, Parik." Zakkhaios' eyes gleamed. "We can go down on the other side. The fallen wall, it tumbled, and the stones are piled one after another. Come with me. We can rescue Æole." He grabbed the man's forearm to pull him along.

"Hold quiet, Zakkhaios." Parik put his finger to his lips.

"For what? It's Æole, and he's in the hole. Don't you care?"

"I care, but I must first listen. Now, quiet." When the breeze shifted, blowing Parik's hair across his face, he reached behind his head and tied the mass securely into a thick knot at the nape of his neck. After a moment of listening, he smiled and nudged Zakkhaios. "Do you hear that?"

"The wind?" There was a low moaning that had started about the time the breeze shifted.

"It's my filius-amicus. Our Æole." He turned to Dulcia and spoke firmly. "We must go to him. You shall watch the ground to give us warning, if need be. Hold the pet securely. He mustn't try to follow." At her nod, he turned back to the youth at his side. The boy must note his next warning. "We'll go slowly. We've no rope, and if you've noticed, others in the city are busy with their own concerns. It's doubtful we'll garner additional aid."

"Yes. I understand. Your words are clear."

"We must make our way to the far side of the hole. You're correct that we may be able to descend there, yet only by testing can we know for sure. Follow me around, boy. We'll see if we can do this."

He and the youth climbed up the street for several steps to go around a collapsed villa, making their way over a small lemon tree that had fallen into the street. Several times Zakkhaios stopped to give the older man a hand, pulling him past tumbled stone blocks that choked their way. Dulcia disappeared from their view from time to time, and then she reappeared across the great pit. Zakkhaios raised a hand and waved, calling to her. Dulcia returned the wave.

Parik instructed him to sit upon the stones that comprised the floor of the house from which the wall had tumbled into the hole. The blocks from the wall formed the irregular steps just below them, and they would drop to the top one first. Then, Parik let himself fall heavily inside. Rocking the block his feet rested on to check for stability, he nodded, satisfied, and called to the youth overhead.

"Boy, are you ready?" He looked up and for the first time paid close attention to the clouds covering the city. They had grown dark. He knew that far across the flooded fields, blue sky must be overhead. The sun still shone there. The gathering storm wasn't a natural phenomenon. The tempest gathering above was for him and would be nowhere else except over the city. He'd lived through this many times before.

It wouldn't help to worry about it, though. At this moment, a youth needed to be rescued, and from the sounds of the moans he'd heard earlier, he was a very injured youth.

"I'm coming!" Zakkhaios slipped off the stone floor, sending dirt cascading awkwardly into the hole. Parik grabbed the youth's arm as he landed, steadying him.

"I have you," Parik said to him. "Now's the time to yell for our friend. He's stopped moaning, and such isn't good. Quick, call to him."

"Æole, it's Zakkhaios. You must answer. We've

come to rescue you. Æole!" He stopped when Parik wrapped his large hand around his shoulder.

"We must listen for his location. Shush." He pointed, showing the youth that their friend might be anywhere, for the sinkhole they were in stretched into the distance on two sides. At various points light could be seen filtering through, the signs that other parts of the city had also collapsed into the labyrinth. Parik whispered, pointing, "The whole city's unsafe. The reservoir has flushed the supporting soil from under much of the middle reaches of the town, and a good deal of the upper slopes, as well, I'm sure." He glanced around at the newly-formed sinkhole they were in. "We must work quickly. Call again, Zakkhaios. Æolus must be here. The blocks will make the sound come from strange directions, but we did hear him. You must make him respond to you."

As Zakkhaios called, Parik began to move across the tumbled stones, looking and listening, finally adding his voice to the youth's. It was the blood leaking from under a pile of stones that drew his attention. He waved to Zakkhaios to join him. At first, the youth's eyes were bright, and his grin was ready to greet his friend. However, when he saw the blood at Parik's feet, all expression of joy dropped away.

"He's dead, then." Zakkhaios' voice was lifeless, and his face was white. "We can't leave him. We must move the stones. Even if he's dead, he can't stay where he is."

Parik placed a hand on his shoulder to calm him.

"Slowly, boy. I didn't say he's dead. It may be the blood of injury we see, and not the blood of death."

Parik hoped life still resided in the youth. If so, he could be healed. He had the power to do that, although at this stage of the game, such a healing from so near death would cost him. For all the good it would do, he knew some might say, but Parik had to think of it a different way. It's all the good he could do, and so he must, even if the youth's respite from death was a short one. For a filius-amicus, he could do no less.

He motioned to the youth at his side, and together they wrestled the first stone off the pile. Underneath, a single bloody hand was exposed. Parik reached, wanting so much to heal this youth, this filius-amicus who had claimed him as a friend, one as close as a father. All it took was one touch, and the fingernail from his goddess mother would warm, bringing healing to his broken body.

Yet, there was hesitation, and Parik drew his hand back. The stones that had crushed the youth still covered him, and to attempt to bring his body to wholeness too soon would be to find frustration, to perhaps cause death outright, or possibly to invite the injuries to form over again even as the youth held Parik's hand. The stones must be removed before any healing could commence.

Then, Parik thrust his other hand in to the youth, the hand with no special powers, other than the ability to tell if warmth, if life still flowed beneath Æolus' skin. He grasped the hand he felt and squeezed gently. Tears flooded his eyes when he felt the pressure returned. He turned his head to the youthful companion at his side.

"He lives, Zakkhaios. Our friend, Æole, lives."

18

THE MOICA PRIEST STOOD at the entrance to his stone viewing platform, the one from which he'd watched the massive footing from the aqueduct sink from sight. He shook his head at the people who seemed to be exploring its depths even as he watched.

"They should attend to more important matters." The words were growled in an angry burst, intended for no one and spoken to no one.

The priest knew the matters he meant, too. The city's infrastructure was under assault, and without it, the temple coffers would suffer. Looking to the sky, he wondered if the temple serving women might have been right after all, and today he'd find the gods did indeed exist. The clouds roiled; and the green flashes he could see within their confines, their otherworldly light illuminating the many internal cloud layers, were unnerving, especially as off to the southern fields, there was still early afternoon sun washing the flooded ground.

He turned back to the temple rooms and stepped inside. With the growing dusk outside, he'd decided to start his divinations early. The acolyte he'd chosen to assist him was in the room, and one of the minor priests was preparing the youth for the priest's special attention.

Only having arrived at the temple complex the previous day, the youth had caught the Moica Priest's notice with his pretty face and his pale hair. It was intriguing to see one of his coloring here in the city. The youth surely must have been stolen from some distant land and sold to the temple by traders who wanted him far from being found. His flesh was firm and of good color, as if he regularly ate well. He might have come from a high-level caste, perhaps a rich man's son. That wouldn't help him here, the priest was afraid. He was now little more than a simple slave to serve the temple's needs.

He'd smelled, though, as did all the acolytes upon first arrival, and the minor priest had him stripped and standing in a pail of water. His skin had scrubbed up nicely, although now that he was unclothed, the Moica Priest was having second thoughts. His face had been so pretty yesterday, already carrying the sharpness of near manhood, but it was now clear that in spite of his height, his limbs were slender, containing little maturity. Pity. The priest's divinations were more satisfying when the acolytes showed physical fortitude. Carrying the heavy pots of meats and the many amphorae of wine was no small task, but he wouldn't send the youth back now. The piping from the reservoir was no longer filling the basins, and there was no more water to clean another acolyte. He'd have to trust there was more strength to the youth than caught the eye. Besides, there were other interesting ways in which the child could be of service before the night was through.

The Moica Priest studied the boy for a moment, as the minor priest at the child's side dipped his cloth in the water and placed it against the boy's skin once again, and he cleared his throat.

"I head to the divination chambers. Dress the child in the divination robes and send him to me when you're finished." He smiled when the priest looked up and nodded. Before exiting the room, he turned once again. "A plate of fruit, also. In addition, wine. A light snack before I begin. The divinations always stir my appetite."

Moving down the steps into the lower chambers, the Moica Priest walked especially hard, stamping his feet at the slightest suggestion of hollowness. He'd heard the stories of collapsing floors in the city, and he'd seen the aqueduct footing sink into the ground. He knew his priests had already sounded out the temple stones, and the complex had been declared safely out of danger. That didn't entirely reassure the Moica Priest. His retinue of temple cronies only told him what he wanted to hear. It was his job to listen between the lines, and the lines this day had become very blurred, indeed. Even so, he was sure his time in the divination chambers would reset his good sense of the world around him, and if not, at least he'd have a pleasurable time trying. He might even let the acolyte share a taste of the meal, that was if he served the old priest's needs very well, indeed.

RENA HUGGED HER KNEES and waited for Kaius to return. She couldn't bring herself to eat the berries he'd pulled for her from a bush. She'd been so very frightened when she'd lain under the stone, and then she'd felt safe when Kaius brought help. Yet, the falling of the floor into the water below had returned her fears more strongly than ever before.

As she and Kaius fled, they saw other places where the stones had dropped far into the ground, and they'd been forced to take circuitous routes to make any progress. Then, the lower city had been flooded—thank the goddess it was nearly drained away—but the fields outside the city gate were impassible. Even a section of the city's wall had collapsed! She'd begged Kaius to take her there for escape, and then they'd been turned away.

She longed for Kaius' return. She'd told him the particulars of their time together, wanting him to know her appreciation. When he seemed puzzled, she insisted, describing it in detail, but still he hadn't believed her. Then he'd gone to see if there was any other way to leave the city.

However, what if he returned, and this place where

she sat was no longer? What if it collapsed into the ground just as the other places in the city had done? One man running by had said he saw one of the enormous footings that had held up the aqueduct, and it simply sank into the ground with no warning, taking a youth with it. Just the thought made Rena's pulse race with anxiety.

Just as she reached to toy with the berries, thinking of trying one, a brilliant green flash lit the street immediately in front of her. The reverberation of cracking thunder enveloped her. Rena screamed and fell to her side, rolling into a ball. When silence returned, and she heard no more than other people's whimpers and exclamations, she dared to look around. It unnerved her to see the place where the green light had exploded just across the street. There was a blackened mark where the stone had split and buckled.

"That could have been me," she said to no one in particular. Her berries forgotten, she wrapped her arms back around her knees and placed her forehead on them. She didn't even cry. She was too frightened. There was no place where she might be safe, not indoors nor out. She wanted Kaius to return. She wanted to feel his arms around her, and she wanted out of the city.

"Kaius," she whispered to her knees. "I need you, Kaius. Come back soon. Please."

THE OIL LAMPS WEREN'T necessary in this part of the temple, for just enough light found its way inside for the old serving woman to observe her charge. She'd been sleeping for some time, but the increasing noises from outside now disturbed her rest.

Chiarina moved her crippled leg, and she jerked, gasping, "Thaddiaos!" Her hand reached out, not finding his warmth at her side.

"Quiet, dear. He's sleeping." He was, too, the old serving woman thought, the sleep from which one never wakes. A withered hand, one old instead of crippled, although at times it seemed the same thing, reached to brush her brow.

"Thaddiaos?" Chiarina opened her eyes, and she looked around the room. "He sleeps? Where?"

"You don't remember?" The temple serving woman took the girl's hand and brushed the smooth skin, thinking how hers used to be as beautiful. No longer, though. She had only parchment for skin, wrinkled parchment that covered bones that always hurt. Raising the child's hand to her lips, she kissed it.

Chiarina's words were barely whispered. "I've been so tired, and I've forgotten how I came to be here. Have I been in this place long?"

Her eyes closed again, and the old woman knew she'd soon be asleep. That was good, but she had a response she needed from the girl. She also needed to see her reaction when she made it.

"A rat has been sleeping with you." The girl's eyes flew open, and she looked at the woman. There was interest there, and the old woman was convinced. This girl knew this rat. This was proof she must have been sent by the goddess, and the rat was her protecting familiar. The old woman had been right to secret the animal away. It would certainly bring good luck to the temple.

"He's gray?" Chiarina smiled when the old woman nodded eagerly. "He comes to see me in the dark, but I've seen him once in the light. I feed him breadcrumbs."

"Ah!" *She feeds him breadcrumbs even when she has nothing herself.* It was another sign.

"He limps on three legs, and I feel for him, for he's crippled like me." The girl brushed her hair from her forehead. "The goddess visits me today."

"Rest, my dear. I've already taken care of that for you." The old woman patted her hand. "The goddess be praised. Close your eyes and sleep."

She was excited, though. It was surely the same rat, although it had four good legs. What if the goddess planned to heal the girl, right here in the temple? How glorious would that be? The one who had protected her would receive the praise, and that would be the one who had sat by her side as she slept and who had defended her in front of the Moica Priest, himself.

This was turning out to be a very exciting day, indeed, and the old temple serving woman rejoiced.

"HE LIVES, ZAKKHAIOS." Parik reassured the youth. "His hand moved in mine, but we must lift the stones to get to him. I can't tell how damaged his body is."

Parik was determined to aid Zakkhaios in this, although he wasn't sure how much strength his weary limbs had to offer. Even so, he'd garner enough to move these stones, curse that old goddess who had birthed this nightmare into being.

"The blood, Parik." Zakkhaios' eyes were wide with concern. "There's so much. Even if he still breathes, how can he continue to live?"

"We must retain hope, even when it seems there's none. If you're with me, ready yourself, boy." Parik moved to a stone. "Grab the corner, and we'll force it aside. Grab securely. It mustn't dislodge yet another block."

"Zakkhaios? Parik? Is Æolus alive?" Dulcia's voice floated to them, accompanied by the sharp, repeated barks of the dog. "You're talking, and I can't hear what you say."

The stone they had in hand tumbled to the side, and Parik sat, winded. He breathed to Zakkhaios, "Call to her, boy. We must have help to move the stones. I can do two, maybe three more, but I fear I'll injure Æole if I should falter."

"But you said there'd be no one." Zakkhaios wiped his hands on his ragged loincloth. "If we can't do this, how will Æolus be saved?"

"Now, boy. Call to her." Parik pointed to the roiling sky above. "See overhead? We must finish this with haste, and help to do so is needed."

The youth stood and put his hands to his mouth. "Dulcia, this is Zakkhaios."

"I know your voice. You're silly, Zakkhaios. Of course, it's you. Is Æolus safe?" Each time she spoke, ChiChi went wild with barking.

"He's alive, but some stones are in the way. Find

someone to help move them."

"You have Parik, Zakkhaios. Have you asked him to help?"

"Please, Dulcia. Just go." He dropped his hands when he heard her grunt of agreement. "She'll do it," he said to Parik. "Can you do another block?"

Parik placed his hands against a stone. "I can do one."

Zakkhaios grinned. "For Æole."

The boy's familiar manner of speaking gave Parik a measure of strength. "For Æole."

Together they lifted, and with the strength of love for a friend, they tossed the stone to the side.

KAIUS RAN UP THE steps, two at a time when he could, taking the flatter parts of the rising street with long strides. At one place there had been no street left, and he'd pulled himself up on a rooftop to get past. It had been like this the whole way. Go up one street until it was blocked, then backtrack until a roof or alley could be found to skirt the damage. Despite the devastation hindering his progress, Rena was waiting on his news, and he knew she was very frightened.

It wasn't especially good news, either. It seemed there was no way out of the city. When the water had partially receded from the city's gate, a number had driven horses and carts thorough, thinking the water still standing outside would let them through. It seemed not. Great channels hidden under the surface of the water had been gouged out by the flow of the reservoir, and the people had dropped out of sight, weighed down by coins and other things they thought important enough to carry with them.

Only the temple seemed immune to the damage, he'd learned, and he'd already decided to take her there. Now, though, he'd been forced out of his way again by the flooding that remained in the lower city. It was going down slowly, but slowly didn't get him quickly to Rena.

As he turned into a familiar street, one that rose with many steps to wind past where the aqueduct had until recently arched high overhead, he stopped in amazement. The massive footing was gone, as if it had been removed by a giant hand. Yet, the stones had been enormous, and it would be impossible to lift them. He shook his head to clear his thoughts, deciding the sight was no stranger than many other things he'd seen this day.

It did surprise him to see a youth of a girl there with a small dog against her chest. He cupped his hand around his mouth and called to her, "Is it safe to pass?" When she waved him up, he smiled and stepped forward to find his Rena. He was surprised a second time when the girl ran to him to stop him.

"Can you help, sir?" Her eyes were desperate. The dog began a torrent of barking, and the girl lifted the small animal to her face. The fluff ball didn't quiet down, though.

"I'm called Kaius. Is your pet hurt? Or perhaps are you lost?" He looked around, not seeing anyone. "I go to the temple for safety. I'm told it still stands without damage." He smiled, reaching out a hand. "I'll take you if you wish."

"No, my friend has fallen, and he needs help." She glanced to the hole Kaius could now tell replaced the colossal stone footing the aqueduct had rested upon.

"In there?" He frowned. If her friend was in the hole, he was lost. "I'm sorry for your friend. You must come to the temple with me. You'll be safe there."

"No!" Moisture pooled at her eyes. "Parik and Zakkhaios have gone in to pull him out. They need help moving the stones. You must help me. There's no one else."

"They're already inside? How did they climb down?" He looked at her in disbelief.

"I'll call to them. Zakkhaios? Parik?"

Her voice brought an immediate response from the hole.

"Dulcia, did you find someone?" It was Zakkhaios.

"Yes! His name is Kaius. Please beg him to stay." Her eyes were still on Kaius, and they pleaded with him.

Kaius took a deep breath and nodded. Others had helped him this day, saving his Rena. He couldn't refuse this request.

"I'll go. Point the way to climb down."

"There." She ran and motioned to the collapsed villa Zakkhaios and Parik had crossed earlier. "It goes to the other side. Hurry!"

He looked at her, and with a smile of encouragement, he threw himself over the debris where the villa had once stood. Once at the edge of the pit, he looked inside to the series of rough steps that ran down the side, and he called to the man and the youth dislodging large stones from a pile.

"You're both uninjured?" At their nods, he dropped to his stomach. "Come here, and I'll pull you up."

The youth put his hands at his waist, winded with his exertions, and he paused until his chest no longer heaved. Then he spoke. "You don't understand. Our friend is underneath, and he's alive."

"No! It can't be!" Kaius saw the red flowing where they stood. "See the blood? You're mistaken. Come, leave him buried. It's a fitting grave. My hand." He waved it. "I'll pull you up."

"No!" The youth turned and reached to his side, grabbing a stone much too heavy. With a grunt of effort, he shoved the stone aside, and it rumbled into the darkness. "I'll save my friend alone, if you won't help. Go away!" Then, winded, he leaned back against the rubble and let his tears flow. "I can't, though. I can't move them all alone."

The old man at his side stood. "I'm Parik, and our friend does live. I've held his hand, and he responds. Please. I'm old, and my young friend here needs help I can't give. All we ask for is your time, and little of that. We're nearly there." He reached to the boy and grasped his arm, squeezing it before letting it go.

Kaius muttered to himself, "And we all die right here when more stones fall in upon us." However, others had helped him in circumstances as dire, and he'd provide what assistance he could. He leaped headlong into the great cavity, landing securely on his feet.

When he got to the pile of stones, his breath was taken away. A youth was there, indeed, still partially buried beneath the stones. Blood splattered his body, and the side of his face was split open. One arm had been mangled, and several stones still covered his legs. The loincloth around the upper part of the youth's hips was soaked with red, and Kaius knew he was standing in the boy's blood. He was fully confident these people were freeing a dead body.

He was here, though, and he'd do what he could. It would add only moments to his absence from Rena, as long as the walls of this unholy hole in the ground didn't collapse around them.

"Which block first?" Kaius turned to the old man for instruction, and catching a clear view of his face, he attempted to place the features. "Do I know you, sir? Your face seems familiar, yet I know no one by the name of Parik."

"I think not, as I'm from far away." Parik placed his hand on one particular stone. "Here. Then this and this." Stepping back, he motioned to the youth. "Zakkhaios will help you. I've used up my final reserves. Thank you, Kaius."

"You're most welcome." Kaius nodded, reaching for the first one. The fallen debris must be moved, and then he could be on his way. The stones were indeed heavy, but with two strong backs instead of just one, the bloody form crushed by the stone was quickly exposed.

"Parik, go to him, now." Zakkhaios stepped back

expectantly. "You can help. ChiChi, and the rat, Dulcia said. You helped them both. Your hand healed me. Without your touch, Æole dies."

"I'll carry him from here." Kaius moved to push through to the bloody form, but Parik caught his arm.

"The youth is right. If we move him, he dies without doubt. You can see the damage. We're lucky he still lives." The old man stepped and knelt beside the broken youth.

"You'll stay down here until he breathes his last?" Kaius was aghast. "This is lunacy. Let me take him up to the sky where he can at least be cleansed."

"How?" Parik looked at him, puzzlement in his expression. "How will you cleanse him? The city's water is gone. The sky overhead," he motioned with his hand, "is green with power. There's disaster all around. He must walk out of his own accord, or he doesn't leave at all."

Kaius snorted. "You're loose in the head. I'll leave you to play your games, but I'll have the priest say a prayer for you. I'm headed to the temple for safety." He turned to climb the blocks to the top. "May the goddess have mercy on you."

"Wait!" Parik implored him. "We'll go with you, all together. I need only a moment."

"Parik," Zakkhaios wailed. "Æole's dying. Please attend to him."

"The youth is again correct. Adults do tend to speak too many words." Parik turned and reached a hand, placing it on Æolus' bloody neck. "His life still flows. Let me ask if he wishes to be healed."

Kaius laughed. "Wishes? With all the dead and dying throughout the city? This is once again absurd." He looked up from the hole, the darkening sky tightening his chest in fear. "I should leave you here, and I don't know why I remain."

"You'll see," Zakkhaios said. "Won't he, Parik?"

"Perhaps." Parik leaned in to speak quietly into Æolus' undamaged ear. "Filius-amicus, I've come for you. You saved your friend, and yet you couldn't save yourself. You're truly a friend to those whom you consider friends. Do you wish to live?" Parik adjusted his hand on the youth's neck.

"I wish for a father such as you, pater-amicus." Æolus' broken whisper could just be heard.

"I'll be that to you for the rest of your days." Tears fell from Parik's eyes. With those words, Æolus drew in a sharp breath, and his color began to return.

"By the great Goddess of Life, how's he doing that?" Kaius' disbelieving question was quickly answered by the youth at his side.

"He's a healer. He heals anyone—anyone who wants him to, anyway."

"I'm watching it, and I don't believe it." The broken places on Æolus' body visibly knitted together as they watched, his skin closed up, and the damage disappeared. "Who wouldn't want this?"

Zakkhaios shrugged, and he carried a wide grin across his face.

Then, Æolus jerked, and his eyes opened wide. He looked around and called out the names of those he could see. "Parik. Zakkhaios. Where's Dulcia?"

"Quiet, boy." Parik's shoulders drooped, and he turned to Kaius, older in appearance than he'd been just moments before. "He's lost much fluids. Also, food will be needed. His body has had to draw upon much of its resources to restore itself. If you'll carry him now." He slumped to the side. "Only a few times have I healed from this close to death, and never at this stage of my own aging."

"Æole," Zakkhaios started, his face dancing with excitement. "You should have seen it. Your skin, it just grew, and your face, well, it's prettier than it was." He snickered. "You can thank Parik for that."

Parik waved his hand at Zakkhaios. "He doesn't remember. The healing, when it's this great, it heals the memories, too. He just knows he's very tired and covered with blood. Zakkhaios, help this good man. Æole needs you to be there for him, as he was there for you. Go. I'll come up when I've regained a measure of strength."

As he helped carry the still-bloody youth out of the hole, Kaius regretted having doubted the old man. He was indeed a healer, a great one, and he couldn't wait to tell Rena all about it. She wouldn't believe it either, not until she saw the blood all over the youth's body. She'd have to believe that.

As Æolus was lifted to the surface, ChiChi broke free from Dulcia's arms, and the animal ran to the edge of the pit once again to call its support to those who had been buried and were climbing back into the world of the living. Once Æolus was at the top, Kaius had to call on Zakkhaios' help to lift Parik out, because the old man had no strength. Finally, standing on the edge together, the four waved to Dulcia.

"His leash," Parik called hoarsely. "Hold it, girl," and then he coughed. "Old age is a curse," he mumbled.

"Better than dying," Kaius remarked, remembering how close Rena and he had come in their room.

"Not when you've lived as long as I have." Parik turned to Zakkhaios. "Please give your shoulder to Æole. He'll be weak." He touched Æolus' chin. "The blood is yours, but it will wash. You're uninjured, filius-amicus. For strength, eat and drink at your first opportunity." He pushed on Zakkhaios' shoulder to get them moving.

"You, Parik," and Kaius looked at him as he remarked on his sudden aging. "How's your strength?"

Parik laughed sourly. "I have reserves I've yet to tap. I feel it gathering all around me." He motioned to the sky and the city.

Just then, a green flash lit the heavens in another part of the city, and all around them green sparks flew from fingertips and any objects close by. After a moment, a thunderous cracking noise whipped past them, lashing their eardrums with pain.

Kaius laughed. "Rain comes, it seems. We must go quickly."

"No," Parik said. "There'll be no rain."

"A storm's gathering. Rain and storms go together, or do you have that touch, also, to order the weather?" He grinned at the thought, and if the old man claimed it,

Kaius would believe him.

"No, I don't control this. However, there will be no rain." The youths had reached the other side, and he turned away. "You're correct, however. There will be a storm, and few will survive."

Kaius frowned at that. This man spoke more like a wise sage than a healer, but maybe he was both. He sure had the healing touch, that was for certain. Kaius had seen it, and he wouldn't have believed it otherwise. No one would, and for that reason, he decided he wasn't sure if he'd tell Rena.

19

"COME. WE MUST MOVE forward." The Muse strode ahead quickly, his sturdy legs and green eyes carrying him up the steep street. The darkness that had overcome the city was of no matter to him, except that it told of the nearness of Parik's rebirth. Green lightning struck off to the side, and the three men accompanying him ducked for cover as one.

After the noise settled, Paulus laughed. "Hey, did that one scare you, also?" He hitched the rope on his shoulder and leaned in between Xerxes and Drakon. "It didn't bother Umaru all so much, such as it might not bother one who's used to it. Strange, is what I think."

"Well, he's off again," Drakon pointed out. "We must be fast as the lynx to keep up." His friends grinned as they moved out. He called ahead, "Umaru, we're still hungry. We must stop and search for food. Please slow your pace."

"You were offered food. Keep up." He glanced back to be certain they were. He didn't feel well, and he knew time was short. It also bothered him that he couldn't track the fourth fingernail when the power was gathered in this concentration.

"The lightning didn't surprise you much, Umaru," Xerxes called ahead. "Green lightning. Not once have I ever seen it. Do you know of it from Africa?"

Drakon reached and slapped the back of his head. "Quiet, Xerxes. Remember the water? He nearly drowned. He'll right himself. Be patient." He turned to Paulus. "Do you need me to carry that?" He pointed to the rope he held in his hand.

"I'm strong." Paulus waved his offer away.

Xerxes snickered. "Just a rabbit to cower at every hole in the street. I'll carry it." He reached to grab for the rope, only to notice flashes of green leap from his finger-tips to the rope. "Did you see that?" He tried it again, and the firefly sparks jumped once more. "Like the lightning."

"Maybe it's been doing it all along. It's growing darker." Paulus reached to Xerxes and watched the green sparks jump.

"Except there." Drakon pointed to the horizon where the sun was shining brightly. "All around is sunshine, except here. What do you make of that?"

The response to his question came from the Muse. "I make that my companions should walk faster." Then, without another word, he made a sour face, and he collapsed to the ground, holding his stomach.

"My friend, Umaru. What's the matter?" Drakon ran to him.

Through gritted teeth, Umaru cursed with sounds the other three men had never heard. Then, he began to lambaste the darkening sky in words more familiar to them.

"Curse you, Parik. You can't let it shake now. I need this body; I need revenge. No!"

As the three remaining friends looked at each other, numerous flashes of green lightning hit the city in rapid succession. If their eyes were to be believed, just as many erupted from the city to strike at the clouds. Then sparks flew from everything around them, and the ground began to shake.

THE MUSE GASPED AND opened his eyes. He was inside now, and his arms ached with weariness. There was someone with him, and from the sounds and smells, a great meal was underway.

He couldn't tell, at first, just which gender he was. If female, some men did prefer wenches to serve their meals. A female would be little good in his plans for Parik. However, if he were male, he wanted to serve no man. He wanted Parik in his grasp, instead.

Then, a voice spoke into his ear.

"So, my sweet acolyte. You're quite good at carrying the meal pots." The lips that spoke the words smacked heavily. "Let's see if you can enjoy our divination as much as I."

The Muse felt a gobbet of meat touch his lips, and he twisted his face away. He yelped when a hand grabbed him tightly around the waist and pressed a cup of sweet wine to his mouth. With the sound of his cry, he knew he was definitely not female, and he wanted away from this man's touch.

He still had Parik to find.

Slamming a much-practiced thrust with his elbow directly into his companion's ribs, he twisted roughly, pulling himself loose, and jumped to his feet, knocking over a great pot of stew.

"You fool," the man at the Muse's side sputtered, as he grabbed at a table and fell to the floor. He yelled with a drunken burr in his voice, "I wasn't ended with my divination, and more pots will have to be brought. To it, boy!"

From the marks on his face, the Muse could see that the man in the room with him was a priest, and apparently very high up in the religious hierarchy. Maybe the Muse had been fortunate and made it into the temple after all. He peered down, surprised to see he was bare. Inside a temple, to search for Parik, he'd need clothing, or he'd surely be cast outside.

The Muse glanced around the space, finding a robe that was open down the front. Slipping it on, he wished for a cord to tie it, but nothing was available. Noticing his exposed legs, he realized the portent of the priest's words; he was little more than a child, for his skin was smooth.

The priest was very irritated, and he growled as he lay on the floor, "I spoke to you, boy. I'm not finished, and I've not given you permission to clothe yourself."

"You're a fool, taking boys for your pleasure." It was a child's voice that lashed out, not even fully fallen into its lowest register. The Muse spat on the floor. "Did you buy this one from a slaver?"

He suspected what would be demanded of the boy when the meal was completed, or else the man wouldn't have been holding the child. It disgusted him.

The priest spat back, this time with words, "I bought *you* from a slaver, and I *own* you. Get back here, boy!"

"Ha!" The Muse wasn't past perverse humor, and he had a word or two to say. Drawing himself up, he spoke as regally as he could in his cracking, adolescent voice. "I'm a messenger from the most ancient Goddess of Life, the one known as Lamahätsu, the ageless Five-Armed Goddess, the Womb of Creation, the Bringer of Life, and the Eater of Essences." Oh, it felt good to call out the old names. "I've been sent to divine whether you've truly perverted the temple sanctions, taking this boy just into youth for your private slave, and forcing him to sate your unnatural desires. You've been found wanting, and you're cursed. Fire and destruction will rain down upon your city, and the earth will swallow you up. Have fear and call to Lamahätsu. She may hear you, yet." The pale-haired youth who was barely more than a child stormed out of the divination chamber with as much stateliness as his slender limbs could muster.

Once outside, he laughed. Lamahätsu! That was a jest. Lamahätsu hadn't walked the face of the earth since the beginnings of all that had been created, but he predicted the priest would spend some nervous moments over the next few handbreadths of time. All the Muse had predicted would come to pass, and it was because of Lamahätsu and her curse. It just wasn't to punish the old priest. It was to punish Parik.

The Muse stopped hard in his tracks, realizing he had no sense of direction in this underground warren. He had to have help, if it could be found. His plan to fight Parik, to kill him, had been seriously compromised with this latest shift in bodies. The motive was still there, as was the intent. However, in this boy-man's body, he wasn't sure he had the physical strength. As the flimsy robe gaped at the waist, he realized he also didn't have the correct clothes. He had some thinking to do, and he'd better do it quickly. That last shaking had been strong, and soon all the energy that had gathered in the earth and in the sky would create a conflagration that hadn't been seen for at least ninety seasons.

Also, his stomach continued to churn, and the stones weren't even shaking. That also carried import for the Muse. It meant Parik's rebirth was so near as to be now.

"THAT WAY. FOLLOW THOSE four men. They're approaching the temple steps now." Kaius slapped Parik gently on the shoulder, pointing with a finger. "You've certainly pulled strength I didn't expect. I must go for my Rena. She'll think I've left her to end in the last shaking. It was a bad one, and its strength I didn't expect."

Kaius now knew he had no choice but to believe in this man, this healer. He'd known when the shaking would occur, calling out to Kaius and the youths to find a secure spot and prepare. Then, lightning had fallen, green lightning, and green sparks had erupted from everything. If this man wished to be a leader in the temple, Kaius would follow him anywhere, do anything he asked. He was truly a holy man sent by the goddess to protect those in the city.

"A few more steps, my friend, Kaius." Parik leaned on the man's shoulder. "The last shaking took much from me, and I fear I can't walk alone. Perhaps the men ahead will assist me after that."

"That far I can go." One of the men was in a fit upon the ground. Perhaps he also was a holy man. Wouldn't Rena be amazed at that? "Wait here, and I'll go to them." He helped Parik rest on a step, and then he strode on ahead.

FROM HIS POSITION AGAINST Zakkhaios' shoulder, Æolus watched the man he'd called pater-amicus. He remembered none of the events at the great stone footing—after the yelling in exultation, of course—but Zakkhaios had described how the house had fallen into the ground, crushing him. Then, Parik had touched him, and his body had been whole again.

During the last shaking, Æolus had seen the green

fireflies of light. They were strongest at Parik. They had flashed and flared around him, while the rest of the company just saw small flickers from their fingertips. Whatever was happening to the city was happening to his pater-amicus most of all, and it was draining his life from him.

Then, pandemonium erupted as three of the men from up the street came rushing down to greet them.

"Parik! The man Kaius told us of your presence. We've searched the city, and here you are, following us all along. I'm your son's friend, Drakon." A strong man with thick legs grabbed Parik's forearm with both hands. "He tells us you're a healer. Several in the city have said so, also."

"My son?"

Æolus could see the astonishment on his pater-amicus' face. He wished to call to him a greeting of congratulation, but he had no immediate energy to do so. His stomach growled, drawing his attention away, and he doubled over with the pain; he couldn't imagine being so hungry.

Before he could gather his strength, a second man stepped forward to steal Parik's attention.

"XERXES IS WHAT MEN call me. Your son's the one on the ground. He was swimming past the city wall, and we fished him in. His mind was lost, and he didn't know who he was. He's searched for you since returning." Xerxes leaned in. "He's not been himself, though. I didn't much like him today. He's been cruel, and Umaru is never cruel. I think his demon's left him, though."

"Umaru." Parik breathed hard, his face collapsing into disappointment. "He didn't take the woman to her people, then."

Drakon frowned. "Xerxes? Paulus? Did Umar say anything in that manner? About a woman?"

"He did!" Paulus erupted with his usual enthusiasm. "Just now as we were coming down. He said he's failed his father, and he doesn't know how he could be back in the city. He mentioned a woman by the name of Zekiye. Also, I'm Paulus." He grinned as if he expected to be teased at his name. He turned to smile at Drakon. "I'm glad to hear you speak of our friend again as Umar, for his demon has indeed left him."

"You say Umaru just righted his mind with the last shaking?" At the three men's energetic agreement, Parik sighed. "I understand, now. The Muse has been with him. I suspect he wanted to kill me."

"No, pater-amicus." Æolus raised an arm in rebuttal, and he made to stand. He collapsed against a fallen stone and leaned his head to the side. Tears formed in his eyes as he whispered, "No one would want to kill you."

Parik smiled at the youth's reaction and called to him, "Some, perhaps, Æole. My son, at least, no longer. Xerxes, ask him to come to me."

"He doesn't want to join us," Xerxes insisted. "He says if Parik's here, he can't."

"He must come to me. Please, men." He motioned to Drakon. "You spoke first. You called yourself his friend. Please explain that I understand, and he wasn't himself.

There was nothing he could have done, even if he'd known. Please."

At that moment, ChiChi leaped from Dulcia's arms, and the animal was off. She jumped to chase it. "Come back, bad Chi. You mustn't run!" She grabbed the leash just as the unruly fur ball reached Umaru. "I'm sorry, sir. My little pet likes to run from me. Are you really Parik's son?"

"I can no longer claim such an honor. Even my friends now treat me as an enemy."

"Please come to him. He healed my friend. He was dead, and Parik brought him back to life. Æolus is my friend."

Umaru snorted, then he shifted his gaze to Parik, speaking to Dulcia with resignation. "I'll go, girl, to meet your healer of the dead. He must be very powerful, and for that reason, perhaps he isn't my father."

She pulled his arm. "You must know he is. He says you're his son. He said you wanted to kill him."

"No! Of course not. I never did such a thing."

Dulcia smiled. "You must tell him, then, and afterwards, I'll introduce you to Æolus. Parik calls him filius-amicus."

A smile crept across the man's face. "That sounds more like the man I call my father. A youth is filius-amicus to him, a youth he's raised from the dead. Perhaps I'll meet this man."

A voice called out, "Umaru! You were curled up, and I didn't know you."

"Kaius, you old drunkard, you. You filled up on

wine in my tavern last eve. Did Rena kick you out of your room?" There was a new level of enthusiasm in Umaru's voice.

"I didn't think I went home. I woke up this morning in the streets, wandering, and the stones were shaking." His words were first spoken in a downcast voice, then, continuing, he brightened. "Rena insists I did come home, though, and that I showered her with attention." He drooped again. "I just wish I remembered it."

Parik grunted and attempted to stand. Kaius stepped to aid him with an arm, only to have Æolus call out, "Pater-amicus, I'll help you." Yet, when the boy made to stand for a second time, he couldn't.

"Nay, stay, Æole." Parik rebuked him gently. "You've encouraged me, giving me strength in other ways. When we reach the temple, and find food and drink, you'll regain your vibrancy. Now, let me speak to another." He turned to the man who had joined them at the stone footing. "You should have told me, Kaius. You were also taken by another, one known to me as the Muse. She can't stay in a body when the ground shakes. She must move on to another. You, too, Umaru. When you came to, the ground was shaking, yes?"

"You're correct, Father." Umaru stepped to Parik. "But what's happened this day? You were little more than my age this morning, and now you're so old you cannot stand. And the city. A great battle has crashed it to the ground."

"My age catches up with me. I wish I could explain further, but it would make no sense. The city? It's a battle greater than you know. Please, let's go to the temple. I need to rest, and the bloody one there needs sustenance. He's very weak."

Kaius snapped his fingers. "Now, I know. I've looked at Parik, certain I should know him, and now I understand. It's you, Umaru. The two of you are the same."

"That's what you kept telling us all day, Umaru. You and your father are the same, and you were desperate to locate him," Xerxes threw in.

"Revenge," Parik murmured. "The Muse planned to use you to kill me, and all for revenge." He pointed to Æolus. "My young filius-amicus could use your strong shoulder. Please, my son."

When Umaru came to him, Æolus whispered hoarsely, "Did you truly wish to harm Parik?"

Umaru frowned at that. "I wouldn't be someone else's pawn in such a game. This Muse, whoever he may be, will know my rage without question."

Those with them were already moving ahead, and as Umaru helped the youth to his feet, Æolus put his arm around the big man's waist. After a slow start, they were soon on their way to catching up with the others.

THE LAST SHAKING HAD stirred much dust from the temple stones, and even a few smaller ones had fallen from the higher reaches to crash to the floor, shattering noisily. Green had sparked from fingertips and holy drapery fabrics, lighting dim passageways and rooms, and entertaining those inside. The temple held, however, to the repeated praises of the priests, acolytes, and temple serving women.

The old temple serving woman worried, though. Her human charge was quite safe, and with the darkening of the sky, a bowl of oil was burning to light the space. The girl's small companion, however, was another matter. The rat was holy, and it was ensconced in one of the deepest parts of the temple, a section that was so old, none except the old temple serving woman ever visited. She felt it was imperative she pay the furred creature some attention.

Filling a second bowl with oil, she inserted a cloth wick and worked her way deep into the labyrinth that wound far into the flank of the mountain. When she found the sloping corridor that ended in the small side chamber with the roughly matched stone, she watched her flame flicker. It had never done that before, flickered here in this most private of chambers. First, she checked on the rat, finding it contentedly munching on a piece of grain. Its black eyes gleamed in the lamplight when she reached to rub it behind the ears. The old woman smiled, knowing someone had trained this rat to enjoy the touch of human fingers, and she guessed she knew just who. Such behavior fit with what the girl had told her.

Then, puzzled, she paused where the old stones turned rough, unlike the others in the chamber. The closer she got, the more her flame flickered. Surely the foundations of the temple weren't being shaken apart, even this deep in the mountain. She shivered. It was growing cold inside the room, and damp. Before, it had never felt cold and damp. It was no longer pleasant.

She looked at the rat, and she knelt to speak to it. "If you finish your grain, feel free to come to Chiarina. Just don't finish it quickly. There are those who wish you harm." Smiling, and satisfied, she stood, and with her oil lamp in hand, she headed back to the part of the temple she enjoyed least of all.

Something did surprise her as she navigated the temple proper. She passed a pale-haired youth, and he walked along very determinedly in a robe open down the front, one that she recognized as an acolyte's divination robe. He wasn't holding it closed, either, ignoring it as unimportant. As the cloth flapped, he muttered continually to himself.

She wondered about that. The youth seemed very self-assured and exceptionally focused. He also looked just like one of the acolytes who had arrived only the previous day. The old temple serving woman was certain he was the youth the Moica Priest had chosen for his current divinations. It was very odd that the youth had been released, because the priest normally enjoyed probing his divinations until much food had been consumed, in addition to the other more intimate activities expected of the boys. The youths were often sent away exhausted, and sometimes in pain. Why, only two seasons past, the old woman had been there to ready the room when a newly arrived youth with flaming hair had divined with the Moica Priest. She'd also helped repair the injuries he'd received during the final stages of the divination. She was grateful this one seemed to have little trouble in that manner.

She laughed to herself, letting her concerns about the acolyte slip away. It was the girl she was pledged to protect, the girl and her rat. The youths that the priest employed she could pity, but she had no control over them. One day, she hoped, there'd be one that would have the capacity to refuse to act as a slave, disavowing the moral degradations that went with such a station, and then the priest would learn his lesson and learn it well. Maybe the youth she passed was the one.

She pressed her lips together, stifling a smirk. One could only hope.

20

"IT WAS THE BEGINNING of time, and in all the blackness that existed in this darkest of nights, not one thing could be found."

The mostly toothless old woman regaled the spattering of children gathered next to her fire. A storm raged outside, occasionally sending waves of thunder rolling through the night, but the cave's walls kept the rain from wetting the flames. The wind was blocked by great fronds piled high and held by rocks too big for one man to carry.

"Nothing?" The word was barely breathed. One small girl, olive-skinned and wide-eyed, sat mesmerized.

All her life she'd been surrounded by things: fire; small gray stones; dry dirt under her feet. To have truly nothing was beyond comprehension.

With one hand waving at the blackened cave wall around her and swinging up to indicate the ceiling far above, the woman grinned. "The blackness was complete. Then, one stormy night, just like the one outside—"

"But," a disbelieving boy called, "you said there was nothing."

"Hush," another boy admonished. He'd come from a different village, and his old grandmother always started her stories the same way. He'd come to see if the tale played out with the familiar events he knew.

The old woman chuckled, her breath hissing through the gaps in her teeth. "The boy is right. This was a storm in the blackness of nothing."

"Rain isn't nothing." An older girl who had heard this story before tested the old woman's proofs. It was raining outside, and the two went hand in hand.

"Again, my best listeners always ask the best questions to test the truth of the tale. To accept without proof is to learn lies. Always question, children. This storm was a storm of blackness, and the sky flashed green."

"Green?" Lightning wasn't green. One child caught the obvious error and called the old woman on it.

"Very good." She chuckled. "You paid attention." The child was the closest to her, and she reached to pat him on the head. "The green was the beginning of everything, you see, and it sizzled through the clouds."

Several of the smaller children who knew this section of the story made a buzzing sound with their lips as she spoke, for this part of the game all could play.

"And it was like fireflies across the land, for the darkness wasn't truly empty. One thing did exist in all the nothingness. One thing was out there, and it was the Goddess of Life, Lamahätsu. She had five arms, and fire flashed from her eyes when she was angry. This night, she was very angry."

The sound of a child's quiet tears could be heard in the back, and a very small voice whispered, "I'm frightened."

"Shush. It's just a story." That was from the older girl. "The quieter you are, the sooner the story will be finished."

"She was angry because the world hadn't yet been created. Lamahätsu had waited patiently for all the eons of existence, and the blackness had finally begun to consume her essence. This night, she knew she'd have to right this injustice herself, and she knew the price she'd have to pay. It would cost her much." The old woman's tongue clicked against the roof of her mouth, and she rocked. The younger children waited with anticipation for the next events to unfold, their eyes on the old woman. The older children knew the story like the stones lining the riverbank.

"Where were her friends? Couldn't they help?" A small girl's voice, of course.

"Silly," a boy's voice admonished. "She was a goddess. Goddesses don't have friends."

"She was alone in the blackness, you'll remember." The old woman's words were grown thick by this time in the story. Her betyl stick had been chewed for many handbreadths of time to release the soporific toxins inside, and she was feeling the effects. Because of the stick, her story had become real to her. "Lamahätsu was the green fire in the sky, and she reached with her Fifth Arm of Death—" The children shivered, their teeth chattering audibly. "—to snatch the green fire, and she gobbled it up. It burned as it went down her throat, and she screamed in the darkness, shaking the stars into the sky."

"There's no stars outside tonight. The storm has eaten them." It was the frightened child again.

"I told you to shush. It's just a story." The older girl reached for the child's hand.

The old woman moaned for a moment, the betyl toxins burning the back of her eyes. Licking her lips, she waved her hand in the firelight to quiet the voices. She wanted no more questions for a time.

"Time had not yet begun when the Five-Armed Goddess began to eat the green fire. In all the heavens was only the blackness that had always been there and the stars the goddess had shaken into the sky with her pain. Lamahätsu floated among the stars and waxed full. Her belly was swollen with the Fires of Creation, and as the ages passed, she could feel the life within her begin to burn."

"Burn?" A quick hand was clamped over the questioner's mouth to still the interruption. No questions were permitted in this part of the story.

"Lamahätsu burned in her womb, and her breasts were swollen with the waters of life. Her screams of pain shattered those stars that had come to see, and her Two Arms of Life fought with her Two Arms of Healing over her swollen belly. Her Two Arms of Healing wanted to return the green fire to the blackness of the heavens, and her Two Arms of Life wanted to birth that which was inside.

"For the lifetimes of many grandmothers, Lamahätsu struggled with this conflict. She railed at her arms, and she railed at her womb. She railed at the stars, and she cried the tears of anguish that still blanket our world when the gentle rains fall. She knew that to birth this that had grown in her would bring the greatest pain she'd ever known.

"It was the Fifth Arm of Death that decided for her. While Lamahätsu was sleeping, the Fifth Arm of Death grabbed a lightning bolt from the sky and flung it between Lamahätsu's legs, breaking open her womb, and igniting that which burned with life."

Each child in the room moaned with the imagined pain, even the girl who had heard the story many times.

"The terrible pain woke the Five-Armed Goddess, and she screamed with all her might. Her fury at what the Fifth Arm of Death had done created the thunder that now rages during the worst of our storms." To add to the drama, the cave's frond-covered opening brightened, and a great crash of thunder drove far into the cave, causing the children to jump. The old woman didn't react, though. The betyl toxins were far along in her system, and she now communed with the goddess herself, gathering the true events of the story directly from the goddess' mouth.

"As the great Essence Eater vented her fury at the Fifth Arm of Death, the pressure of her scream broke her womb's hold on that which was between her legs, and with a second scream, this time of pain, the fires that created our world poured from between her legs."

A small set of hands began to clap, and they were quickly silenced. "It isn't over, yet," a voice whispered to the overly enthusiastic applause.

"Lamahätsu was exhausted, but her work wasn't done. Her birthing wasn't yet complete. With her Two Arms of Healing, she held the flaming place between her legs, willing the pain to end. In her Two Arms of Life, she gathered up the Fires of Creation and formed them into our world. It was still red-hot, and she had to breathe on it for many generations to get it to cool.

"Finally, growing weary, she grasped her swollen breasts and squeezed them with all her might, flooding the surface of the world until it began to grow firm. As the waters from Lamahätsu's breasts boiled for longer than long, the clouds were created, and that's why great storms thunder across the land today. The coals from the beginnings of time even now boil the water from Lamahätsu's breasts, making the clouds above, and when it cools, it fights to get back to the earth where it belongs, giving us the storms that flood the land."

The old woman sat still for a time, and the only sounds that could be heard were the distant rumblings of the storm and a small rivulet of water that had begun to run down the cave wall near where she sat. The storm was waning, and the children would soon be set free. However, the story had one last chapter to tell.

"The great Lamahätsu had created the world." The old woman's voice was a mere whisper now. This part of the story was intimately hers, and she knew it was real. She was in this part of the tale, although she'd never told any of the children just which part she played. "Lamahätsu was still lonely, even though people ran to and fro. Many of them worshipped her, those that remembered her existence. Others had forgotten, and Lamahätsu knew others would also forget until she was no more. For this reason, Lamahätsu created a son."

"Like me?" A small boy's voice piped his excitement.

"Shush," was the answer to his question.

The old woman continued, "He was a man, tall, with the green eyes of the sky's fire, and hair of darkest night. His skin was the olive on the tree, and he was loved by all women." She knew. She'd loved him once, still did, in fact, and had never taken a man. The child she'd birthed had had no father, and she'd killed it as it was born, wrapping its cord around its neck before it could breathe its first breath. All the other young women—and girls, too—who had been at the son's celebration had, without exception, also birthed children that very same night. Some had done as she had, wrapping the cords, and others had kept their babies hidden away so the village men wouldn't dash their heads upon the stones. The children were abominations, cursed demon children from the pits of the earth, and none could be allowed to pollute the village's purity.

The old woman knew, though. She knew exactly which of these children were from the demon bloodlines. She'd killed the child that had grown inside of her, and she'd watched those who had hidden theirs away. She knew each one, and she watched the children of the children to keep her people safe.

The old woman had known Lamahätsu was a goddess from the moment she heard her speak. When she opened her mouth, the leaves spoke for her, or the winds whispered her words. The old woman had wanted Parikshit that night, and he would have been hers. However, when his mother, old Lamahätsu, had touched her side, she'd known what the goddess had done. By the time the child was born, Parikshit was gone, and she never saw him again. However, she never stopped loving him. Never.

By this time the storm had passed, and the children saw the old woman had fallen asleep. Released from this enforced story time, they sprang to their feet, and in a rush of dusty footsteps, they burst into the night, stomping and splashing the puddles of water left by the rain.

The girl who had shushed the small child watched her run into the night. Her hand was still damp with the child's fear, and she wiped it absently on her clothing, shivering in the aftermath of the storm.

21

THE MUSE STAGGERED AGAINST the wall, and as he sank to the floor, the side of the acolyte's tunic he wore caught on the rough stone, pulling it away from his body. He cried out in his high-pitched youth's voice as his stomach roiled inside.

"No! I must not shift again!"

He knew, however, he might have no choice. The intensity of the churning once again told him the final events of Parik's rebirth were at hand. The next shaking the city would have to endure would surely be the last, and then all the forces that had gathered would be unleashed. It might take the Muse many seasons to find

Parik, if he were shifted to a far land. Revenge was needed now, and Parik had to know the Muse's fury.

The old temple serving woman turned at the voice to find the pale-haired youth shrunken against the wall. She knelt to give him assistance. She tugged at his opened tunic, hiding his exposed loins.

"Cover yourself, boy. We're in the temple, and your nakedness is unseemly. With this robe you wear, I can see you've been with the Moica Priest, and you've surely slaved hard." She tugged the tunic to, muttering, "And I'm equally sure you've been forced to endure the priest's moral turpitude."

The Muse looked at her and forced a laugh, quickly letting it sink to a grimace. "What that priest was doing to this youth was unseemly, but this body is as of yet undefiled. My troubles are of a different sort. Help me up, woman." His stomach still churned, but he'd not been thrown into another body. Also, he noted, the stones around him hadn't shaken. He knew then that the power in the green flashes of light would no longer leave him in peace, even between Parik's attacks. He'd lived it many times. It was another sign the end was very near. He must move quickly to make Parik pay.

The old woman pulled her hand away and rocked back on her feet. "You're a youth, and yet you speak with authority. You don't carry the look of the usual acolytes, either, with your pale hair and light skin." She stood and reached a hand to him, holding him steady as he rose to his feet.

"I'm looking for one named Parik." He held one arm

against his stomach as if in serious pain, and still he looked at her expectantly. "Is he here?"

"Have you been sent by the goddess?" The old temple serving woman gathered the neck of her tunic as she formed her next words. "I've a child, one who needs healed of a crippled leg."

The Muse sighed. "Then I know he isn't here. He'd have healed the child, already. I've come to the wrong place, all because of a rat." He chuckled, then began to laugh.

"You find something amusing?" The old woman glanced around, only to discover there was nothing and no one else around.

"Yes." The Muse held his side, finally coughing in exhaustion. "This child's continually cracking voice in this barely grown body. How do these unformed males tolerate the indignity?"

"It is as it always has been," the old serving woman intoned.

"I don't suppose a gray rat has come to see you. That's why I'm here, and if not, it's been a useless chasing I've done today. Now, look at what I've become, a mere youth who is more boy than man standing here with my loins exposed to an old woman."

The temple serving woman fell to her knees. "I now see you as you must be. You're a god, sent to help us in our time of need. You speak as a man, yet your voice is that of a child. You know of the rat. Will you heal the crippled girl?" She dropped her face to the floor in supplication.

"The rat?" The Muse reached to pull her head up. "A rat has come? When? Where is it?"

She dropped her head again. "Please, Holy One."

The Muse smiled at the woman's words. He did, indeed, miss the old names.

"You must first go with me to see the girl. She's had a very hard life. She's crippled beyond walking, and it causes her great pain. Also, her brother died just this day."

The Muse sighed with resignation. He was in a youth's body, and his beard wasn't yet sprouted. However, he did like the term "Holy One." He would humor this woman.

"Many have died from the falling stones, old woman. Why should this girl's brother be different than all the rest?"

"O Holy One, he was dead before the stones fell. It was from starvation, Holy One, a slow and lingering death." She touched his bare feet. "Your feet are those of a rich man's son, one who wears sandals all the time, and your nails are neatly trimmed. Only a god who has just come from the sky—or from underground, if you wish—would have feet so perfectly formed." She leaned forward and kissed them.

The Muse laughed. This was too much and very appreciated. For someone to kiss his feet, he'd grant her any request. It was the best thing that had happened to him in centuries, and it was certainly the best thing he could count on ever happening to him in this body, what with immature loins and limbs that surely could best no one in a fair fight.

"Rise, good woman," he entreated in his cracking, most god-like child's voice. "Take me to this girl." It occurred to the Muse that if Parik had sent the rat here, as the story of the old woman in the street had earlier suggested, then he might also travel to the temple himself. To find Parik, it seemed that at the side of a crippled girl was possibly the best place a boy-god could be at this time, even if the boy-god's only real power was to be able to shift his presence to another person's body when the need arose.

Yet, he knew even that minor power wasn't available to him for a time, what with Parik's energies drawing together underneath the city. The processes gathering for Parik's new life were far more powerful than the Muse's meager shifting ability, and when Parik was reborn, the gathered energies could easily vault the Muse much farther than across the city—unlike the Muse's pathetic skills that only allowed shifting to someone close at hand.

He'd become a poor god, indeed.

With condescension, he helped the woman up, and patting the hand she offered him, he motioned for her to lead him to the girl. Her lined face smiled at him ghoulishly before turning once again to stride ahead.

"IN WHAT WAY CAN I help you?" The presence of a flame-haired acolyte in a simple tunic drew the attention of the supplicants who had gathered at the temple steps. Freckles blazed across his face.

"Food, please, and protection." Drakon knelt in front of the red-haired temple youth. "We three wish to return to help others in the city," he motioned to Xerxes and Paulus, "but there are two of us who need a place to rest." Zakkhaios had his arm around the bloody Æolus, and Umaru now supported Parik. "The other two must also stay to lend their shoulders for strength."

"Grain we have, and bread we can provide. Drink is in short supply. The reservoir has emptied, and no water flows in the pipes." The acolyte's head bobbed. By his voice and height, he was older than either Zakkhaios or Æolus, but he was still an unshaven youth. "Not many have come to the temple, but you're welcome to join those who have."

"Water, please," Zakkhaios pleaded. "For my friend, to wash the blood."

"He's injured badly?" The acolyte stepped to him, a slight limp in his carriage, looking for damage. His own arms were covered to the wrists, with only his neck and face showing.

"No longer." Zakkhaios paused, glancing for a moment at Parik. "Just hunger and thirst. He's well, but he needs to be cleansed. Something to drink, also, and soon."

Peering into the dimness of the temple and then back at the group of refugees, the acolyte spoke quietly, "I recently carried a large container of water to the Moica Priest's chamber, one intended for washing of an acolyte new to the temple. I've not removed it, and it's possible the youth can cleanse the blood there." Motioning to

Zakkhaios, he whispered, "This way. Your friend must come quickly."

"He's weak. He can't move on his own." Dulcia knelt in a quick curtsey. "Please, sir."

The acolyte stepped up and put his shoulder under Æolus' free arm. "I'll help you, but no one must know. We go to the priest's chamber, but he, um, your time spent at the temple will be more pleasant if he doesn't see us there."

The acolyte had spent time in the divination chambers. The man was a beast, one who took boys for the purpose of slavery, often dragging them into base deeds that could never be undone. It had been the cause of the acolyte's own troubles two seasons ago when he'd served in the divination chambers. After the Moica Priest's night of gluttony, the red-headed acolyte had refused to assist the man in further endeavors, and he'd been punished. This bloody youth clearly had need to be stripped and cleansed, but it must be done without the priest's awareness.

Moving up the steps towards the priest's private chamber, the acolyte motioned for Zakkhaios and Æolus to wait. "I'll see if we're free to proceed. Also, I'm called Rufus, as you can see by my red hair." He nodded quickly and made to walk off when Æolus weakly grabbed his tunic.

"Æolus," he tapped his chest, "and this is Zakkhaios." He sank back against the wall, closing his eyes as he did so. "I'm sorry. Even speaking exhausts me."

Rufus clasped his bloody shoulder. "Æolus and

Zakkhaios, I won't forget." He grinned. "I'm good with names. I'll see you get care." He slipped away silently, returning after only a few moments, whispering, "The way is clear." He put a hard roll in each of the youth's hands. "For nourishment. Let us move now, for we must progress rapidly. I've put a fresh loincloth out, and there's a cloth for the washing." He looked at them intently. "Please be quick. I'll guard the door and discourage entry. Are you prepared to move?" At their nods, he wrapped Æolus' arm over his shoulder, and they traveled the rest of the way with as much speed as they could muster.

Once inside, Rufus helped Æolus sit and stepped quickly to show them the container of water on the floor. "Here. Stand and wash. A mug and more water are on the table. Use it for drinking, only. The water no longer flows from the spigots, and we must conserve." He smiled and shrugged in apology. "I'll be outside. Finish and dress with haste, please. For your protection, the Moica Priest must not see a youth in his chambers. We wouldn't want to arouse his, um, interest."

He stepped away and through the door. When he pulled the door drapery behind him, it crackled with small green fireflies.

"THE SPARKS, EVEN HERE." Zakkhaios commented on the light as he handed his friend the cup of water.

"Green sparks," Æolus whispered. "I saw them outside."

"Don't talk, not now, Æole. Drink, first. Parik said

you must." Zakkhaios pressed the cup to his friend's mouth. He smiled with relief to see Æolus greedily consume it. "More?"

Æolus shook his head and pointed to the container on the floor. "I do feel better, but I would be clean. Help me stand."

The water looked used, but it was better than being bloody. Æolus held his hand out, and Zakkhaios helped him up. Brushing his friend's skin with his hand, dried, encrusted blood flaked to the floor.

"Crusties, Æole. You have crusties." Zakkhaios snickered with a grin. "However, we must be quick. Our new friend Rufus has said so." He reached for the washing cloth. When he lifted it, green sparks flew. "More sparks, Æole!"

As Æolus released his bloodied loincloth and stepped out of it, the youths heard a commotion at the doorway. Rufus' voice came loudly through the draperies.

"The Moica Priest won't deign to be disturbed. Go away, I said." Then more loudly, "Priest, I'm very sorry. Your privacy is now assured."

Æolus grinned at his friend. As he reached for his roll and stepped into the container, he tore off a big bite. Between chews, he whispered to Zakkhaios, "I'm certainly glad to have Rufus outside the door. I wouldn't want for a strange person to walk in at this moment."

"I feel the same, Æole." Zakkhaios wasn't so pleased, though, and all discussion of the unusual green sparks was forgotten. He was scrubbing the blood from

Æolus' body, and the water had turned very red, indeed. His stomach didn't like that at all.

WHEN HE SAW KAIUS walk in with a very pretty woman under his arm, Parik waved weakly to get his attention. He tapped Dulcia's leg and pointed. Once ChiChi saw Kaius, the animal leaped from the girl's lap, barking, and ran toward him.

"Small dogs should have small voices," Umaru groaned.

"Just go retrieve it." Parik reached to a small mug of wine his son had procured, satisfied to see him step toward the dog. He sipped it, knowing he'd get only small improvement from the refreshment. His weakness was as much from the last shaking as it was from the healing of his filius-amicus. With more churning now in his stomach, it would be only a short time before the next assault on the beleaguered city. It would be the last. He could feel it. Then, everyone would die, and he'd be young again. It was a youth he didn't relish, not at the cost of those who had become his friends. Now he wished Æolus and Zakkhaios would return. He worried about them.

"This is Rena." Kaius beamed, stepping forward to greet his new friends. He named those he'd helped while away from his woman, motioning to each one. "Parik, Umaru, and this is little ChiChi." He squatted to pet the dog where it stood on the stones at his feet. "ChiChi belongs to Dulcia." He put the ball of fur into her lap, handing her the loop of Parik's makeshift leash. "Hold it well. Some are hungry in this room." He laughed when she grabbed the animal firmly, frowning at him in dismay.

"Don't tease, Kaius." Rena took his arm as he stood. "Where are the rest? I want to see the youth that was nearly dead."

Parik glanced up, not entirely pleased. "You shared with her?" He sighed. He preferred his deed not be told. If the Muse were in male flesh and readying for a kill, Parik didn't need his presence announced. With the gathering power, Parik remained hidden from the Muse. It had always been so in the past. He didn't wish to help the Muse by advertising his location.

Then, a disturbance was seen across the space, taking away the opportunity for a reprimand. Parik motioned with a weakened arm.

"There they come, and a new youth is with them, the temple acolyte from our arrival."

The red-headed acolyte with the two youths stepped up to Parik. "You're the healer?"

Parik sighed again and closed his eyes. It seemed the two youthful friends had also been sharing. Time was short, however, and it surely couldn't matter strongly at this point.

"Yes." He looked up. "My filius-amicus is clean. Thank you." He smiled in gratitude.

"And fed and watered, pater-amicus." Æolus grinned.

With the healing, Parik knew the boy's body was in finer condition than it had ever been in his entire life.

Even old wounds and bloodline flaws were now wiped away.

"And very much a man," Zakkhaios hissed, poking him in the side. "I've seen so, and too closely for my liking."

Æolus' face reddened, and he looked around. "There were three others with us. I remember them from just outside the temple. Where did they go?"

"Back to the city," Dulcia piped in. "Others needed their help."

That was when Æolus really took in Umaru's visage. "You," he pointed, then looked at Parik. He laughed. "You're the same. How are you related? You must be, you see. You're exactly the same."

Dulcia piped in again, "Parik is his father. Umaru's now helping us."

"I don't see how." Umaru dropped his head. "I've failed in all I've promised, even to betraying my friends."

Æolus knelt beside him. "You should be pleased. Your father has protected us. My friend, Zakkhaios, tells me I was very near killed, and Parik brought me back. I'm well, you see." He held up an arm that had been en-crusted with blood and ran his hand under his armpit and down his side. "No wounds can be seen." His eyes caught Parik's then looked back to Umaru. Placing his hand on the man's leg for reassurance, he said to him very seriously, "Parik is my pater-amicus, and I trust him. If you're his son, I trust you as well."

The acolyte reached and clapped Æolus on the

shoulder, interrupting them. "I've someone for you and your healer to meet, Æolus." He pulled the youth up and spoke to the adults. "I would borrow this one to go and retrieve her. She's watching over someone in another chamber."

"This is Rufus." Æolus flashed a smile to those who had arrived at the temple with him. "He's an acolyte."

"They can tell." Rufus looked down and pulled at his clothing. He leaned in and whispered to Æolus, "My tunic names me as such." He turned to Parik. "May I bring this person to you? She's caring for a cripple she believes will be healed. There was an argument over a rat, one that stays with the girl, and it isn't resolved, so the woman watches over the cripple herself. If you're a healer, she'll want to meet you."

Parik felt his spirits lift. "A rat and a crippled girl?" Perhaps she was the girl he'd hoped to help earlier. In all the destruction that was coming, he wished to do this good deed more than any other. "I would go to them, instead. Help me up, please." He put out his hand, and Rufus reached for it.

"It's some distance away, but I'll be glad to take you." The acolyte turned to lead the way.

"I'm going, too." Dulcia jumped up, "I have Chi-Chi's leash. He won't get away this time."

Umaru stood. "I think we should all go. We've faced much today, and I, for one, wouldn't that any of you get out of my sight. Kaius?" He motioned. "Your Rena, too. This way, Rena, and you may speak with the newly-alive youth and see if my father did a good job." He chuckled, leaning toward her, speaking sotto voce. "I can see in just these few moments why my father has become attached enough to this boy to name him filius-amicus." He winked at the youth.

"Let's go, then. It's in the temple serving women's quarters, but there will be no men there today. It isn't yet dark, and with the damage in the city, perhaps not even tonight will the men come." Rufus motioned with an arm, showing them the way.

22

THE MOICA PRIEST STUMBLED into the small antechamber where his red and gold tunic lay, gasping with pain, and he cursed the pale-haired youth. He did so in his head, though, unsure whether there could be any truth to the boy's words. Out loud, all he gave was a tight-lipped snort of frustration.

Could it be possible the child was indeed a messenger from the goddess? He'd been very helpful with the meal, although frightened at first, and that had made the priest work him more. Then, the youth had become someone else entirely, taking on the aura of one used to deference and authority, and shocking the priest into insensibility. His beauty, the perfection of his skin, and his pale hair certainly gave credence to his claims that he was a messenger from the goddess, one come to the priest in mortal form. No acolyte during the priest's time in the temple had carried such looks.

If the youth's words hadn't rung so clearly, matching with the events taking this city by the very throat, the priest would have leaped to him, grabbing his wrist, and would have beaten him into submission. However, if he was truly a messenger from the goddess, that perhaps wouldn't have been the wisest of courses. The priest was immensely glad he'd taken no further liberties with the child. He shuddered to think about the justice that might be meted out for such actions against a messenger of the goddess.

Pulling his tunic over his head, he felt searing pain return, and he cried out with agony, doubling over and unable to move. The youth had hit him hard, but goddess, the continuing pain was torture. He was certain it must be a snapped rib. Was the youth a trained expert at inflicting injuries with nothing more than his bare elbow?

His patience exhausted, the Moica Priest began to rage. Messenger of the goddess or not, for this pain, the youth would be beaten, his skin lashed until it bled streaks of scarlet. When the youth's pale hair was red with his own blood, then the priest would ask him if he had any additional words from the Goddess of Life.

Underneath his fury, though, the priest remembered two of the names the youth had used for the Goddess of

Life. One had been the ageless Five-Armed Goddess, and the other had been the Essence Eater. He'd not heard those names in fifty seasons, and he wondered just how the youth had come upon them.

Even so, for the pain in his side, the youth would suffer, and it would bring great pleasure to the priest, great pleasure, indeed.

SMOKE FROM BURNING OIL wafted toward the Muse, and he felt remnants of the old days when he was truly worshipped as a deity. When the smoke hit him in the face, he coughed, reminded that this smoke came from an earthen bowl lined with a cloth wick, meant to do no more than light the depths of the cavernous temple.

"Sweet child, I've brought someone to see you." The old temple serving woman stroked the brow of the crippled girl called Chiarina.

"Does Thaddiaos walk again?" Chiarina opened her eyes, letting them rest on the old woman. They opened wider at seeing the youth. "Are you from the goddess?"

"Thaddiaos?" The youth questioned the old woman. Each time after shifting to an unexpected host, he was forced to struggle with finding his place in the surrounding environment. He was used to that, but he also knew he had little time. Still. This Thaddiaos. Was he important? "Who is this Thaddiaos?"

The crippled girl shifted position, and as the Muse watched, sparks rippled along the edges of her clothing. His stomach also still ached from its earlier attack, and its intensity reminded him the upcoming rebirth was very near.

This Thaddiaos, though. Had Parik performed this healing, for the boy to walk? His importance would come only by questioning. It seemed stupid that the people didn't notice one thing that should be a signal to even mere mortals. The great energies from the beginnings of time were gathering in this place, and the flashes of green lightning, along with the sparks that flickered each time two objects grew close, these were the fireflies of death to these people, the harbingers of the end.

Even so, the Muse also accepted that the humans hadn't been there at the beginnings of all that was created, and they hadn't reached out into the darkness and eaten the fire in preparation for birthing the world into existence. If they had, they would run from such signs, run to the hills for protection from the upcoming conflagration that would soon truly leave this city in ruins.

The old temple serving woman placed her hands on the Muse's feet, answering his question. "Most Holy One, the crippled girl had a small brother, and he now sleeps the permanent sleep. He's the one I told you of earlier. Please, just touch her skin, and she'll be healed." The woman leaned forward and kissed each of the youth's toes. With each kiss, she whispered her innermost thoughts, speaking them aloud in a repeated phrase. "Blessed is the goddess," she intoned in her inimitable fashion.

The Muse laughed in his youth's adolescent voice. "If I only had Lamahätsu's powers at my command!"

Kneeling, he spoke kindly to the old woman, his essence stirred by the memory of enjoying such worship in the distant past. He also thought of a way to have this woman search for Parik. "I'm a herald, only, good woman, sent to direct the healer. One named Parik must be found. I'll wait with the girl, giving her comfort, and when you bring the one named Parik to me, his touch will make her whole."

That was the truth, too. Parik's touch would make the girl whole. Of course, she'd almost immediately die when the energies that had assembled under the earth burst forth to greet those gathering in the sky.

The old temple serving woman raised her head, her eyes filled with tears of gratitude. "Afterwards, I'll take you to see the holy rat that's become the girl's companion." She grinned ghoulishly with a secret shared. "I've hidden it away."

"Good sir?" Chiarina called to the pale youth. Carefully, she sat up on her elbows, and she reached a hand to him. "Am I truly to be healed?"

The youth that was the Muse moved to her and smiled. He spoke words of blessing, although they were designed for the old woman's benefit.

"Child, you've suffered enough, and the goddess has chosen to smile on you. There's a healer in the temple," he hoped so, anyway, "and he must be brought to you. I'm here to ease your time until he arrives."

"What may I call you?" Tears began to flow down Chiarina's face.

"I'm known as Muse, and I'll be here until I'm

called to move on." That was the truth, also, as far as it went. "Please lay your head and rest."

The Muse realized he knew this girl. This was the cripple Parik had spoken with from time to time. Her hovel had been just up the way from their quarters in the city. With that realization, he had no doubt Parik would indeed be here.

Painting a smile on his face, he looked to the old woman, and he spoke in the most urgent voice this youth's body could muster. "Go. You must bring me Parik. He must know there's a cripple to heal."

Watching the old woman leave, the Muse turned and smiled at the crippled girl. Her presence would soon be unimportant to his end purpose. He'd allow Parik this healing. Then he'd burst upon him and take his life. He'd do that, even though this tunic he wore gapped, he wore no loincloth, and his voice was that of a child not yet changed into a man. These things weren't the Muse; they were inconsequential. What mattered was death, Parik's death. In the old times, the Muse hadn't been called the Giver of Death for no reason.

He chuckled, and it wasn't a pretty sound.

THE GREAT CITY HAD been shaken to its very core.

Now, green fire lanced at the foundations of the wounded behemoth, sending great waves of green fire-flies to spark across those buildings still standing. Manganese had flowed to where it was needed, and calcium was there in abundance. So were gold and phosphorus and copper. Small amounts of tin and nickel and silicon were laced in with the others. The assemblage burned green with the fire of life, the same fire the great goddess Lamahätsu had eaten at the beginnings of time in order to form the world in her womb.

The Fires of Creation were all that was lacking. When the magma surging along the mighty fissures beneath the city reached the surface, the final elements of creation would be in place. Green fire would meet green fire as that in the heavens welcomed that in the earth. All in between would be swept away, and only Parik would remain.

The time had come, and Lamahätsu's curse would soon wreak havoc upon the innocent once again.

PARIK WALKED BETWEEN HIS son and Æolus, each giving him strength in his own way. He was grateful, too, for without their help, he was certain he couldn't have made it so far. The temple interior tunneled far deeper into the mountain than he'd imagined.

Rufus paused when he came upon the old temple serving woman in her white and red tunic walking in the distance. He turned to his troupe of followers. "It's she, the one I lead you to. She moves urgently and so must be on a mission of some importance. Even so, the healer stands at my side, and she must be informed." He raised a hand to let her know he wished to speak, and she slowed at his movement.

"Yes, acolyte. You're Rufus, I believe. Is there urgency that I must be made aware of? I look for a man, one who is unknown to me, and I must search quickly."

"Just a moment of your time, please. We came looking for you, and you've found us."

He turned with a motion of his hand and indicated all those with him, pointing at one after another as he mentioned their names.

"Kaius and his woman, Rena. Dulcia with ChiChi." The dog barked repeatedly with the mention of its name, and the girl immediately pulled the animal to her face to quiet the sounds. Rufus grinned and went on. "This is Zakkhaios and Æolus, who was healed."

The old temple serving woman's eyes widened, and her urgency to get by these people seemed less.

"I was just here earlier today with Dulcia," Æolus interrupted. "I'm sure you must remember me."

"Friend of one called Loukas." The old woman drew in a sharp breath. She reached to touch his arm, lifting it to peer at both sides. "You've been healed?"

"Parik did it," Zakkhaios burst in, breathless. "Æole was killed."

"Almost," a deeper voice rumbled, one crinkled with age.

"You look perfect." She stroked his arm and then ran her hand down his chest, stopping at his navel. "Better than perfect. Was the injury inside?"

"He was crushed by stones. His head was smashed, and all over there was blood. Everywhere." Zakkhaios leaned in to whisper to his friend, "I'm sorry, Æole, to embarrass you." He turned back to the old woman. "You should have seen it, though." He nudged his friend's arm and grinned.

"He had to be cleansed of blood that covered his body." Rufus ducked his head in respect. "However, you were headed on an errand of importance. We will no longer detain you."

"The boy spoke of Parik." The old woman looked hard at the acolyte. "He did this healing?"

Rufus ducked his head once again. "I'm remiss. There are two more with me, Parik and his son Umaru." He motioned with his hand as he called each name, only to see the old woman sink to her knees as she turned to the elder man.

"Your messenger foretold your coming. You must return with me. A crippled child needs to be healed." She reached to touch his feet as she had with the pale-haired boy.

"Messenger?" Umaru turned to his father. "You have messengers now?"

"It would seem so." Parik smiled tiredly. "Up, woman. Take me to this child. I may be able to do nothing about what's happening to your city, but I can speak with the girl."

"You'll heal her?" The old temple serving woman's eyes were red with the emotion of the moment.

"I'll see her. I can make no promises other than that."

He sighed. He'd heal her—if she wanted. Perhaps she could have a few moments of wholeness before her world came crashing down. That wouldn't be long, he knew. There were green fireflies everywhere, and his stomach had once again started to churn.

Parik walked as quickly as he could, albeit that meant very slowly, as the old woman led the group deep into the temple complex. His slow steps were an extension of what he felt inside his heart. The time was short, and the coming of the devastation couldn't be far away. Those around him had little time to live, and then they would all die. For that, he had only himself and Lamahätsu to blame.

23

THE MUSE LOOKED UP to see the old woman returning, and he was surprised. She had quite a retinue with
her, four youths and as many adults. Then, with excitement flooding his limbs, the Muse saw Parik. He was
taken aback, though. The man was still filled with youth.
The Muse had enjoyed this man's attentions just the previous evening, running the female's fingers through his
hair, and afterwards resting by his side. He knew his
look, and as well, he knew that the shakings that had
torn the city should have attached their power to his essence, draining his youth from him in preparation for his
rebirth.

Then the Muse's eyes caught the old man next to the one he'd thought to be Parik. They were the same. So, he chuckled, the man the Muse had been much of the day had found the old man. The younger Parik was in reality Umaru, the one the Muse had embraced three times while outside of the city, implanting the man's seed inside the woman's womb next to the betrayal Parik had thought to be unknown.

With satisfaction, the Muse considered that Parik had never seen him in this body he currently wore, and with the energies of the man's renewal pulling at the very air around them, he wouldn't be able to recognize him, wouldn't be able to read the signals that always drew them together, just as the Muse couldn't now read the fingernail Parik wore.

With that realization, the Muse knew how to bait Parik, in order to torment him, although he'd probably not be able to kill him. He was no more than an unformed youth in this body, and Parik had brought a band of reinforcements that would surely overpower the Muse's youthful host if an attack occurred. Oh, for the remembered power of Lamahätsu, when his simplest thoughts were the storms that rolled across the heavens, and lightning flew from his eyes! If that power were his again, he'd fling fire with his Fifth Arm of Death, and all those in this chamber would expire in an excruciating demise worthy of the old goddess.

The pale-haired youth with skin the color of clear sand sat at the crippled girl's side and smiled. His countenance reflected a practiced appearance of welcoming adoration. Despite his expression, the youth who was now the Muse felt no romantic interest in Parik. As a male, he was always driven to kill Parik over and over. That's why his blood boiled especially hot as he watched the man approach.

His voice, however, was filled with charm.

"Welcome." He stood, aware that his acolyte's tunic was unbelted and uncaring whether they saw he was yet to be a complete man. It would mislead Parik, and that would serve the Muse's purpose well. "Old woman, have you found the healer?" He didn't need her answer. She had. The Muse knew that as well as he knew the old names she'd called him. After all, Parik stood at her side.

She rushed forward and threw herself to the youth's feet. "Holy One, I've brought you the one you seek. He who has the healing touch is the aged personage stand-ing before you. The boy in the loincloth was very near death just today, and the healer brought him back." No-ticing a movement at the crippled girl's side, she point-ed. "The rat I told you about. It's come to greet you."

The rat, however, no longer interested the Muse. He had what he needed: Parik.

The youth who was the Muse stood tall, opening his arms in a gesture of welcome, this time ensuring they saw his body was little more than that of a boy. They had nothing to fear from him, a boy-youth with no weapons or reason to harm anyone. He was simply here to guide the healer to this crippled girl. They wouldn't realize his plan was to kill the healer until too late. At least that had been the plan. It still would be, if the opportunity presented itself. Now, though, the Muse knew he'd have to tread this ground carefully. Parik must not know who he was until the very end.

"Healer, how are you called?" The Muse smiled his most beatific expression. It was one learned from eons ago and very useful when convincing mortals to bend to the will of a goddess.

"Parik is how I'm known, youth." The timbre of Parik's voice told of his tiredness as he turned to his son. "Umaru, please lend me your arm. I must draw near the crippled child."

"Of course, Father." Umaru took his arm and helped him forward.

As Parik knelt at the child's side, he reached and touched her face. He turned to Æolus. "Æole, filius-amicus, where did you and Dulcia find this girl?"

The youth who hosted the Muse felt his jaw tense with understanding. This youth, the one Parik had healed, was his filius-amicus. How Parik would suffer if the youth suffered, too! The situation only grew sweeter.

"In the side street, pater-amicus."

The Muse's eyes narrowed at the returned term of affection. The boy treasured Parik, even as Parik offered him affection. Never had Parik used those terms with him, never in all the lifetimes they had shared as the most intimate of companions.

Æolus continued, "It was four steps from the flat street where the carts roll."

Parik returned his gaze to the girl and whispered,

"Your name, child."

Her eyes looked at him, unknowing who he was for a time. Then her mouth widened in a smile. "Chiarina, good sir." She lifted her hand and placed it on his.

"Your brother, Chiarina. He lives?"

"Can you heal him?" Her eyes flooded with tears.

"He's here in the temple?" Parik looked up, his eyes finding the old temple serving woman. She shook her head, indicating he lived no more. He brushed Chiarina's face, pressing his fingers to her neck.

"I can't. I see you're full of sorrow for him. Do you wish to know healing for your sorrow?"

Her voice surged with heartbreak. "Thaddiaos! I miss him so!"

Parik pressed her, "Do you wish this healing?"

Her tear-filled eyes found his, and she nodded her head. Immediately, a smile crept across her face. Parik's nail began to glow as healing was drawn into the girl's body.

"Look at that!" Umaru's voice was incredulous. "Her leg is changing." It was, too, lengthening and becoming straight in the manner of a normal limb. He turned to Kaius who only smiled in satisfaction, having seen this already.

The old temple serving woman fell to the Muse's feet, kissing them repeatedly, and the pale youth smiled. This kissing of his feet he enjoyed immensely, even if it wouldn't keep him from lashing out at Parik once this was done.

Rena and Dulcia cried tears of joy as the leg continued to grow and straighten, while the two youths who had traveled the day together just grinned.

Æolus whispered to Zakkhaios, "Of course Parik can do this. He's the one who's come to save our city."

IT WAS THE RED-HAIRED acolyte who had the most remarkable response. He still carried the scars from his divinations with the Moica Priest. The time the priest had taken him to the divination chambers, the red-haired acolyte had fought his attempts to force him into an unspeakably perverse form of slavery. He'd injured the priest in the process, and his punishment had been meted out swiftly with pots of boiling foods poured over his arms and legs. Then the priest had wielded a blade and taken from him his manhood. The red-haired youth was now scarred and partially crippled.

The acolyte dropped to his knees, tears flooding his face, and he laid his hand over the one on Chiarina's neck. "I wish to be healed, also."

Parik cried out in agony, and Æolus fell forward to grasp his pater-amicus by the shoulders, holding him erect. "I'm here for you, pater-amicus. The shaking of the city took my mother, and you're all I have. I'll give you my strength for your own."

Finally, Parik withdrew his hand. He collapsed to the floor as those around him looked from the girl's leg to Parik and back again. What they had seen was impossible, but it had occurred just the same.

Chiarina sat up, feeling of her leg. When the old temple serving woman threw her arms around the girl, tears flooded down Chiarina's face.

"I don't hurt. In here," she tapped her chest, "or here." She reached for her leg. "I'm filled with joy. Thank you, sir."

Rufus didn't have to touch his arms or legs to know he was whole, yet he did, anyway. Then, he fell to Parik's side and grabbed his hand, kissing it. "You've given me back my youth and my manhood." Tears ran down his face. "The Moica Priest scarred me when I refused his advances, and I've been a near-cripple since. You're truly a god."

The Muse laughed with his child-like laugh, and he did so loudly, shattering the scene before him. "A god! How fitting, Parik. You're now a god!" The pale-haired youth with the beautiful skin stepped to Æolus and looked at him with disdain as he spoke to Parik once again. "You're a god who takes the mothers of the city's youths, and then you claim their boys for your own. Is that how it is?"

Æolus frowned at the words, and he turned to Parik. "What's he saying, pater-amicus?"

"Pater-amicus!" The Muse laughed again in his child-youth voice. "You're a murderer, Parik. Have you told them that?" He knelt at Parik's side and took his aged chin in his smooth, perfect hand. "You're so old, Parik. Are you ready for new life? It's coming, you know. You'll wear the freshness of youth, with hair barely on your face. You'll live long, too, and then you'll kill again. You heal these people, and to what purpose? Have you told them they will die, and in only a mere handsbreadth of time? This filius-amicus you brought back from the edge of death, this Æolus, will die in that same short handsbreadth of time, and you'll have killed him, as I'm sure you killed his mother. Have you told him that, my dear Parik?"

The Muse patted Parik's face and stood, looking down at him, a new hardness in his eyes. "If I had a blade, I would drive it into your heart for gifting your child to that woman, Zekiye." He saw Umaru's face jerk to look at his. "Yes, Umaru. I was Zekiye, and then your day disappeared from you. I was you, driving your friends to find Parik. You found yourself where, outside the temple steps? That was where I was when the ground shook once again, and then I was shifted to this youth's body, this boy whose voice hasn't yet dropped and whose loins are still smooth. You, also, will die, Umaru. Has your father told you that?" Then the Muse staggered, grabbing his stomach. "Not yet, Parik. I'm not through."

However, at that point, the Muse had little say in the matter, and that was his own fault, even if he'd made that decision many lifetimes in the past. It was one he could never undo. He didn't have to like it, however.

"Parik!" he yelled one more time.

PARIK CLOSED HIS EYES wearily. With the boy's words, he knew what the others didn't. This one, his messenger, was no messenger. It was his Muse, and he'd found him. What would the Muse do to torment him, now?

I would this were over, coursed through his mind. His rebirth was at hand, and all this would be finished. Rest wasn't to be his, though, he quickly discovered.

"Father, what's this?" Umaru dropped to his knees at Parik's side.

Parik breathed his answer with exhaustion, feeling the roiling in his gut. "It's the Muse I told you of." He looked to see Æolus in tears, and he motioned for the youth to draw to him. Taking his hand, he squeezed it tightly. "You're my filius-amicus, and I'm a father to you always. Never forget."

"I won't, pater-amicus."

The Muse, doubled over in pain, let out a high-pitched laugh. "I tell them the truth, and they still worship you, Parik. Will they continue to care for you when the world around them burns with green fire, consuming them with the pain of your rebirth? Will they love you then?"

"Always," Æolus cried in a forceful voice.

"May I?" Umaru put his hand on Parik's blade.

Parik knew it no longer mattered. This youth only hosted the Muse, and all would be dead shortly. When Parik didn't respond, Umaru whipped the blade from its sheath and dropped into a fighting stance.

"You'll die, Muse. You used me wrongly today. Now you mock my father, and you don't deserve to live." Umaru advanced on the boy.

"He can't be killed." In compassion for the pale-haired boy the Muse used so meanly, Parik called to Umaru to cease his advances. "Leave the boy be."

"This blade will kill him!" The big man's words growled his assurance.

Parik painfully pulled himself to stand. "You'll kill the boy, but the Muse will live, becoming one of you, perhaps. Kaius—"

The man at Rena's side cried, "No! I've entertained the Muse already. Don't kill this boy if that may be the case."

"I misspoke, Kaius. The Muse rarely takes a person twice, and only then if they wish it. You, too, Umaru are safe." Parik shook his head. He didn't wish the Muse to take Æolus. He'd grown to care for the boy, and to be taunted by him, he couldn't bear it. Better that this boy with the pale hair continue to host the Muse. He motioned, "The youths are not safe, nor Rena. Leave the Muse be. He can only mock me. He has no real power."

Parik grasped Umaru's arm as he felt the world twist. He attempted to call out a warning, but it was taken from him, and the stones around them began to shake once again.

THE MUSE STAGGERED AND closed his eyes. His side burned like fire, and he knew he'd shifted once again. He looked at the hand extending from underneath his gold and red tunic, and he understood that he was old, no longer the beatific youth with immature loins. That was some improvement. The pain in his side wasn't.

The massive blocks from which the temple was built were coming apart this time. The Muse brushed roiling

waves of dust from in front of his face as the stones under his feet heaved, keeping him from standing properly,
and he saw the flickering of green fire among the cracks
in the blocks, lighting them from deep within.

"It's here, Parik." He screamed his words, and they
came out in a quavering, old man's voice. "You've
shifted me again, but your time has come. I've told them
the truth, now. You'll always know the pain of their
doubt. I've won again."

The Muse realized with satisfaction that in this body,
he might still kill Parik. This was a man's body, not that
of a shapeless youth. He began to stagger forward
against the continued shaking when several lesser priests
came running drunkenly up to him.

"Moica Priest, are you injured?"

The Muse recognized that term. He was in the elder
priest's body, the one who had been offering sustenance
to the youth the Muse had just left. He knew, then, the
pain in his side. He had hit the man roughly, and now he
was certain he'd broken something. Good, he thought.
He just wished he didn't have to endure the pain for him.
It would be short-lived, though. The green fire was already here.

"A girl. There's a crippled girl. Take me to her." She
was crippled no longer, but these men would know to
whom he referred. "And a blade. I need a blade."

"A blade, Holy One?"

The Muse liked that reference.

"Yes. A blade. And each of you, all. Blades. We
have an enemy to vanquish."

Panicked looks formed on the minor priests' faces. From their subdued whispers and hand signs of obeisance, it was clear they had never handled blades.

"Holy One. Surely . . . in the temple."

The Muse was out of patience, though. The stones had shaken, were still shaking, and he had to get to Parik. Now that he had an appropriate host, plus a position of apparent authority, he needed those around him to give him cooperation. His anger lashed out with a threat that surely would apply, even if he was unfamiliar with the details of this temple's workings.

"Do you wish to be assigned a duty that handles the cleanup of the temple's necessary sanitary bins? The acolytes who have drained the temple coffers with their cost have performed adequately in that function until now. However, I'm certain there are those who would be very pleased to move up to a position in the priesthood. Do I have volunteers to relinquish those positions? If so, I'm quite confident I'll have no difficulty locating acolytes who can find blades and use them."

There was a moment of surprised consternation, and then, in a scramble, the priests voiced their acquiescence to the Moica Priest's request. Before they could leave, the shaking of the stones in the temple stopped, and each of the minor priests paused in the silence. Then, billowing volumes of dust sifted from the ceiling directly overhead. Without warning, two wooden support columns splintered, and a great stone slab from immediately above them fell onto one of the minor priests, killing him before he could cry out.

"The goddess has given you a warning," the Muse called to them. In a sense that was true. It was the goddess' curse that had set this series of events in motion.

It was only moments until the Muse felt a blade pressed into his hand, and he looked around him to see six additional blades at his side. One of the priests called to the others, and with careful steps, they moved to find the crippled girl.

THE PALE-HAIRED ACOLYTE stumbled as the stones shook, and the clattering of Umaru's blade against the floor startled those gathered around the healed child. Parik was now curled on the ground, and green fire arced over his body. Spitting green fireflies raced throughout the room, exploding onto whatever they hit. The very stones of the building shifted against each other, and dust filled the air.

Screams were heard from the outermost part of the temple, and as the shaking continued, the reverberating crash of falling stones punctuated the panicked moans of those within the great edifice. When the moving of the stones finally stilled, green streaks of fire much like cloud lightning continued to arc between the massive building blocks, each time returning to reconnect with Parik's body.

Æolus crawled toward him, only to have Parik cry a warning.

"No, Æole. You mustn't touch me." Even as he spoke, violent green fireflies danced from his body, some exploding in midair, and others flinging themselves across the room before fading away.

"Pater-amicus, what is this?" Æolus' eyes were wide, and alarm was in his voice. He turned to the pale-haired boy, only to find him huddled on the stones, his eyes terrified with confusion.

"The youth needs your protection, Æole," Parik admonished, as the green fire jerked his frame anew, each time sending dozens of fireflies flying. "The Muse has left him, and he will be frightened."

"I'm frightened," Umaru called. The others were huddled in pairs for emotional support. Who knew when the shaking would return, and in several places, blocks had fallen from the temple's ceiling. More might die, and there was no place to run.

"The rat," the old temple serving woman called. "Look, it has stayed through the shaking." Sure enough, it was at Chiarina's side, as if protecting her after a fashion. "It came to her from its secreted place deep within the temple. It knew she was to be healed today. I knew it when it came to her. I knew it." She appeared gleeful, despite the most recent twisting of the temple's foundations.

"Deep within the temple?" Kaius questioned, releasing Rena and crawling to Umaru. "If there are secret places deep within the temple, they're bound to be far into the side of the mountain. They might provide us some safety."

"The reservoir, Kaius," Umaru reminded him. "It's on the other side of the mountain. If the bed of the reservoir were to crack, it would certainly flood anyplace we go, especially deep into the mountain. How is that safe? We must go to the gate and run to the fields. We can do this. I'll carry someone, and you, Kaius, another. We will be safe."

Kaius grabbed his arm for emphasis. "You haven't been yourself this day, Umaru. You haven't seen that the reservoir has drained under the city already, flooding the escape beyond."

About that time, a stone support in the center of the space turned loose, and it shattered as it hit the floor. Several refugees from the city screamed as a large section of the ceiling let go, tragically trapping several people underneath, including a small child. Moans of pain could be heard from under one side of the stone.

Rena cried, "Kaius, we must go somewhere else. We'll all die if we stay here." She crawled to him and locked one hand on his arm in a death grip. "We can't stay in this place. Remember our room when the floor fell? I don't want to die today."

He grabbed her and pressed her head to his shoulder. "We'll be safe, Rena. Trust me."

Umaru motioned him over. "You say the reservoir has flooded the fields outside the city?"

"And washed away the city's foundations. The boy, Æolus, was crushed when a footing from the aqueduct sank far into the ground, bringing another wall of stones down upon it. There's no safe place in the city. The stones in the streets simply drop from underneath your feet as you walk. Even in our room—" He closed his eyes and didn't go on.

"I see." Umaru was quiet for a moment, thinking. "North? Over the mountain? If the reservoir is emptied, it might be possible. After a distance, there's a path that will return to the plains. I've traveled it many times before."

As he finished, a clamor could be heard, and the Moica Priest arrived in his gold and red tunic, interrupting the discussion with six armed priests and a blade in his own hand. None of the six seemed particularly proficient, but the Moica Priest obviously knew his blade skills well. He did seem to be protecting his ribs on one side, however.

"Parik, there you are. Now you die." The Moica Priest pointed his blade at the man wrapped in green lightning and began to stride confidently forward.

The red-haired acolyte, Rufus, scrambled to lift Parik's fallen blade. "No," he cried, jumping between them, his youth and fresh healing giving him some advantage. "You won't harm him. I may not be the best with a blade, but I've held one on occasion. I'll match you, old priest, and if not, I'll be glad to die trying."

"Move, temple acolyte." The priest advanced, although he continued to favor his side. "If it comes to a real fight, even against an inexperienced youth, I might not win. However, I have six blades besides mine, and you'll die. Then I'll kill Parik."

"I think not," Rufus cried. "You took my youth and made me a cripple, stealing my manhood in the process, and the healer has given it back. Now I'll be the man you wouldn't let me be, and you'll die, priest."

"Then," the Muse cried, "you'll give up your life for your impertinence." He motioned for his priests to move forward. "Prepare, acolyte, to meet your end."

"Nay. Your end, Moica Priest." Rufus' blade flashed in the light of the surrounding lamps, and green sparks ran wickedly along its edges.

"UMARU," PARIK CALLED WITH all the strength he could muster. "You must find some measure of safety, even if that's deep in the mountain. Gather everyone, or all will die." The fireflies had grown more numerous, and it was now difficult for him to talk. Each time he opened his lips to speak, green fire filled his mouth.

"You must come with us." Umaru stepped toward him, his eyes transfixed by the green fire. In his hesitancy, he seemed unsure what to do, and that was very unlike the big man.

"You must leave now. Quickly, to some place of safety. The acolyte will protect me. His blade is strong. I'll meet you there." He wouldn't, but these people must be convinced, and now. When Umaru didn't move, Parik continued in his exhortations, calling more forcefully, "The others can't fight, and you must rescue them by finding a place of safety. Go!"

Parik dropped his head, as new waves of the green fire ripped into his body. When they slowed, he whispered hoarsely, attempting to convince the man with yet another argument. "Among those who have come to the temple seeking safety, there's only one blade, and the acolyte has it. It's useless to dream otherwise."

Umaru's expression cleared, as if coming out of a daze. "Your wish, Father. I'll once again do as you say. I don't like this hiding, though." Umaru began pulling people to their feet. "Old woman," he hissed when he was close enough for her to hear. "Where's a part of the temple that will protect us? You mentioned a secreted place."

"The rat knows. We must shadow his path. He'll lead us to safety." Her eyes gleamed as she pointed to where the rat had already begun to head down a stone corridor. The girl, Chiarina, had risen and was following.

Umaru nodded, muttering unhappily, "More likely, a rat will lead us to the nearest pile of grain, but with seven blades against one, the grain seems a better choice than a death from blade strike."

"THE PASSAGEWAYS WIND DEEPLY into the mountain. It's the only way. All others are blocked. Go." Rufus called to those he protected, verifying the old woman's claims, as he brandished the sword, the brilliant fireflies flying from the edges like drops of green-stained rain, spattering when they connected with the floor.

"You must come, too," Rena pleaded.

"I'll protect the healer. Get the others to safety. The acolyte, too. He's been freed of his demon."

Rufus pointed the rat's direction with his free hand, directing those who had come to the temple with the healer. He motioned to the sandy-skinned youth who had so recently taunted Parik, determined to protect one who was where he'd stood barely two seasons ago.

At a fresh taunt from the Moica Priest, Rufus turned and lifted his blade, letting it flash through the air. A new level of green fireflies leaped from the edges, lancing to the ceiling and floor, and exploding into showers of sparks wherever they touched. He grinned when he saw green fireflies on the blades coming towards him, also. He stepped forward, laughing when the minor priests fell back at his approach.

"Ai-ee," he cried, as the last of the group he protected scrambled down the seldom-used corridor. He flashed his blade once more, and charging ahead, soon had it bloodied with the red of the Moica Priest.

However, this was to be no quick death. The man who had given the acolyte so much pain would die slowly, very slowly. He'd suffer until all Rufus' pain was assuaged. The priest had long ago taken something very important from him, and this day was Rufus' chance to right that wrong.

24

THERE WERE MANY TWISTS and turns as the group navigated far into the temple. The path was discerned more by the old temple serving woman's memory than by sight or even the sound of the rat's toenails on the stone. From time to time, they had to navigate around fallen blocks, and finally, at one point, the old woman called for them to stop in the darkness. She made sounds as if looking for something, and then there was the sound of two items being struck together. After several tries, a small light glowed, then grew brighter as she held up an oil lamp with a cloth wick.

She grinned in the wavering light, and her smile was

ghastly.

"There's grain just ahead, and the rat travels to it. It's a place no one goes, an old well from the temple's earliest days, some say. No one will find us there."

In the distance, a muffled booming told of stones in the temple structure still falling, even though the shaking had long since stopped. The old woman pointed down the corridor, giving Umaru her lamp.

"Go. I have another lamp I can light, and I'll follow. I know the way, even in the darkness." She waved him on with her hand.

"I don't like the thought of running to hide in a place with no escape. Is there a way out to avoid being trapped?" Umaru hesitated.

She smiled and patted his hand encouragingly. "This is a place of safety. In the seasons since my coming to the temple, my hands have gone from youth to wrinkled parchment, and yet this place has always stayed the same. Go. I'll join you." She said nothing of the wind that had come through the last time she visited, for the excitement of the healing had stolen that from her.

The sound of ChiChi's barking resounded through the corridor, interrupting their discussion, and Dulcia cried out in alarm. "Come back, ChiChi! Someone! He'll be lost in the darkness. The light. Please bring it. Please, someone, help me." Her voice echoed against the rock, and already the dog's barking was fainter.

"Go!" the old woman admonished. "I'll follow. The new acolyte, too. Tell him to close his tunic, as well." She chuckled. "I've grown an affinity for the youth. He needs care."

The big man nodded in agreement.

UMARU STEPPED AWAY, the oil lamp held firmly in his hand. Soon, though, the barking grew louder, and after a time, rounding a corner, he found ChiChi. The dog's snout was worrying at the presence of the rat, although the rat was paying the animal no mind. The rodent was gnawing away at a kernel of grain, ignoring the barking ball of fluff.

Chiarina moved forward and knelt at its side. "I know you. You do have four legs, little rat. Parik healed you, too, just as the woman said." Her hand went out to pet it across the top of the head just as a thundering crash sent dust billowing into the room.

Zakkhaios ran to the corner around which they'd just come, followed by Æolus. The first youth stopped abruptly, and his friend crashed into him, nearly knocking him down. They turned to the other six in the room, their faces ashen.

"The ceiling has fallen," Zakkhaios whispered. "The corridor is gone."

Æolus whispered something even more important to him. "Pater-amicus. I've lost you forever."

"SO, YOU BLEED AS any other man." Rufus had swung his blade with all the strength he could muster, for his tortured memories fueled his anger.

When the six priests saw the acolyte thrust his blade at the Moica Priest, they dared to believe the temple leader would prevail. He was wearing his red and gold tunic, and the goddess would surely empower him. However, as they watched the blade exit through the back of the priest's tunic, clearly the goddess had abandoned them, and being simple minor priests forced into servitude as soldiers, they immediately dropped the metal they carried and ran for the perceived protection of the upper temple complex.

As the priest collapsed to his knees, his hands grasping the blade, he coughed, and blood seeped from between his lips. Rufus strode to him, his anger strong and his revenge incomplete. With a strong foot, made even stronger with Parik's healing, he raised it to the priest's shoulder and pushed hard, knocking the man to his back. Stepping on his chest, he placed his foot firmly on the hated red and gold tunic, and he braced himself, removing the blade from the man in one swift pull.

Rufus leaned close to the hated face. "Do you know me, priest? Even at the cost of my manhood, I'm glad I fought you. You're why this city dies. I'm glad to give my life protecting the healer, if I only take you with me." He spat in the old priest's face.

The man's lips worked for a moment, finally managing to speak. "The city dies because of Parik. He kills all of you. Kill me, boy. I would that you release me from this body." Pain wracked his features, then a series of coughs brought up more blood.

"So, you're this Muse the healer described. You must die to be released, is it so? Don't answer, because I know it's true. I won't release you. Suffer. If the healer makes this city die, then so be it. You're forced to enjoy your suffering until he does. I spit on you again." This time he spat on the old man's loins, a telling statement to anyone who was familiar with the priest's regular divinations.

Across the room, the brilliance that surrounded Parik drew Rufus' attention. The green light filled the space, forming a wall around the healer, and it flowed through the air as sunlight filters through water. Parik was encased in it, and he seemed to be in great pain.

"Healer!" Rufus dropped his sword and leaped over the old priest, drawing as close as he dared. "I would help you. What can I do?"

Parik arched his neck, revealing great pain on his face, and he held up one hand for the youth to stay back. "The forces have gathered, and my time has come. I'm everything the Muse proclaimed me to be, and I'm not proud of it. I'm sorry, my defender. You will die. I can't stop what I'm to do." He dropped his head with an audible groan.

"Let me come to you." The acolyte made as if to push forward, but the wall of green light kept him back. "I can give you my strength."

"Stay. To come will cause you much pain, and you've endured enough. Make your peace with your gods, if you have any."

"I've no gods, none except you. You gave me back what the gods of this place took from me. I would come to you, if you will."

"Be ready for much pain, if you choose that path."

Parik lifted a hand to invite him in. "I'll be glad to have someone at my side. Press hard against the light. It will fight you, but it will relent."

Reaching Parik did cause Rufus much pain, searing him to his very essence. However, as Parik had suggested, it was less once he had the healer in his arms. He sat with the healer's head in his lap as the green lightning lanced Parik's body more and more frequently, jerking him with torment each time. The fireflies had long since fled, for the green light filled the space where both a crippled girl had been healed, and the Muse lay drowning in his own blood.

Rufus was content to die. He was most blessed on this day, of all the people in the world. He'd vanquished his enemy, and he held his god in his arms. No man could ask for more, even if he was only sixteen seasons old.

ICE AND FIRE. Fire and ice. Far under the tortured city, magma reached long fingers to toy with the snowmelt from the reservoir, and the snowmelt had no place to hide. It twisted and fought, finding cracks in the bedrock, cracks that had been fractured by the shaking far above, as it sought escape. The magma had a thousand probing fingers, though, and there was no fleeing its touch.

As the magma wrapped its sure grasp around the snowmelt, it sizzled and flashed into steam, rising through even smaller cracks back towards the surface. Teased by its first tempting tendrils of success, the magma surged faster and faster upwards, turning the remains of the reservoir into steam more and more quickly. Soon, the superheated vapor billowed up faster than it could be contained in the rock. Reaching the surface, it found the natural catacombs created by the flushing action of the reservoir as it had scoured the underside of the city's foundations. There, it collected, and as the pressure built, the temperature of the steam rose higher and higher.

Those still alive amid the crushing devastation in the city first felt it as a warming of the paving under their feet. Soon, those isolated buildings still standing were sizzling ovens, and the water in the fields outside the city began to churn with heat. Some few people decided that to make a go for it was better than roasting alive in the city, but halfway through the fields, they floated in the water as the skin on their bodies blanched away.

The green in the clouds was constant now, and it flashed continually to the ground. There was no longer any mistaking the lightning that flashed from the city streets back to the clouds above. Whenever it leaped skyward, the lightning took whatever was in its way, dropping it afterwards back to the city below, blackened and lifeless. Quite a few people happened to be standing in just the wrong places at the wrong times, or maybe the lightning was there because the people were. Or, maybe there was just so much lightning that the people were bound to become casualties one way or another.

In the temple, roiling waves of green lightning swept through the room where Parik lay. The red-haired acolyte had given all he had to comfort Parik, continuing to live long enough to observe the Muse's death, even as the old reprobate's voice had screamed in pain. The green lightning had lanced through the old man repeatedly, arching the old priest's body as he'd writhed in excruciating torment.

Now, Rufus was long since dead, and the priest's body was a charred lump.

In all the city, only Parik was destined to live. However, to see him at that point, no one would have called him alive. He was a mass of writhing, green energy, and only one thing was needed to bring him back to youth once again: the Fires of Creation, and they were on the way.

CHIARINA HUDDLED AGAINST the glow of the oil lamp, holding the rat in her arms for comfort. Beside her, Dulcia smoothed the fur on ChiChi's head.

"I have your two coins." Dulcia smiled and glanced at the creature in Chiarina's arms.

"Coins?" She had no memory of coins.

Dulcia pulled them from her tunic and held them out in her opened palm. "From when we found you. I forgot to leave them with the temple serving woman."

Chiarina reached for them. "Someone left coins for Thaddiaos, and I never knew. He was hungry, and he never got to eat." She grasped them in her hand for a moment, then handed them back to the other girl. "He doesn't need them now. Please keep them."

"They're yours."

"Please." Chiarina pressed them into Dulcia's hand. "For my brother." Then she closed her eyes and let out a deep sigh. "If the city is truly in such chaos, the coins are useless, anyway. Yet, your generosity touches my heart. I think of you as a friend, already."

Dulcia slipped the coins back into her tunic. "The coins are yours if ever you have need of them. Don't hesitate to ask."

A bond had been formed, the two becoming sisters in kind. It was one that would serve them well if ever they escaped their stone prison to see the light of day once again.

However, stone was forever. It always had been, and always would be, and nothing could change that.

"AT LEAST WE HAVE air." Kaius grinned, looking at the girls conversing normally even in their current situation. "Does anyone else feel it?" It was quite a torrent, too, and damp. "We won't suffocate. If the rat will share, we won't starve, either, at least not tonight."

"Kaius, there are children present." Rena rebuked him as she knelt by the two girls. "Ignore him, Chiarina and Dulcia. My man always manages to be inconsiderate."

"Bah," Kaius chortled. "Come, Umaru, let's discuss the merits of our situation." He stepped to the adjacent chamber and motioned with his hand for the other man to follow him.

"I'll be glad to join you." Umaru stood and moved to the small chamber where the air flooded in around the rough stones. His eyes traced the steps that hunkered in the shadows, circling the chamber and ending at a roughly finished plaster ceiling. "However, I hope you don't wish to discuss our entombment in this mountain. I now regret our decision to find refuge here. At least in the city, we would have had a chance. Here, we're trapped in solid rock."

"Nay, not entombment. Air." Kaius grinned. "Escape."

Umaru spoke slowly as he replied, "I understand there's air coming in. However, we're not mists, to seep through small cracks in the stones." He reached a finger to run it where the air poured in. "We need escape. The stones in the corridor, they could be moved, perhaps."

"And I'm the healer." Kaius continued to look at him with mirth. "This was reputed to be an ancient well, or so the old woman said. There's air, and it's very damp. If we could break this loose?" He reached and hit one of the roughly hewn stones.

Umaru clapped the other man on the shoulder and held his hand there, digging in his fingers harder than necessary. Then, he released him and laughed, slapping the shoulder once more. "Now we're able to survive many days. We have air and water. Food, too, if we steal from the rat. Also, we have a task to keep us busy. To think like you should be the goal of everyone in this prison." Despite his laugh, his smile quickly faded away.

Kaius sighed. "You wish to climb the steps with the oil lamp again, leaving everyone here in darkness? Was there not a ceiling above, one just like this?" He tapped the stones through which the air leaked, chipping away small bits of remaining plaster that had long since crumbled to the floor.

"You're correct, my friend, and I offer my apologies. Your idea is better than none at all." He turned at the sound of footsteps beside him, reaching to put a hand on Æolus' shoulder. "Welcome, boy. I see your shadow at your side." He nodded at Zakkhaios and then smiled as he ran his hand around Æolus' neck. "I see why my father considered you his filius-amicus. He was fortunate to have found you."

"We're afraid, Umaru." Æolus glanced at his friend and back. "Zakkhaios and I, we're afraid, yet we wish to help. What can we do?"

"Knock these out?" Kaius hit one of the stones. "It appears the steps may go down. If air comes up, a way must be possible."

"Kaius, give it up." Rena chuckled sourly as she called to him from the other chamber. "False hope isn't better than no hope."

"Move," Zakkhaios said. "I at least will try." When the men stepped aside, he slammed into the rough stones with his body, raising stone dust and causing Kaius to cough.

"Fair," Kaius nodded. "Umaru, what you do think? There was much dust. Am I still so dense?"

"Æolus, you must have a try." Umaru looked behind his father's filius-amicus and crooked his finger at the youth with no name. "You also, boy, must make an attempt. After Æolus." When the pale-haired youth refused to move, Umaru bent over and looked him in the eyes. "I need a name. I can't continue to call you boy. You're known by what?"

The youth looked away, and tears welled in his eyes. However, he didn't cry. "It's the first time someone has asked my name since I was stolen for a slave."

"It won't be the last, if you give me no answer."

The boy straightened his shoulders proudly and turned back to Umaru. "I'm called Al-Aricus, son of Al-Aric the Freed, second only to High King Reynaldus. My father and mother have been killed, and now I'm only called Al." His proud look faded, and his shoulders fell once again.

"Al?" Æolus clasped his shoulder and questioned. "Is that your true-friend name?" When the youth looked puzzled, Æolus grinned. "True-friend name, the name those intimate to you use. Zakkhaios calls me Æole. It's my true-friend name."

Al frowned. "I'm no longer Al-Aricus for the reason I'm no longer a son. My father and mother are dead. They've been placed in the ground, and I'm a slave." His eyes were full again, though.

Dulcia called from her place by the lamp, "I have no father or mother, and I'm not a slave."

Standing, Chiarina supported Dulcia's remark. "I also am alone, and no one owns me, no one but me." She bowed her head slightly and sat back down.

Zakkhaios slapped Al on the shoulder and encouraged him. "Æole and I have no one, either. We've cried at our parents' deaths, but we're still alive. See, we're all the same, and we're not slaves."

"Coins were handed over by the temple, and now I live there."

Kaius pulled him apart from the other two youths. "Al, there's no temple left. You were not yourself for a time, correct?" A frown passed across the boy's face. "I see you know. You were taken by, um, by a messenger, and he spoke through you, telling us all would be destroyed. The city and temple are gone. You can't be a slave to a temple that no longer exists. So, do you wish to be known as Al or Al-Aricus?"

"My father won't return from the ground. I can be only Al."

"Al it shall be. Your strength is necessary to us. I wish all three boys to hit the stones. I wish one of the stones to fall. Before our oil is gone, we must at least discover if there's a way out. Zakkhaios caused dust to stir. If dust stirs, the stones will move. Zakkhaios? Æolus? Will you help Al?"

The youths' bodies were sore by the time they got the first stone to loosen. They listened as it tumbled many times before hitting the bottom.

Umaru turned to Kaius. "Do you feel the steps perhaps go all the way down?"

Kaius drew in a deep breath. "I trust so, friend Umaru. I have nothing from which to make wings, if they don't."

"You've done well, boys." Kaius reached and clapped them on the shoulders, holding the pale-haired youth's for a moment. "You, especially, Al. Now, we need to break another stone loose. Soon we will know if we may descend to safety."

However, before that could take place, a great gust of wind swept through the new opening, filling the room, and the oil lamp fluttered and went out. In the depths of a darkness that was complete, ChiChi started to bark frantically, and the scrabbling of the rat's feet could be heard on the stone. The men and boys followed the barking into the main room to comfort the others.

"Umaru? There are no green sparks down here."

"I'm just now aware of that, Kaius."

"Kaius? I'm frightened." Rena's voice was high, and it broke as she spoke her final word.

Before he could reach her, though, the whole mountain began to shake, knocking the men and youths to the floor. It was bad, too, the worst they had experienced that day. It didn't stop, either, and it seemed as if it never would.

25

SUPERHEATED STEAM, THE VERY same water that only that morning had fueled the homes and graceful fountains spread about the city, found itself now trapped in the catacombs beneath the city. It burst free in a cataclysmic series of explosions such as the world had never seen.

Great blocks of stone were thrown into the lightning-laced air during one explosion after another, until finally, with a great rumbling noise, the entire city was lifted dozens of handbreadths into the air by a massive discharge of released energy. The stones seemed to pause at the apex of their flight, and then in a slow motion reversal of their leap for the skies, they shivered in a great way and fell, crushing through the tortured foundation rock that no longer had the strength to support the weight of those very stones that had long made up the city.

Dust flew, dimming the green lightning for a time, and when it cleared, a great cavity lay where the city had once been. Only the temple, built onto the solid rock flank of the mountain that rose in the distance, still remained, its facade cracked and askew but recognizable. As the temple continued to thrust into the darkened sky, defiant and unwilling to fall, the surging magma that was the final piece in the puzzle vomited into the great caldera that had been the city, bringing with it all the minerals needed for Parik's rebirth. It roiled among the stones that had fallen, crisping lemon trees, and pulling the final screams from the few people who remained.

As the heat built in the caldera, the lava that the magma had become created a vortex of superheated wind, sucking in cooler air from the countryside, and fueling the great cloud that refused to dissipate from over the city. Instead, it darkened, and the green lightning increased, dancing across the surface of the lava-filled lake. Sky had finally met earth, and the remaking of Parik could commence.

Inside the tortured temple, the great edifice standing defiant to the last stone, the winds that were more than just ordinary winds tore through stone rooms, shaking the very blocks the building was made of. As if a great fist reached from the sky, the vortex increased, and the winds began to peel the temple apart one stone at a time, flinging each one into the lava pit at its base. Soon, Parik, writhing in his green cocoon of light, was exposed. The storm had found him, and it was time to remake him into the man he'd become.

FAR AWAY IN THE WINE country, a youth named Loukas stood on the wooden cart he rode through the vineyard fields. His hands were stained with the grapes he'd piled high in the cart, and his loincloth, an old one too tight for a youth who had been to the temple serving women for intercession, wrapped his hips. His mother had told him he'd throw it away after this day. Stains were her excuse. The tightness was the reason.

He knew where the city was located, and on a clear day, sometimes he could catch a glimpse of the temple as it caught the evening light. This day, there were storm clouds churning across the sky, and the temple couldn't be seen. Green lightning could, though, a strange green lightning that unnerved the youth, especially as the late afternoon sun was shining everywhere else.

He watched as the bottom edge of the clouds began to glow red, faintly at first, and then brighter and brighter. Then it seemed the strange cloud mass swirled in upon itself, and with a great green flash that made even Loukas cover his eyes, the great storm quieted. With relief, he stood for a moment, watching as it gradually dissipated, until nothing was left. He looked for the temple. He knew exactly the glimmer he should find, and it was odd to him that it wasn't to be seen.

He sat in the cart, and clicking the reins, the small horse began to move forward. There were two more rows of grapes still to pull. Thinking of the green storm, Loukas grinned. He'd ask Æolus all about it. To have experienced such a storm in the city, what luck! Loukas wished he were there. No, instead he had to be here pulling grapes from the vines, and this was the most boring way to spend his time that he could imagine.

Lucky Æolus.

There was something else making Loukas wish he were back in the city. When he'd assuaged his misdeeds with the temple serving woman, after she'd asked him the rote questions and he'd answered them all, she'd whispered fondly remembered words in his ear.

"You must come back to visit again, Loukas, my handsome youth. Come back to me, soon." Then she'd administered the ritual washing, and with special care, too.

He'd return, and if Æolus hadn't yet made his pilgrimage there, they would go together. He was saving the coins his father gave him for working in the vineyard for just such a purpose, for he could be certain of one thing. Æolus hadn't done anything interesting to be worth atonement and would probably never see the inside of the temple, if Loukas didn't take him. It would be the only way for his friend to become a man.

Glancing back once more to find the temple, he noticed the supply cart from the city coming across the lowland. The dust of its trail rose far into the sky. It was quite some distance away still, but it would arrive before dark. He must tell his father and mother, and they'd surely understand if he abandoned the final two rows of grapes. He must be there when the driver was handed his coins, otherwise, his father would never think to ask of news from the city.

Lucky Æolus, he thought, not for the first time.

THE STONES WERE ONCE again still, and it seemed a lifetime had passed.

"We remain alive," Rena whispered.

The dog began barking frantically, and fighting Dulcia's restraining hands, it tore from her grasp, rushing to the pile of stones and rough timbers that now filled the lower half of the small space where the three boys and the men had tried so hard to create a way of escape.

"We won't go down now." Umaru laughed when he peered at the rubble blocking the dog's way, but it was a laugh of frustration. "I'd almost begun to trust Kaius' vision."

Not getting anyone's attention, ChiChi left the chamber and ran to the corridor through which the group had first entered their oppressive prison. The barking echoed against the fallen stone that held the group penned inside. Then, the animal ran back to the small chamber filled with yet more stones and began to bark anew.

"Your dog," Chiarina pointed, "likes to see what's unknown." The rat was content in her lap, and she stroked its new leg.

Dulcia groaned. "My dog likes to bark. I'll retrieve

him." She brushed stone dust from the front of her tunic and made as if to stand.

"No. I'll go. Please." Al stood, entering the small chamber, and his pale skin seemed to glow, even in the dimness of the room. He scrambled to wrap his arms around the small animal.

"Umaru, do you see with your eyes the same thing I see with mine?" Kaius' voice was filled with excitement.

"That your idea will no longer work?" Umaru shook his head, and dust flew from his long hair. It was coated and looked like an old man's.

"No. Light. Look at the youth's skin." He stood and took Al's arm in his hand. "He glows. There's light within the small chamber. We might climb the steps, if you're willing to try once again, even without the lamp." He broke into a smile. "If there's light, there's surely an opening."

Æolus laughed. "It's a well, truly, as the temple serving woman said. It surely went to the top at one time, and this corridor was made for access directly from the temple."

"My father often had old wells sealed to protect our flocks." Al placed ChiChi on the floor and climbed on the tumbled stones that filled half the small chamber. "My father's servants did that once, covered the top of a well with stones. He said others might fall in and be injured." He looked up, holding his hand in front of his face.

"And how do the stones look to you, my young friend?" Umaru leaned forward to peer into the niche.

"Do they offer more than false hope?"

"The steps don't stop as far as I can see." Al's eyes were red with impending tears, but a smile was on his face. "I wish to be free again, as my father was free. Will anyone else follow me?"

It only took a moment for the others to respond, and in a scramble of dusty feet, seven additional people, one dog, and one rat headed towards the light. The eighth was already there. Freedom did look good to them, and after being underground, they were certain they would find it smelled even better.

THE SUN WAS LOW in the sky, and the air was clear. It was hot, though, as a young man, one with fiery green eyes and hair the color of darkness, stood. The stone all around him was blackened, and far below, the red glow of crusting lava could still be seen.

He breathed in the air, and it felt good. Youth was invigorating. However, he didn't feel refreshed, not inside. This had been the hardest rebirth he'd ever experienced. The centuries had taught him that each new birth would cause him pain. The sudden old age wasn't new to him, and when the time grew near, he expected the green lightning that would lance his body, bringing excruciating torment as it worked its wonders of creation. Yet, this time other factors had proven to be the difference that had torn his essence wide within his heart, and he knew it would be a very long time before it would heal.

This time he'd cared.

Dulcia, Zakkhaios, and ChiChi. He smiled at the thought of the small dog. Then, he pictured the boy who had claimed his love. Filius-amicus. Æole.

Tears filled Parik's eyes. He'd lied to the youth, to all of them. He'd let them believe he'd save them, when he could have told them the truth. They wouldn't have listened, but he could have told them.

Despite his remorse, he knew his self-pity was just that, self-pity. They were gone. The city was gone. No one ever lived except him. And the Muse. He snorted at that. He and his Muse, bound together throughout all the ages. *Curse you, Lamahätsu.* He raised a fist and shook it at the sky.

Yet, he knew the centuries of reality. He'd lived them all. This place was dead, and he must find food and water. Yes, and clothing. He must begin to build a new life. The Muse would return, flitting from person to person, teasing him, sometimes attacking him, intent on his death, and at other times as an intimate, washing his senses with the most intense of pleasures.

Freshly reborn, however, he'd have freedom for a time. If the Muse were far enough away, he might even have seasons or decades of seasons. Turning his attention away from the glowing remains of the city, he looked for a way to the plains. He'd go south. The coastline there was far away, and he'd see if Zekiye had truly escaped. If her man no longer wanted her, Parik thought he might like a try at her heart. She'd been beautiful, and she'd be a pleasing first step into this new life.

As the evening sun kissed the horizon, Parik did

make it to the plain, now devastated and dry. As he walked forward, his bare feet stirred dust that was lifted in the gentle breeze and drawn the direction of the city, finally carried to the sky by the heat of the slowly cooling lava, all that remained of a once-thriving city.

It was as it should be, that all had died so that Parikshit Aagneya, the Tested-One Born-from-Fire, could live once again.

NOT ALL THE STEPS were there. Some had been broken by the falling stones, and others had been torn loose when the mountain itself had shaken in the onslaught of the final conflagration. Yet, there were sixteen strong arms, and the eight people who had thought themselves buried forever far underground really wanted to reach freedom. Hands were held and feet were steadied, and after much coughing and crying, Al pressed his face into the evening sun.

"Freedom." He scrambled out, calling back into the hole, "It's a recess in the rock, open to the south. It's freedom." He reached his hand for Rena, helping to pull her out.

"We're at the edge of the reservoir." Kaius followed Rena up, looking around. "This is a familiar path. I've walked here many times, sitting in this very recess for protection from the sun. It was an old well all that time, and I was unaware." He turned and reached for Chiarina's hand, and then he took the hands of the others, one after the other, pulling each free.

Umaru was last, and he stood in the golden glow of

the setting sun. "Light." Then he laughed, looking at Kaius. "I'm glad we climbed up, friend. I wouldn't have liked climbing down."

Æolus held one hand over his eyes and peered out where the city had been, and from there to the freshly baked plains that were no longer green. A dust trail could be seen, and just barely, he could tell a distant figure walked toward the south.

"One has survived," he called to the others with excitement. "See? Walking on the plain? The words of the Muse were wrong. One did survive."

"One." Umaru put an arm across the youth's shoulder. "One out of ten thousand. It should have been my father. I would have enjoyed learning his life."

"My pater-amicus. He died so we could be saved." Æolus reached a hand and wiped the tears from his eyes.

Umaru stood by the youth, his arm still on his shoulders, and he spoke his next words carefully. "I have no filius-amicus, Æolus." He held himself stiffly, his emotions strong in his voice. "I'm not my father, and I sorrow that your pater-amicus lives no more. However, I would fill his place, if you would permit me. May I be that for you?"

Æolus stood quietly for a moment, and then his arm stretched around Umaru's waist. He looked up, grinning. "You must call me Æole. If you call me Æole, then you're my pater-amicus."

The two stood in the fading light, until the rest of the group of eight survivors decided they must begin the walk to the plain to find shelter for the night. Chiarina was the last, and she remained alone, staring at where the lone figure had been. Rena went to her.

"We must go, Chiarina. What are you watching?"

"It's my Thaddiaos we saw walking there. He walks from the city, and he walks to happiness. I stand here wishing him to find the happiness he never had."

Rena brushed the girl's hair from her forehead. "You loved him very much, did you not?"

Chiarina reached a slender hand to her face to wipe away a tear. "I love him, still."

Rena hugged her. "You've grown today. Your Thaddiaos wouldn't know his sister with how much she's grown."

The girl stepped with Rena to follow the others, but she had one more thing to say.

"Thaddiaos would know me. He'd know me by my love for him. Thaddiaos would always know me."

Epilogue

LOUKAS LIFTED THE BASKET over his head and dumped it into the cart. He still wore his purple-stained loincloth from the day before. When the man with the supplies told his story, Loukas had refused to believe it, and even, to his father's dismay, called him an untruthful man.

Then, later, when his mother came for the offending loincloth, he refused to give it to her, saying he'd worn it when leaving his friend Æolus for the final time. He'd wear it still. He'd wear it for Æolus.

Still, this noon, his father said the final two rows must be gleaned, and so Loukas gleaned. His eyes were frequently moist, however, and he hadn't been able to see farther than the basket in his hands. That was why a familiar voice calling his name surprised him so.

"Loukas! Amicus!"

Loukas looked up to see a face he'd thought dead, and another and another. Other faces were there, also, but there were three he knew by heart.

"Æole! You live! How can this be?" He threw the basket into the cart and ran as fast as he could, slamming into his friend, throwing his arms around him and slapping him enthusiastically on the back. "The man with the supplies said all was destroyed by a great storm. I saw it, too, even from this distance. You survived, and you, Dulcia, and you, Zakkhaios." He gave them his greeting hug, also.

"And I." Umaru stepped up. "I must see the severed toe. Æole has described it to all."

Loukas looked at this companion, one who clearly accompanied his newly alive-again friend, and grinned, pulling his foot up as he hopped on one leg. "It was Æole's fault," he claimed.

"Untruth." Æolus laughed and pushed him over to land in the dirt. "Ask Dulcia. She saw." Dulcia was gone, though, once again chasing after a dog that found freedom more interesting than a makeshift leash that never seemed to keep the animal within arm's length.

Loukas jumped back up and threw his arms around his friend once again. "You're alive again, Æole!" He backed away, his hands still on Æolus' shoulders, looking in his friend's face. "I learned you were dead, and now you live. I'm exceedingly glad."

A hand slapped Loukas on the shoulder and turned him around. "You've no idea just how true that is. You're Loukas, clearly, and I'm Kaius. There are more for you to meet, and then you must take us to your parents. Æolus tells us there are workers' huts we might use for a time."

"Of course," Loukas said. "Come, and I'll show you." Then he laughed. "Of course, if you stay in the workers' huts, my parents might expect you to work."

Umaru laughed, also. "Work, we might, but water and food, first. We've walked a very long way. The huts will wait until later."

ÆOLUS TURNED AT A hand on his shoulder, and Zakkhaios pulled him away, wrapping Æolus' neck in the crook of his arm, hissing intently into his ear.

"Why am I never just Zak to you, Æole? Am I not your friend?"

Æolus looked at him with surprise, not having ever thought of it. Zakkhaios was just Zakkhaios. Then, with his newly minted enthusiasm for life, he grabbed Zakkhaios' face firmly with both hands and planted an overly dramatic, juicy kiss right on his cheek.

"Now, you're Zak. Wa-hoo!" He threw his arms in the air and ran through the rows of grape vines, jumping and yelling, "Zak, Zak, Zak!"

Kaius stepped to Umaru, pointing to the youth. "That's something I don't understand. We've walked all the way from the city, and he has the strength still to do that. How?"

Umaru laughed. "He's a youth who's been given his life back. We should all find it so easy to rejoice." With that, he lifted a hand, closed his eyes, and yelled to the sky, "Wa-hoo!"

Without warning, a youth in a loincloth slammed into him, knocking him to the ground. When Umaru looked up, Æolus was sitting on his chest, and he grinned as he looked him in the eyes.

"We think the same, pater-amicus."

Umaru grinned back. "Yes, we do, filius-amicus, and I'm glad."

Then, Æolus leaped to his feet and was off again. "Wa-hoo!" His legs carried him through the field, and there was no grapevine too tall for him to jump.

PARIK RESTED QUIETLY IN the heat of the night. The air was thick with the aromatic fragrances of a tropical world where life, where love, was there for the taking, if one simply reached out a hand. The sounds of the seas beat at the cliffs in the distance, and the moonlight littered a room that had become more than a temporary stop along Parik's unending journey through the ages.

There was life in this room, and soon there'd be more, Parik's gift of life, as well as the twin that had been given by the Muse. The great belly that was between Parik and the woman he'd grown to love carried both, and soon it would set them free.

He'd know his children this once. For a time, if necessary. For a lifetime, if possible. The Muse must have been cast far away. There was no throbbing in his fingernail, no sense of his—or her—closeness, and Zekiye was safe, Parik hoped. She knew of the Muse, had hosted his—or her—presence, and with such foreknowledge, would always be free of his—or her—influence ever again.

Parik had sensed the Muse's revenge, though, the second child, its wrongness; and with his skin resting against the woman who loved him simply because he was Parik, he whispered into her ear, "Do you wish our children to be perfect?"

He knew the concerns she pushed aside, the worries that came to her at the edges of waking when the morning sun first shattered the quiet of the night. When he'd first found her, he'd seen the misshapen thing that would be born. Only one child would be perfect, Zekiye unable to know which was Parik's son, and which was its twin. He hadn't told her, but she knew. They felt different, she said.

Parik sensed the building of Zekiye's pulse, the throbbing just underneath her skin, as it raced through her body at breakneck speed.

"Of course, I do," she whispered in return. Her voice carried the breathlessness of hope, and it also throbbed with an undercurrent of fear. It was clear she wanted that more than anything in her being.

As Parik's hand, newly youthful and smooth, touched the side of Zekiye's belly, the fourth fingernail began to glow. Heat burned his finger, as deep inside, the thing the Muse had planted in the woman's womb straightened, its limbs becoming true, and its body becoming strong. It became a true twin to the gift Parik had bequeathed that night so long ago in a city that could now be visited only in the dreams of a few.

"They will be," he whispered, as he held his hand against their children, and then his voice was taken from him. All he knew was his love for the woman at his side, as he gave himself to her wholly and completely. After a time, exhaustion gave way to the night, and all was still.

As the moon rose, casting shadows over the sleeping lovers, there was something else quite intangible with them in that room. With this woman, with these children she'd bear, Parik had finally found a love that was his and his alone—and of course, he'd freely admit, Zekiye's, too.

THE MUSE WRAPPED HER fur-lined animal skin around her shoulders and screamed her frustration to the frozen sky. She had no idea where she was, and she couldn't sense Parik anywhere. There were only a handful of people in this frozen wasteland, and all they did was hunt for seal. She couldn't eat another meal of the atrocious food, and she couldn't sense another host within shifting distance, at least not one that would allow her freedom from this frozen hell in which she'd been marooned. She groaned as she realized the tribe, the People, were breaking camp once again, and she had no idea where they were going.

"Medicine woman," a quiet voice whispered at her side. A goddess of some persuasion or another had come to live in the People's old religious figure, and they were now afraid of her. "We require you to bless our journey." She must do that for them, the People insisted, or no seals would be found to nourish them on their hunting forays.

Once again, the Muse screamed her frustration to the sky.

Did you enjoy this book?

Find more books by Farley Dunn

at

◦❀◦ THREE SKILLET

www.ThreeSkilletPublishing.com

The Center's Child

The Destiny Changer

The Electric Minute (short stories)

And the exciting and fast-paced *Se'Yan't Chronicles:*

All Fall Down (Book 1)

Exiled on Rant (Book 2)

400 and Counting (Book 3)

The Grandmothers (Book 4)

and more . . .

www.ingramcontent.com/pod-product-compliance
Lightning Source LLC
Chambersburg PA
CBHW071214250626
47159CB00001B/303